Feet shuffle, voices rise, and a woman approaches the front.

"What is this?" I whisper to Zane as if he'd know.

He leans toward me, a fresh clean scent wafting to me. "Testing."

I got that, but I wanted to ask how and what kind since I expected our second batch of work would be psychological. What can be done without a one-on-one interview? I can't be the only one who's curious as the volume in the room has grown more and more, I wonder if other people think the same as me.

The doors suck shut behind us, and all sound ceases.

PERRY ROAD

EMI GAYLE

MM&I

PERRY ROAD

Published by MM&I
www.emigayle.com

ISBN 978-1-937744-47-2

First Printing: September 2013

To the United States of America,

It's not over until it's really over.

1

"Did you get it?" Cam sits next to me waving her PCD through the air. She's been antsy for the last hour, reminding me all about her invitation—one she received at precisely nine A.M., two months, three weeks and six days ago. On her birthday. With her brand new personal computing device.

Not that I'm jealous, or anything.

"Still nothing." I've been waiting for my invitation all day. *All* day.

"Check again."

I refresh the screen, but, again, nothing shows up on my P-Comm—my old, ancient, decrepit communicator. "Nope. Nothing." When I say I received nothing, I mean *nothing*. Cam gets countless messages, both text and voice. Me? Nada. May be normal, but someday I want to be more like Cam. Popular. Interesting. Someone people want to talk to.

"It has to come today, Eri," she says for the hundredth time, as if I didn't hear her the first ninety-nine. "It will come today. It's your birthday."

"I know." *I know.* Her reminders aren't helping my slowly dying self-esteem.

"Maybe if you upgraded your equipment ..."

Like that can happen.

"Or maybe it's just late." She says it as nonchalant as always, and as if she didn't just insult my P-Comm.

What she hasn't yet mentioned, and I'm waiting for her say to because she will, is that someone probably left my name off the registration list. On purpose. By accident. Who knows? It happens.

"Check it again," she says.

I tap refresh, and again, I get zilch.

Cam hops up and thumps her way toward my dresser and back. "You're eighteen. Everyone gets an invitation when they turn eighteen. It's the rule."

"It's not technically a ru—" Her glare stops me. There is no point arguing with Camelia J. Hopper the third—the only girl I've ever known to get numbers in her name.

"It *will* come. And you'll be with me, Eri." She wraps her arms around me, blonde hair spilling into my face. "You have to be with me. Who's going to brush my hair for me? Who's going to help me fold my clothes? And no way am I sharing registration amenities with some chick I don't know. You barely take up any room. I have to go with you."

Spitting out a strand of her hair as she pushes away, I say, "I could be a fluke."

Cam's serious expression comes complete with scowl; I wonder if her mother ever said her face would stick because I'm pretty sure it's going to some day. That's how often she gives me *that* look. "Erianna." Her hands are on her hips, and she's definitely giving off the mom vibe. "You're not a fluke. Only . . . *flukes* are flukes. You wouldn't be my friend, if you were a fluke. You will get the invitation. Now, check again." Her green irises bore into mine.

"Fine." Yet another hover and tap and the little loading animation flips and spins and flies on my screen as if trying on my behalf, or maybe to shut Cam up itself, to pull even a junk message to the surface.

I may not be as popular as Cam or as beautiful, bubbly or fun, but she is right.

Everyone gets the invitation.

It's not a rule. It's the law.

Unless the person is a fluke.

Which I could be. Don't want to be. Really, really, *really* don't, and staring at Cam in her new clothes without holes, her clean hair cut by a professional and the fact that she's my friend reminds me why: Flukes are poor. I should know. My mom is one.

The animation keeps going as if it's really trying for me— not that it can. I drop my P-Comm to my leg just as dark words appear on screen. My heart picks up speed, and a tingly tension takes over.

"Well?" Cam asks.

For some reason, I don't want her to know. I want to find out by myself if I'm going to get a real life, or if I'm destined to wear hand-me-downs from twenty years ago until I'm ninety. I want to prepare, to plan, to cry if we don't get to go together, or if I'm not like her.

I'm not, of course—in any way like her. Who am I kidding?

After what seems like hours, but is only seconds, I say, "Nothing."

"Damn." She throws her arms up in the air. "Figures. And it's almost five. So, you know, I gotta go. Mom's sure I'm going to be chosen to pop out babies like she is, so she wants to make sure I know how to cook before the fake chefs get ahold of me to 'teach' me." Cam gives me a dramatic eye roll and places a hand to her forehead. "Like, oh, my Oz, Eri, you know? We have people to cook for us for a reason. Duh! If I learn to cook, what job am I going to give someone like your mom, you know? And why would I get picked to be fat and ugly when I look like this?" She bats at her blonde curls.

Wanting to change the subject—to anything but the woes of Cam's perfect life—I walk to her, give her a hug and a quick pat on the back. "I'll ... call you when I get it, 'kay?"

"You better. We only have two days to shop for the perfect outfit. Why couldn't your birthday be October twenty-ninth instead of December?" She snatches up her coat—preparation for the winter blast that will tear into uncovered skin. "And ... you're not a fluke. You will get in the white house, and when January first comes, we'll be official!" She boogies her way out, hips wiggling. For someone who's not happy about the prospect of becoming a baby factory, she's awfully chipper.

I know it's because she's waiting to hear my fate. To prove I'm not a fluke. To validate my relevance as her friend—the one girl Cam can give backhanded compliments, and, for that matter, insults all day long, and still walks back in with a smile as if nothing happened.

Cam heads out through the hallway and says goodbye to my mom who's probably still working at her makeshift office in our miniature kitchen—trying, I assume, to avoid the whole days' events. As much as Cam wants me to *not* be a fluke, my mom *wants* me to be one. If I'm like her, nothing will change. Like Cam, I'll be the same old Erianna, just one day older and as useless as all the other flukes in the world.

The front door opens and closes, and I move to the window. Once Cam disappears from view, and only then, I turn over my P-Comm and touch the one message that sits inside.

The one that says: "Invitation for Erianna Price Keating."

⊂━✦━⊃

After closing the privacy shade on my tiny window, I walk

to my door and shut it, making sure not to let the latch click.

If Mom knows I've closed it, she'll assume I've gotten my letter and demand to know what I've found out, which would promptly set her off on an emotional roller coaster. She's been waiting as anxiously as Cam, just without the giddy excitement or the bouncing.

Unlike Cam, though, I've managed to keep Mom away all day by waving my P-Comm and telling her the truth—no invite.

With shaking hands, I click on my name.

To Miss Erianna Price Keating,

It sounds so formal with the whole thing there. A deep, unsettling anxiety roots in the pit of my stomach.

Maybe I didn't want this after all. Maybe being like Mom wouldn't be so bad.

No. I can't think like that. Change is good.

Returning to the invitation, I read on.

The National Archives, Records and Citizen Administration of the American Union cordially invites you ...

Invites. I should be relieved, yet invite is such a huge lie, and everyone knows it. My heartbeat speeds up again, and my palms break out in a clammy sweat. I wipe them on my jeans, careful to avoid the side seam that I'm sure is going to break the next time I wash them, and scan lower.

... to this year's Registration Service Ceremony for all candidates born in the calendar year 2132.

I skim some more.

All I want to know are two bits of detail.

Registration begins on January 1, 2133 at exactly 06:00 at the 61C Perry Road location.

61C. *61C?*

Oh, no. That's not where Cam's going.

I flop back on my bed as tears well in my eyes. Cam and I want to go together. We filled out our life preferences and evaluation materials together, checking off all the same boxes to make sure of it. Biology, anatomy, history options. All of it matched.

Turning to my side, worry builds up and trembling adds to my racing heart.

Who's going to help me when I don't understand a question? Who's going to help me through the tests? Cam and I planned forever to be together. She convinced me we would be. *No way this will keep us apart, Eri. We're totally in,* she said.

I flip to my other side, holding my pillow with its fake lavender scent, and dry my tears on bunny's ears. It's stupid of me to cry into a stuffed animal, but I've had her—and only her—all my life.

'Only babies cry', Mia, my sister, said to our Mom when she *didn't* get an invitation.

On a sniffle, I spin again.

The light from my pink lamp illuminates the side table, where I store the three books my dad had in his closet and Mom let me keep after he died. They're paper—the only paper books I've ever had my hands on. I've spent more of my time with my nose in Huckleberry Finn, Alice in Wonderland and Little Women, than all the other reading material available to me. Huck wouldn't have a problem getting through the week-long registration, testing and orientation, to adulthood. I should be more like him. Adventurous. Carefree. Ready to take on the world.

Who am I kidding?
I can't do this.
Yes, I can.
I can do it.

"I can," I say aloud.

Semi-convinced, I wipe away the tear stragglers and scroll all the way up on the message to start again, ready for the details.

Eighteen years I've waited for this moment. Everything is going to change, and that's all I've ever asked for.

2

Eyes to the screen, I begin reading my letter again, forcing myself not to start sniffling again over the thought of being separated from Cam.

Per section 134.53.654, all male and female citizens living within the latitudinal and longitudinal boundaries of . . .

The gobbledygook of numbers is one geography lesson I must have missed. In this case, I doubt it matters. The American Union stretches from the east to west coast of North America. Somewhere in the middle, a twenty-ish-foot tall wall separates us from the United States, so it's not like we're going to mix with them just because we used to once share land. Returning to my message, I get back to reading.

. . . and having turned eighteen within the months of January through December of the same year, must register and be evaluated in their local precinct.

The letter reads as if I didn't already know the rules. It seems stupid that they have to explain something that's been the law for a bazillion years. Rules are rules. We either follow them or chaos reigns.

The southern part of our continent is a testament to what happens when people get in the way of popular progress. They probably don't even have registration, since, according to history, the U.S. is a bunch of crazy capitalists only focused on making money. They probably train their kids from day one to make a credit—or whatever they call credits. I know where I live. I know registration is how I get a job. Why do they have to tell me who's included?

Please bring all the following documents: birth identification number, confirmation of nationality, educational eligibility certificate and ...

The list of stuff goes on and on and on. That part, I skim. Our counselors at level three educenter went through the packet ages ago. Cam's had her folder ready since the start of our senior year. Technically, I have, too, but not for the same reasons; I just didn't want to be caught off guard if someone asked for it or if I turned out to be a fluke.

Should you be hospitalized, incarcerated, disabled, or exempt at the time of your appointment ...

Sometimes, I wish I had an excuse not to grow up. I want to, but the idea of just staying home, curling up with my blankets and closing my eyes forever, is kinda inviting.

'That's just the shy girl talking, Eri', Cam would say, while trying to shake the living daylights out of me.

She's right, though. If I want a new life, I have to go through registration. Not that I want to stay and be like Mom, but I don't want to leave her, either.

Sitting up again, I stare at myself in my dresser mirror with its plain white paint and the remnants of past stickers still attached to the glass. My reflection, though, with mousy brown hair, ugly brown eyes, blotchy skin, too-long legs and a flat chest has never, and won't ever, be reason enough to keep me home. I haven't been sick in ages. I'm not disabled, either—not physically or mentally. Nor have I been jailed, though I know a couple guys in my level three educenter who have. A few times. Guess they'll be going down path number two. Letting the lottery choose my entire future is not something I'd want. Ever.

Nothing will keep me from being drafted into a job, a career, a livelihood for the rest of my life, but at least going through registration, I'll have a say. A choice.

With a huge sigh, I scroll down the page more.

No late registration will be allowed, and the penalty for failure to attend includes involuntary commitment to your state's lottery.

Yep. A shiver zips through me. What started off—in my head, at least—as a welcoming messages has grown more menacing with each additional word. I'm glad I've read it by myself, where I can let it sink in without Cam's gaze boring holes into me, or Mom begging me to find an excuse not to go.

Flat on my back again, I stare up my ceiling; the white plaster is bumpy where Mom and I did repairs when the rain leaked through. I may not know what I want in life, but with the letter, I've confirmed two important points. First, like Cam said, I'm not a fluke. Second, I'd rather take my chances with NARCA than get put in the lottery.

Back to my device, I scan through again, my earlier unease calming. So far, nothing is out of the ordinary, and the excitement Cam had at reclassification from kid to adult reaches inside and begins to root.

I could get excited about it all. I should. I will. I am.

Two more days and my future won't be unknown, but laid out right in front of me.

In two days, I'm leaving and will get everything I want.

It's time to tell Mom.

○══╪══○

My heart pounds in my chest and my palms have gone all clammy again. The anticipation as I walk through the hallway from my bedroom toward the kitchen is worse than waiting to go down a roller coaster's first hill. If I get roller coaster maintenance as a job, I'll have to beg for mercy and plead for something different.

From my spot in the middle of the hall, I can see the whole rest of our house, including Mom, who sits at her desk in the corner.

Stand here forever or get on with it.

Suffering from my own mental volleyball game of go or no go, I take a deep breath and step.

The floorboard creak sounds through the house, and Mom spins around. "Hey, baby." Her face is the picture of happiness with her smile and bright eyes. I'm pretty sure she thinks I'll be overlooked, since I haven't run crying into her arms, yet.

"Hey, Mom." I shuffle closer.

She claps her hands together. "So … dinner. We could do something nice. I've been saving up." The twinkle remains in her eyes to the point I don't want to deflate her happiness.

What would it hurt for her to think something different than I know? I'm sure she does that to me—or has. I'll have time to tell her later, anyway. "Uh, yeah. Okay."

Mom quirks up an eyebrow. That usually means I've taken too long on my answer.

As she stands and comes toward me, she places her palms to her cheeks. "I'm so proud of you, Eri."

My cheeks flame.

"You've grown up to be such a responsible, thoughtful, beautiful—"

Is she really talking about me?

"—young woman. Tonight, you deserve some indulgence. What do you think about Milton's?"

My eyes widen. "But … that's our super-special …"

Her lips curve higher. "Honey, this is the first day of the rest of your life. I want you to celebrate."

"Yeah, but—"

"No buts." She pats my cheek three times. Translated: *this conversation is over.*

Guilt runs rampant through me. I should tell her, but she's so happy, and it doesn't seem right to spoil her day. Instead, I smile and say, "Dinner at Milton's would be awesome, Mom."

Lucky for us, Milton's is within walking distance of home. Most stuff is. She and Dad bought our little shanty with that in mind, and since she hasn't had personal transpo since Dad died, the location works for us. Groceries are three blocks east. Public comms center is four blocks west. My educenter is only seven blocks north. Even if we had enough money, nothing is far enough away for me to need my own transpo.

Of course, if Mom weren't a fluke, she'd have either been given tram credits in the inner district, or her own vehicle if she'd been assigned a house farther away from her job.

Flukes, though, they're on their own. Alone. Outsiders. If they don't make what they have work, they starve to death on street corners and in alleys—some prostitute themselves for food or try to marry in so they'll get assistance. Mom kept herself way above those standards even without any assistance from the A.U., and for that, I have to thank her.

Doesn't mean I want to do the same thing. Who wouldn't want to have more? Who wouldn't want Cam's life over mine?

"Other than dinner, what can I offer you, baby?" Mom asks as we stroll along the sidewalk.

"Maybe a T-shirt?"

For December twenty-ninth, the weather is warmer than I thought—at a balmy forty-four degrees. It had been crisply chilly when Cam first came over. For our region of North America, it seems every other day is different. Every few hours change, even.

"I'm thinking we'll need bikinis by February, if this weather keeps up." Mom cracks a smile and nudges me with her shoulder.

February. After I get my official papers. After I get my job assignment for the next ten, twenty or thirty years. A job with actual credits and a place to live that doesn't have holes in the ceiling or appliances on the verge of breaking. I really need to tell her my summons came. "Mom—"

"Ooh!" She stops me just outside Milton's door, the basil and oregano scents reaching deep inside me. If it could, my nose alone would probably drag me forward. "What if, this summer, we save all our credits and go to the beach for a whole week."

Guilt wracks up, and my hands tremble. "Mom, I—"

"Surprise!" Voices spring from the doorway as Cam, Jen, Clark and RK file out. "Oh, my Oz!" and "Happy Birthday!" and "Isn't this awesome?" follows.

As I'm surrounded by my friends, Mom stands just outside our circle, grinning like Crazy Sally who lives in the tram station by the commerce center and totes a red plastic cart full of who-knows-what everywhere.

Mom waves me on and steps back. For a moment, my heart flip-flops. I don't want her to leave, but as she keeps going, I realize she's dropping me off, not staying. She's giving me freedom and independence. She's leaving me to be an adult, with my adult friends.

Cam threads her arm through mine. "Isn't your mom awesome? She set all this up."

I glance over my shoulder and find Mom with her back to me, walking away. "Yeah, she's ... awesome."

"So, come on!" Cam says. "You don't want to get left behind, do you?"

⊶――◆――⊷

I love the smells in Milton's. What wafted outside intensifies as I walk in, and I soak it up, breathing in and savoring the warmth of fresh baked bread and seasonings.

RK ushers me to a table where a couple more of Cam's friends already sit. He kisses the side of my neck—slobbering, if the cold that wafts over it is any indication. I want him to go away, but he says we're dating, and no one else ever asked me out, so I accepted and am stuck. "Hey, baby. So, did you get it?"

I see him for the first time all day and he asks me that? On my birthday? "Um ..." His cologne, something I've never been able to remember the name of, overpowers the Italian smells. If I don't turn my head, I'll start sneezing or gagging, or if I wait long enough, I'll end up puking all over him. It happened once before, only I managed to turn my head to the ground. That's how strong his scent is.

Cam drags me away. For whatever the reason, I'm grateful. She pushes down on my shoulders until my butt lands in a chair.

"So, Eri, happy eighteenth!" Jen says, handing me a small, wrapped, pink package.

"Awe, thanks, Jen. You didn't have to do that." Even as I say it, I slide my finger under an edge and rip the recycled plastic covering.

"Of course I did, I mean, what with your Mom and being poor and—" She buttons up her lips. Jen always has good intentions, but sometimes, her mouth works before her brain engages. At least she recognizes it. Cam, on the other hand, just doesn't.

"It's okay." I return to the package and slide the box out. If I didn't know better, I'd think she bought me jewelry. Which would be totally weird for a girl to do.

RK sits next to me, grabs a napkin and drops it on my lap, taking my attention away from my gift for a moment.

"Open it, already," Cam says. "We all went in."

My jaw drops open for a second, but I shut it. They all used credits? What am I? A charity case? Hesitation grips me. I want to open the present. I want to accept it, but at the same time, something is off. It is my birthday, but they've never bought me anything before.

"Oh, come on." Cam grabs it from me and flips open the top.

A silver heart with a ruby in the center sits in the middle of the box. No way it would be real. None. Thank goodness.

Still ... wow. The thoughtfulness alone should make me giddy.

Cam lifts it out and drapes it over my palm.

RK leans toward me, his shoulder bumping into mine. "I put in an image for you."

Prying open the little clasp takes a few tries, but my fingernail, as short as it is, does the job. Inside, one half of the heart is empty. The other has RK's formal photo, one I know he paid to have retouched. His brown hair's a little lighter, brown eyes a little brighter, and no one would know he has acne scars along his left cheek by looking at it.

"Um ..." I bite my lip, wanting to be thankful, but again, not understanding why they all went in on jewelry, and hold my breath the closer RK gets. "Thanks. A lot." Still not inhaling, I turn to RK. "Thanks for the photo, too."

He smiles at me, and I return the expression, but as his lips near mine, I spin toward Cam and give her my 'what's going on?' signal, hoping no one else notices I've just dissed RK.

Facing our crowd, she says, "Who's ordering what?" and opens her menu, hiding behind it. Back to me, she mouths, 'Nothing. Why?'

There is something going on. I'm not stupid, just dirt poor. Mom's dream of saving for a beach trip is a big problem, and it makes me wonder if Cam knows about that idea. Why would Mom even consider that option, knowing we have nothing to spare in a week, let alone a month or a year? Sand, surf and sun may only be two hours away, but that's with a long-range tram ride or a really long walk.

Back to my menu, I don't even have to search for my dinner. It's the only meal I ever order because it's the cheapest.

Clark and RK start with appetizers as Cam leans into me and whispers, "Your mom said to go big. She transferred twenty credits to me."

Twenty credits? When has Mom had twenty credits to spare? In the last year, every appliance in our house has died and either not been replaced, or we found a refurbished, older model. I haven't bought new clothes in at least two years, but the ladies at the Hand-Me-Down shop know me and even save some of the better more 'in fashion' pieces for me. Twenty credits could have fixed a few of those pieces and bought me a new wardrobe.

There is definitely something going on. Remembering my manners, I finally say, "Thanks, Cam." *But I'm going to stick to the spaghetti.*

With food selection over, and Gabby, our waitress, off with a giant list of dishes to prepare, the chatter in the room starts up again.

Clark talks about how his dad's company just won some big,

major deal that means everyone in the office gets the standard increase in pay. Whatever that is.

Jen waves a breadstick around while she goes on and on about how her mom is up for some big prize at her office— something about breast cancer research, I think.

"So, Eri," RK says, "Did you get the invitation ... or are you officially a fluke?" He asks like our entire relationship hinges upon the answer.

Cam leans around my shoulder. "And? So? Did you?"

They'll hound me until I give in. I have a horrible time lying to people's faces, and I've already not said anything for too long. On a long sigh, staring at RK, I say, "Yes."

Cam hugs me from behind as RK reaches in and does the same from the front. Being sandwiched between them isn't exactly the spot I want to be on my birthday, and the gag hits me hard. Cam pulls me away, and I heave in a clean burst of Italian-scented air.

"I knew you weren't a fluke," she whispers into my ear. "See? Just because your Mom is doesn't mean anything."

I know she's not being mean every time she brings it up, and normally, the reference doesn't bother me, but in the last week she's mentioned that part of my life at least eight hundred times. Perhaps knowing for sure that I'm not like my mom distances us more. As much as I'm ready to start my life, I don't want her to be far, and I don't want Cam to think she can pick on Mom.

"So, what's your house? RK asks.

"Um ..." All the faces around the table angle toward me. I know they're all waiting, whether excited or afraid, I don't know, but curious for sure. "Red. The red house." Saying where I'm going out loud makes it even more real. Scarier, too.

The people in front of me say nothing.

They turn their heads, gazes reaching each other but no longer toward me.

Cam leans to my ear. "Are you sure?"

Blinking back my confusion, I say, "Yeah, why? I know we're not together, but—"

"Let me see the invitation."

I pull my P-Comm from my bag and hand it to her. Cam has no problem accessing my message, even though my device is six years old. Her eyes shift a little tiny bit as if she's scanning or reading. On the other side of me, RK inches away, a coolness reaching the skin of my bare arms where he'd been up against me.

"Well," Cam says. "She's right."

Of course I am. I know the addresses, just like everyone else, but I don't understand the blank stares.

"So, you're a red?" RK folds up his napkin and lays it on the table.

"Well … yeah."

"Sorry, but I gotta go." He slides from his chair and takes a few steps away.

Jen grabs his arm. "RK, that's not fair. This is Eri's birthday."

His head angles toward her, body poised to bolt. "Stay, then, but anyone who's going to the red house goes there for a reason, and not one you or I—or anyone else here—should get involved with." He yanks his arm from her grip and stalks the rest of the way out.

3

Tears prick my eyes and burn worse as Cam rubs my arm. "So you're going to the red house. It's ... no big deal."

My relationship with RK may have been on the outs, but why did the red house bug him so much? It's just a house. We go. We register. We test, get assignments and plans. The houses are separate so not everyone goes to the same one.

Right?

"I gotta go, too." Clark pushes back in his chair and stands. "He's my ride."

"Me, too," Bailey says. "Happy Birthday, Eri."

"Sorry, Eri." Jen shrugs and jumps up. "We all came together."

With no one left except Cam and I, the party's over, but what's before me is what I'm used to. Me. Cam. A plate of spaghetti—when it arrives.

Elbows propped on the table, I drop my head into my hands. "What did I do, Cam?"

"Oh, sweetie." Her tone goes back to that motherly one. "Forget about them. RK doesn't deserve you as it is. Ignore him."

Gabby walks up with three plates of food while another waitress follows her with the other three. "Everyone coming back?" she asks, placing my plate in front of me.

"Um ..." I start.

"Probably not." Cam accepts her plate of lasagna.

The rest of the dishes are taken away, though the frowns on the two employees faces have to reflect my own.

"So eat." Cam points a fork toward my plate.

My appetite disappeared when Bailey stood up.

Confusion still reigns in my mind. RK's going to the black house. Jen to the white. Clark to the white. Bailey to the black. Cam's going to the white house, but she doesn't have any issue with me, and no one else has an issue with her.

Does she? Do they?

I eye her as she eats, twirling pasta on my fork. My P-Comm buzzes against my plate. I tilt it up, giving myself something else to do.

Sorry, A. Think we should break up. -R

He's direct, I'll give him that.

"Was that your mom?" Cam asks.

"Um ..." I don't know what to think. I'm not happy. I'm not sad. I'm just blah.

She sets her fork down and shifts toward me. "You can't let this bother you, 'kay? I mean, RK's a jerk and ugly. Clark's his best friend and has to follow him. Bailey's just ... Bailey. She could have called her dad to pick her up, and Jen ... well ... she's just a Bailey clone."

Swirling more of the noodles, the red of the sauce making a hypnotizing set of concentric circles, a tear falls onto my plate, breaking the path of one of the lines.

The huge sigh next to me lets me know Cam's seen it. "Seriously, Eri, you haven't been this emotional since, like, the sixth grade. What gives?"

I tilt up to her, the entire day running through my mind. Everything weighs on me like some monstrous brick that spans both my shoulders. My birthday doesn't usually suck, but it's never been as bad as this one. No one's ever left, probably because no one's ever joined in. "I'll be fine." Managing those words is like pulling out my own hair one strand at a time. I know, in two days, life will be better, but at the moment, the constriction in my chest has reached a peak I'm not sure I can handle.

Rather than wait, I dig for the locket and flip it open. RK's photo stares back at me. Grabbing the fork, I stab his tiny face, puncturing the photo, and root around until the edge comes up. With one swift flip, the picture goes flying.

"Wow. What was that for?" Cam asks.

"He broke up with me."

"That was him? Fugly broke up with you by your ancient P-Comm?" She huffs. "I expected you to dump him any day now, but how un-cool. He could have, at least, waited until tomorrow. We could go egg his house or something." She says it as if it's a normal occurrence, a daily activity or just something to do.

A small laugh bursts from me. I never should have thought less of Cam. She may not be totally tactful, but she's always been my friend. Can't afford the eggs for the prank, but I'll take her being with me over the extra effort to pay RK back. "No. It's okay. Maybe we should box this up and just go to my house. Mom probably made some sugar cookies."

Cam runs a hand through her hair. "One of these days, I'm just going to buy you a chocolate cake. It's your fav, Eri. Why don't you just ask for it?"

The stupid pain in my heart, head and eyes returns. People with money don't understand. Yes, chocolate is my favorite, but sometimes, that's not what matters. The thought, the time mom puts into the cookies has to be enough for now. Once I have a real job, with real money and real food, I'll buy myself a cake. "I'd really just like to go if we can."

"Yeah, sure." Cam waves at our waitress, who's standing at the bar.

She comes over, a giant smile on her face. "Ready for dessert?"

"Nah, we just need to box up her dinner and leave," Cam says as I stare at the gift—one my so-called friends shouldn't have gotten me.

Three steps away and three back, the owner, Mr. Milton, joins Gabby.

"How are you, girls?" he asks.

"We're good," Cam says.

"You'll be paying for the other food, right?"

My jaw drops open. Mr. Milton knows I can't afford six meals, and the twenty credits my mom apparently gave Cam won't cover it, either.

"Oh, yeah, sure. We got it." Cam nods his way as she rifles through her bag.

Mr. Milton smiles. "We'll have it boxed so you can take it all home, then. Thanks for joining us tonight, ladies."

As he leaves, Cam gets really close to me. "Okay, listen. I have enough for you and me. I seriously wasn't expecting them all to bail, so after I give her my card and pay that, I'm giving her this one." She pulls out a card I don't recognize. "And when she goes to swipe it, we're outta here."

"But you need to get your—"

Cam shakes her head. "It's a dummy, silly."

"What?" I can't believe what she's said. Dummy credits have no funds attached to them. They look real, they process real, but they're totally illegal since they have no way of being tracked, and eventually the credits are deducted. No way can we use that. "We can't—"

"Yes, we can, or we're both going to be here doing dishes, or something gross that we shouldn't have to do."

"But—"

"No buts, Eri. We haven't gone through processing. We can't work, so we can't pay for this. You got—" She reaches for the bill, holds it up and flips it toward me. "Eighty-five credits?"

"No, but—"

"I said no buts." She glances toward the bar and smiles. "Sometimes, you just gotta do what you gotta do."

Gabby brings out the boxes and refills Cam's drink.

"Can you run as much as possible off this account?" Cam asks. "And twenty off this one?" She hands Gabby the credit gift Mom must have given her. That one, I know, is legit. Mom would never, ever use a dummy. "And let me know what's left?"

"Sure can." Gabby takes Cam's real credits with her back to the bar. We sit for three whole minutes, and Cam stands as Gabby returns. "You've got a balance of sixty-one, forty-two," Gabby says.

"Okay, cool." Cam holds out the dummy. I reach out to grab it, but she yanks it back. Her eyes narrow before widening. "I insist, Eri."

My heart drops into my chest, but I can't let her hurt Milton's, and I can't let her get in trouble because of me. Eventually, someone will backtrack to the video, find us at the table, see Cam hand over the dummy and come after us. They'll match up the day, the purchase and the people in less than forty-eight hours. "No, really," I say as my heart hammers in my chest. "Remember, you used up that one getting cans for the soup kitchen."

Gabby's head swivels back and forth between us.

Cam's glare penetrates my soul. After a second, she raises

one eyebrow. "Fine, Eri. Dinner's on you." With a huff, she turns and storms away.

The four white boxes stacked in front of me add to that weight from before. My mom gets stiffed too much for me to do that to someone else.

Cam's through the exit before I even move, the bell sending a sweet chime back toward me.

Shifting toward where Gabby's standing with me, I know what I have to do. I lift the four boxes and heave a few sighs. "Um … I think I'll need to talk to Mr. Milton."

Unfortunately for me, the man I need to talk to waits at the end of the bar. Gabby motions me right on over.

As I approach, he lifts his head, hand poised with pencil above a large tablet. "What can I do for you, Ms. Keating?"

"Um …" Sliding the boxes onto the counter, I draw myself closer.

"They left you the bill, didn't they?"

Somehow, I manage to nod.

Mr. Milton hangs his head. When he meets my gaze again, he says, "What should we do about this?"

"I have ten credits." It's everything I have saved for over a year. "I know that leaves me fifty something to cover, but I'm willing to wash dishes, or clean up, or do whatever I can. I know I can't work on the books, but I'm free right up until I have to go, and—"

He holds up a hand. "You'll cover the rest of the bill by yourself? Why not make your friends—"

Shaking my head, I say, "It's not their problem." Though it really is, but something tells me they aren't going to help. Ever.

His pen slaps against the screen. "Okay, then. Eight hours should cover it."

"May I take this back to my mom first?"

Mr. Milton slides the boxes away from me. "I'll just put these in the chiller, and you can take them home when you're done. We close at eleven tonight, so that's a solid three hours you can fit in now."

"Okay." I sound just like the nickname I'd once been called: Mouse.

"The bathrooms need to be checked first, though." He points toward the back.

Happy birthday to me.

Eleven thirty couldn't come fast enough. Mr. Milton let me go after I extracted what seemed like my thousandth dish from the washer and stacked it. The only good part of the situation came in the four boxes of leftovers that Mom and I can eat for dinner for the next week, at least.

A creak accompanies my opening of our front door, and the soft yellow light of the living room.

Mom tilts up from the divan, where she sits with her Comms unit in hand. "Hi, baby. How was your night?" She smiles, expecting, I presume, an awesome report, given how long I stayed.

I raise the boxes with the intent not to answer. "I brought leftovers." With a forced smile, I take them into our kitchen, teeny-tiny compared to Milton's. "We've got dinner for the whole week, Mom."

A squeak sounds behind me as I lay the boxes on the nearly empty shelves. Glancing over my shoulder, I find Mom at our kitchen table, her elbows on the flat surface, chin balancing on her clasped hands. With the fridge door closed again, the kitchen darkens.

"Come, sit with me, Erianna." Her tone tells me she needs

to talk about something serious.

My inner anxiety meter shoots up to high as I take the only other seat we have. Palms to the fake, plastic wood, I slide my hands left and right, wiping off nothing. We may not have much, but it's ours, and Mom and I both keep the house clean.

She takes a deep breath, green eyes darting side to side before stopping, focused in my direction. "Honey, I just want you to know that, as an undocumented citiz—"

"Mom . . ."

Her hands lift. "Let me finish."

I try hard not to let my shoulders slump or to let the guilt-o-gauge overtake the anxiety meter.

"As an undocumented citizen, what you teens call a fluke, life isn't always this tough. I just . . . I didn't pursue additional education, and when your father . . . left us, I just couldn't bring myself to go back."

"Mom—"

She shakes her head. "Please, baby, let me finish. Okay?"

What can I say? 'No, Mom, don't tell me about your life because I'm not going to be like you?' Instead, I tuck my hands under my butt and figuratively zip my lips.

"Just because the government doesn't support . . . flukes, doesn't mean you won't have many, many opportunities. And, if it's something you want, you can apply for a number and try to get status, but, baby, it's just not necessary." Mom closes her eyes, her lids quivering.

I know why she's hurting. Mia went after her application like a fire to dry brush. She wanted an invitation. She begged for one, even going down to the registration office and telling them they'd overlooked her, that she wasn't meant to be a fluke.

After a moment, Mom opens her eyes again. "I'm sorry, baby. This isn't about her."

Her. The girl, who, once she did get her acceptance, never came back.

If I didn't hear the emotion in Mom's voice, the glossiness in her eyes tells me Mia's absence is still Mom's biggest open wound—worse than Dad dying the summer before I turned four, leaving her on one income, with two kids.

Mom swipes a hand under her nose. "I shouldn't be talking about this on your birthday." Her lips curve up. "Today is a happy day." She pats the table. "Well, happy night. In another few minutes, it'll be tomorrow, and your adult life will start." She breathes in deep. "Now, off to bed with you, and in the morning, we'll start thinking about what comes next."

I'm still trying to get up the nerve to tell her how wrong she is and how we won't have anything to talk about because the national service agencies do know about me, they have me in their system, and like Mia finally did, I'm going to leave.

Unlike Mia, though, I'll be back. I want to promise that I will, because Mom deserves to have one of her daughters around. I want Mom to move in with me, to get out of our rinky-dink living space. I want more so she can have more.

Mom pushes back and stands. She holds out her arms in that way she does when she wants a hug but wants me to want it, too.

I always do, so I get up and move to her and lean in, wrapping my arms around her. "I love you, Mom."

Her hands rub up and down my back. "I love you, too, baby. Always have. Always will."

I hope so. Even thinking it makes my heart hurt. When I get around to telling her, I'm sure she'll still tell me she loves me, but the disappointment will be there. The ache running through me is already powerful, but making her feel bad will be worse than anything I have to go through.

Maybe there's a way I can go and not tell her. Go and come back and her not even know. Go, get a job, credits, and surprise her with something she's never had. Yeah. That's what I need to do. Show Mom I can do this. For her. Not like Mia did.

"All righty, then. Off to bed with you, my adult girl." She ruffles my hair and extracts herself, her hands moving to my cheeks. "Still can't believe you're eighteen, but I couldn't be more proud."

Yup, going to have to keep this one a secret.

"'Night, Mom." I turn away, fighting with my heart to stop the pounding.

By the time I hit my room and close the door, my chest is tight.

Flopping onto my bed, I curl up with bunny and stare at the screen of my P-Comm.

Guilt, lies, falsehoods, whatever it is, presses down upon me like an anvil-sized burden.

4

The sun brings a new day and Mom's voice drifting from the living room where she's teaching some kid from somewhere else in the world, on some subject I have no clue about. Mom once told me that most teachers work in the schools, but they have set hours. Since all teachers have to be documented citizens, they're limited to thirty-five hours a week, leaving Mom with a great opportunity: tutoring. Nights, holidays or when someone needs her help for a test, are her busiest times, but we never really know who's going to call or when they will.

Or if they'll pay. That's the bad part.

At least she's not a hooker or a bag lady like crazy Sally. For a fluke, Mom really has done a great job with our life.

Morning also finds Cam back in my room, apology made, but wonder nagging at me. Despite the fact her house is three times the size of mine, she almost always comes to me. She says it's more peaceful. I can understand that, since her family qualifies for in-home support services, and someone's always there being noisy, cleaning, cooking, doing laundry for her or her five brothers. It makes me wonder why her mom wants her to learn all the mundane household stuff if she'll always have help.

"Why did you stay, Eri?" Cam files away at her nails, sitting on my bed.

This is a first. Cam never, as in ever that I can remember, brings up what she calls 'bad memories'. Walking out without paying and leaving me qualifies in that way—at least to me.

"I had to talk to Mr. Milton." It's not a lie, so it leaves my lips without much additional guilt build up. Besides, what am I going to say? *You're a cheating scumbag using dummy credits to pay for the meal that you ate.* I can't do that. She's my best friend. The one who stood up for me when everyone in my level two educenter picked on my holey shoes at the start of second grade, saying it didn't matter what anyone wore if they didn't have any money, just that they were nice.

She turns toward me, her file stopped mid-pull. "I waited for, like, ten minutes and had to walk to the PTD all by myself. Luckily, Jen got a ride and was coming back, so she brought me home."

Now, I get it. Her comment didn't relate to me and paying for the food, but in Cam getting a way home—not alone.

I pick at the hangnail on my finger.

"I'm really sorry about RK, too." She flops back on my blanket, her hair spilling out around her head. "He's a real jack-donk for dumping you on your birthday." The swish-swish of the emery board resumes. "You're not better than him, but he's just fugly."

I really want to say, "I know someone else who wasn't very nice on my birthday, too," but I keep silent. As I always do. Better to not rock the boat, especially since I'll need Cam's help to get to registration without my mom knowing.

"And, you know, the whole birthday thing ... we all really thought you'd like the pendant, you know."

Her gift is still in my bag, on my shelf. I did like it but still don't understand it. None of them have done anything like it in eighteen years. Why now? Why, when they had to know they'd ditch me if I didn't get into their houses? I still don't understand why the red house is so bad, either.

"We're good, right?" she asks, as if there's really not dozens of reasons for me to be irritated with her.

"It's okay. Life happens." I can't believe I've let her off the hook. Then again, Mom always says some arguments aren't worth having and some fights aren't worth fighting.

It's better, sometimes, just to forgive and forget.

"What should we do today? Wanna go to the commerce center?" Cam flips to her side, facing me. "We have to buy some new clothes so we can make really good impressions on the evaluators."

Here we go again with the clothes. Cam's got a closet full, dozens more than the thirty-three items normal people get to purchase each year—outside of our educenter uniforms. "I'm just going to wear my—"

"Noooo!" She jumps up and grabs my hand.

I end up sliding to the edge of the bed and toppling over onto my knees from the force of her yank. I'm stuck as Cam lowers to me.

"Oh, my Oz, Eri! I didn't think you'd fall off! Have you lost fifty pounds or something?"

Shaking my head, I adjust so I'm sitting on my butt, cross-legged. At least that way, I won't fall again.

Cam mirrors my positioning. "What's going on? I can't go tomorrow, you know. Mom's got this whole goodbye dinner thing planned."

Goodbye? We go to the address on the invitation. We listen to information, and for seven days we're evaluated mentally and physically on our various abilities, told what life's going to be like at the end, choose our profession based on interests and skills proven, and we get assigned housing, a mentor and whatever else to get started. It's not like we're going away for-ever. *Right?* I realize I've scrunched my brow through the whole thought, and I run my hand over it to relax my face.

Cam slaps my knee. "I mean, who makes a party to say goodbye to *childhood?*"

Childhood. Now I get it. That's the important part of the conversation, too. Cam obviously couldn't care less about what happens after registration. "Right, I know. That's so babyish." Something inside me longs for a party for me—not a surprise one, and not one with people who ditch me because of the house I'm supposed to go to.

Her head flops forward, and she fiddles with the laces on her shoes. "It's kinda sweet, though, too, don't you think?" Her tone suggests she's looking to me for confirmation, something Miss Confident does all the time, yet I'm not sure she ever re-ally listens.

"Oh, yeah. Your mom's sweet like that." It's all I can come up with. Lame, I know, but it's an agreement of some sort and might be all I can give her, unless she tells me why she had a dummy credit.

I realize, as I think it, that I'm not letting go, not forgiving, and I've not been invited to Cam's party. Me, the girl she's been friends with since before level one educenter isn't invited.

With her gaze on mine, Cam says, "So can we go to the commerce center, then? We can catch the PT—"

Which doesn't cost money, thankfully.

"—eat over at the food court—"

Which costs a little money that I no longer have, or none if you show them a meal card, of which I don't have.

"—shop 'til we drop and get some new drapes for our bods,—"

Which will cost way too much.

"—and be home by four so you can ..." She waves her hand through the air. "... do whatever you do, and I can go help my mother."

Work to pay off the rest of the four boxes of food I have in my fridge.

"C'mon, Eri. I need to get out. Mom's acting like I'm about to die, not find out what I'll be doing for the rest of my life, and I know it won't be baby making. I'm too smart for that."

What can I say? 'No, Cam, I have no money, no extra job, am working to pay off your mess from last night and, oh, by the way, my mom doesn't know I got my invitation, so there is no party for me, and I can't fake it either.'

I should. I really, really should. "Yeah, sure. And—"

"Woo-hoo!" Cam grabs my hand and jumps up.

Rather than have my arm get torn from its socket, I stand, too. I know I'm acting like some major push over—worse than normal; I just can't seem to say 'no' or hurt anyone's feelings at all these days.

"Two more sleeps, Eri, and life really gets started! We are going to rock the world!"

That or it's going to eat me alive.

A shiver runs through me, but with Cam's infectious laugh and her constant tugging, I'm out the door, waving bye to Mom, and on the sidewalk waiting at the public transpo stop in less than a minute.

Someday, maybe someday, I'll find a way to tell my friends exactly how I feel. *Right. That'll happen.* A laugh bursts free.

"What's so funny?" Cam asks, rubbing her arms where the chill of winter's air must have touched her skin before we reached the warmth of the waiting booth.

"Just thinking to myself."

"And you're funny now?" She nudges me with her arm, a

smile on her face.

"Yeah, I think I am." Better than being sad. Or mad. Or depressed. All of which I could be.

Someday, it might be nice to get new friends.

⚬══━══⚬

Cam and I pile onto the tram, dropping our butts to a shared seat and squishing up against the window. Sometimes, I wish Cam would get clearance for a personal vehicle. Her parents have offered, but she refuses to learn, and Cam won't let them or her brothers transport us.

Then again, RK had his own transpo, one that had been turned in from a junkyard before it went to recycling. I hated riding in it because it used energy like nobody's business; his parents must have had to pony up some serious credits to keep it going.

Around us are kids our age, women with babies, men in suits and a couple of old grannies with birds I hope are fake in their little hats. Staring out the window, I watch the roads, houses, buildings, everything go by—like I do every time—as Cam gabs about whatever's on her mind.

After fourteen gazillion stops, which is really only five, the intercom reminds us we'll have to change trams or head back toward home. Cam and I wait as the grannies go first, followed by the lady with the kid that started screaming one stop before.

Something tickles my neck as I stand waiting for the guy in the suit, and I run a hand under my ponytail, expecting the tag in my jacket is poking me. My finger hits something, and I tremble as I grasp it, preparing to swat away whatever has crawled into my coat. I glance down, searching for the offending bug, hoping it's not a cockroach, and pray my stomach can handle whatever I find.

Once, when I turned ten, Mom bought me a jacket at the Hand-Me-Down store. She hadn't checked the pockets before she gave it to me, and thanks to the giant beetle that crawled out when I slipped my hand in, Mom checks all my pockets first now.

Cam's already in the aisle and halfway out as I turn to see what I wiped off me and onto the floor. I may not want to know, but I have to, just in case whatever it is would breed in our house. Or worse, on me.

On a shiver, I search the seat and find nothing—except at the seat's edge, a note-chip sits tucked between the brown vinyl. Since I don't have any chips, Cam must have dropped it, so I grab it, and my bag, and hurry away, swiping at my hair more. Nothing else tickles my skin.

"What took you so long?" she asks, as I step down the last of the three stairs onto the sidewalk.

"This was between the seats. You must have dropped it." I hold out the one-inch-square chip to her.

"Not mine. I only use pink ones."

"Your brothers? Did—"

"It's not mine, Eri. Now, c'mon." Just like she did at my house, she grabs my hand, dragging me forward a few steps.

"Maybe I should give it back to the driv—"

"If someone lost it, they're just SOL."

I yank free from her hold and start back toward the tram, but it's already pulling away, and they don't stop once they get started unless a leg or arm is caught under the rail. I'm not willing to risk my life for a note-chip.

Cam's tapping her foot as I spin back around. "Really? People lose those all the time. They cost, like, nothing."

Yeah, Cam, to you, they cost nothing. "Fine, let's just go already," I say.

The commerce center is packed with people. Given we're just a day from New Year's Eve, and a few days past Christmas, it shouldn't surprise me. Loads of voices among the four floors of the CC ratchet up the decibel level, though the scent of baking bread hits me first. The sniff I take is involuntary.

Cam giggles next to me.

"What?" I search the area in front of us but don't see anything that would make her laugh.

"You do that every time we come here, you know?"

"Do what?"

She lifts her nose and makes an audible sniffing sound.

"Oh." I walk toward the smells as my stomach grumbles. We'll pass the store, but since Cam doesn't eat bread, won't stop, not that I could buy anything. I can at least lust after the cakes, pastries and other sugary yumminess in the display cases.

Walking by, I take a huge whiff, doing my best not to let Cam know I'm inhaling the scents to try and stop more growling. If only smells could feed people.

A quick peek inside reveals luscious items stacked on shelves. A couple sits at a small table-for-two, sharing what has to be a muffin as big as my hand. A girl leans against the entrance frame, the latest PCD, a model several years younger than my P-Comm in one hand and something chocolate in the other.

More grumbles take over in the pit of my belly.

Move on, Anna, or you're going to go in that store and try to buy something with no credits.

With Cam tugging me on, I glance back one last time and inhale the heavenly scents. A girl with dark black hair to the middle of her back turns, her profile illuminated by the counter lights, and I freeze.

It can't be.

My stomach squeezes and tightens as if I haven't eaten in days.

"Come on, Eri," Cam says.

Standing there an extra moment, I shake my head, but the face I grew up with has etched itself into my mind. "Mia?"

"What?" Cam asks.

Mortified that Cam even heard me, my entire body heats up. "Nothing." People bustle out of the shop, but not the lady with the hair. If my sister lived, worked or shopped, anywhere near our house, she'd come visit. *Right?* Even if I haven't seen her in four years, she wouldn't stay away. *Would she?* Would she even look the same after four years? That long ago, I had super short hair after a bad experience with one of the many hair irons Mia acquired from who-knows-who. She could have cut it, or colored it, or done anything since then.

And I wouldn't know. Because she never came back.

The jerk on my arm pulls me from my thoughts and growing brood. "What *are* you doing?" Cam asks. "We have stores to hit. Clothes to buy. We have to look good!"

"Sorry. Thought I saw someone ... uh ... from the educenter building."

"Well, duh, it's break. Everyone's here. What else do we have to do?" She slides her arm through my crooked one and pulls me away. "Why can't we have more than one commerce center per district? Huh? You know it would be so much better not to have to share space with some people. Especially S-D-eleven people." She's weirdly whiny, considering we're southern, district eleven people.

As she speaks, I can't help but glance back, wondering if I'll see the woman walk out—to either confirm my vision or prove just how crazy I am.

It's all because you earned your registration that you're think-ing about her.

Yeah, that's it. Has to be.

Cam heads straight for Rise21, her favorite store—ever—bypassing every other shop to get there and taking me from my ghost sighting.

Inside the store, the brightest colored shirts hang on racks, the pinks, fuchsias and azures laying claim to my inner de-sires. I bought a shirt from Rise21 two years ago, and I still have it in my closet. It was a season behind the trends and on the ninety-percent off rack. Thankfully, what I'd saved for a whole year covered it. For anyone else, it still would have cost a month's clothing credit. It's probably the shirt I'll wear for my interview, too.

"How can we help you, today?" one of the clerks asks.

"Oh, we're just looking," Cam says, pulling me toward the middle racks where her favorites usually wait for her. "Oooh, look, Eri." She holds up a super-bright blue blouse with a shell neckline that I know will fit skin-tight to her size-two body.

"It's pretty." I wouldn't wear it, even if I could, and given last night's episode with the dummy credit, I'm wondering why we're even in the store. I've got to ask her, otherwise, I'll start shaking which will eventually turn into an outright panic attack. "Cam—"

"Or this one?" Both hands are up with shirts in each, one purple, one strawberry complete with weird polka dots.

"Um ... sure, but, Cam, I need—"

"Ooh!" She hangs them both up and stalks off to another rack.

Like the good little doggie I am, I follow.

She turns with a shirt and holds it out. The raspberry is so pretty and the neckline is a simple V. I reach out and slide my fingers along the soft fabric. Clothes lust takes over.

"You should try it on." She thrusts the hanger and item at me.

"I can't—"

"Of course you can." With a roll of her eyes, she grabs my shoulders, turns me around, and pushes me toward the back. On the way toward the dressing rooms, she grabs the two she'd first picked up. "In here." Cam pulls the door tight.

We've tried clothes on in the same room before, so it's no big deal, but even trying on a shirt that would eat up a month's credit from working at Milton's can't be smart. No way can I afford it, and if I rip, it, I'll have no way of paying for it. There's just no reason to try it on—to tempt myself.

Cam thrusts it into my face. "I have extra credits."

She's said that before, but I'm not sure I believe her. The cost of dinner would have been about the same as the shirt. I narrow my eyes, waiting for the admission. "About that . . ."

"Oh, give it a rest, Eri. You're so rigid. Live a little." She whips off her shirt—one she probably bought a month ago, and slips on the first. Flattening out the wrinkles, she stares at herself in the mirror. "I'm not sure about this one." From right to left, she turns her hips as if considering. "What do you think?"

"It's pretty." I'm still holding the shirt she found for me, the soft fabric running between my fingers. "But, Cam . . . the credits. I mean—"

"Nah. Not worth it. Try yours on." One of her manicured fingers angles toward me, a Cam-like order, if ever I've been given one.

"I really shou—"

Cam glares at me, complete with pursed lips. "Seriously, Eri. If you think those evaluators are going to take your mousiness as confidence, you've got another thing coming."

Fighting with Cam is like tearing down a brick wall with a spoon. There just isn't any point in the exercise. Since it's obvious Cam's going to avoid any discussion about money, and since I know I can't afford the shirt and it'll end up back on the rack, I could live a little. I could just try it on.

Lifting my T-shirt off, I drop it to the chair. Switching to the hanger, I strip off the new shirt and slide it over my torso.

"Oh, my, Oz, Eri! That is gorgeous on you!" She forces me into a spin, the material hugging my nothing-of-a waist and flaring out just a little over the top of my old jeans. "Now, where's your pendant?"

"Uh ... in my bag."

"I want to see the whole thing on." She digs through my stuff and pulls out the box, before extracting the necklace and clasping it around my neck.

It is beautiful, and the deep red of the jewel adds some color to my otherwise pale complexion. An instant pang hits my heart. *This was stupid.* I shouldn't have tried it on.

Next to me again, with her hands on her hips, she says, "That is *too* gorgeous. I'm buying it."

My headshaking begins as soon as she says it. "You can't, Cam. Not with what happened last night." The only reason she might have a dummy is if something happened and she ran out of money. There's no other logical reason.

Cam flashes the whites of her eyes at me. "Really, Eri?"

"Really what?"

"You've got to lighten up. That was a one-time dealio. Just wanted to see what it was like. I was going to pay them back later and just lie and say the account had a problem."

I cocked my head. "For real?"

"Of course. I'm not that mean. Now, this." Her extended

finger traces a line up and down my upper body. "This . . . you have to have it for the interview. Have to, Eri."

It's too much of a gift. I'll never have anything to give back to her and could never make it up in a million years.

Man, I want this shirt.

But it's not right.

With a heaviness in my chest, I take off my I-wish-my-life-was-different shirt and attach it to the hanger.

Cam's lips turn down, but she grabs her second shirt, tries it on and decides she doesn't like either. With her selections and mine, she walks up to the counter and holds out the two toward the clerk. "Do you have these in a size two? I didn't see them on the rack, and these don't fit me."

Don't fit her?

The clerk takes both from Cam. "I think so, actually. Thought we had them on the rack, but let me check in back." With a giant smile, the lady walks toward the back door.

Cam grabs my hand and pulls me toward the exit.

"What're you doing?" I'm walking with her for no more than two seconds when it dawns on me. "No, Cam, stop!" I can't get her fingers from around my wrist.

She barrels ahead, me slipping on the flat surface and failing to get a good grip, and stepping out and through the doors.

As I break free, the alarm sounds, and Cam takes off but glances back with a huge frown.

I follow her gaze. The shirt she'd had in her hand is in mine.

5

Sitting in the administrative offices with the head of security, and waiting for my mom, is a situation I never once thought I'd find myself. Ever.

"Now, young lady ..." He pushes the identification pad toward me.

With my thumb to the screen, the system says, "Erianna Price Keating. Eighteen years, one day."

The officer switches toward a bigger, desk mounted screen for a second before returning to me. "You haven't yet been through selection?"

"No, sir."

He hangs his head and sighs. "Still technically underage, then." His hand flops onto his PCD—a much larger and more sophisticated-looking P-Comm. I have to wonder how much it can do since mine pretty much only accepts and sends out-going audio and text. PCDs can do it all. Of course, it makes sense for the head of security to have one.

Cut it out, Eri. Stay focused on the situation not the gadgets. Focusing on the situation, though, makes me shake, so I return to staring at his fancy personal comms device.

After a quick touch with his thumb, he brings the unit to his ear. "Mrs. Keating, this is Don Handle. I'm the head of security at—" He pauses, I presume as Mom freaks out jumping to conclusions. "Yes, ma'am, we have your daughter here in the off—" With the second pause, he turns his big burly, bearded face toward me. "She's just fine, ma'am, but we'll need you to come down and discuss—" Another pause earns Mom an eyeroll she won't see.

I wish he'd increase volume so I can hear both sides of the conversation. Just to prepare.

After another stint of silence, he says, "Thank you," and lays the device on the table.

"Now, Miss Keating, let's chat. Shall we?"

By 'chat', I expect a crucifixion, but since I've never, *ever* been in this situation, I expect my imagination is running away from me.

"Tell me what happened in Rise21, today."

As a fluke, Mom says the best defense is silence, because what I don't say, the authorities can't hold me to. Of course, they can see everything, so I'm not sure her logic works. "What about the video?"

"We'll have that queued up in a few minutes." A knock at the door has him turning, and the clerk from Rise21 enters.

"I've made my statement to your assistant." She glares at me. "I'd like a copy of the video prior to her release, please, and I'd like a ban on both that girl and the other—"

The officer holds up a palm to the clerk. "We'll take care of all that part—"

"She's a shoplifter!" Her hands fly up in the air and land on her thighs.

The officer pushes back from his desk, nudges the clerk toward the door and closes her out. He meanders back toward me and clasps his hands. "We'll take care of that later. For now, since you're not a legal adult, we'll just wait for your guardian."

Sure we will because then the day will get better.

I can't even laugh at my own internal sarcasm.

Mom barges in thirty minutes later, I presume because she had to finish her work and catch the tram. "What the hell is going on?" Her face is red, dark hair up in a ponytail. She looks so much like Mia, it's scary—whereas I look like an emaciated version of Dad, or the one photo I've seen of him.

Security Officer Handle, as I learned while we sat and stared at each other, stands from behind his desk and extends a hand. "Have a seat, ma'am."

She doesn't leave the frame, glaring at me. "Explain yourself, Erianna Price."

I want to say, 'Cam was going to buy my shirt, but then she decided to steal it', but I can't get the words out. I know that makes me the stupid one of the two of us, but throwing her under the bus, as the old saying that Mom uses goes, seems wrong. My answer is a shrug.

"Erianna!" Her voice ratchets up. "Shoplifting? Have you learned nothing about small businesses and how they survive, whether owned by a fluke or not?"

You have no idea, Mom.

"Ma'am," Handle says, "perhaps we could calm down a bit. Your daughter is not actually in trouble."

My head tilts up. "What?" I ask as Mom does, too. How does he know? Did he learn something and not share when he went out for five minutes? He didn't mention anything before.

Handle waves her toward the chair next to me. "Have a seat, and I'll explain."

She lowers to the chair, her handbag with the ripped corner landing on her lap.

He steeples his fingers and drops his chin on the upper

point. "The young lady with you ..." He pauses as if I should fill in the blank.

Mom turns to me. "Who was with you?"

"Ju-just Cam."

Mom faces the officer again. "And?"

He turns the screen that's been facing away from me the whole time. The view is of me and Cam. He taps the screen. The color video replays Cam grabbing my hand and pulling me toward the exit.

"What are you doing?" I ask in a voice that has never sounded like my own. I walk with her for no more than two seconds when I say, "No, Cam, stop!" and claw at her hand around my wrist.

She forges ahead, my stupid plastic shoes making me slide right along with her. Heat creeps into my cheeks. It's embarrassing enough knowing Cam got me twice in two days, but now everyone knows my shoes are the cheapest of the cheap.

Out the door, Cam goes, me in her wake as the alarm blares, and I'm free, standing there in the opening, holding the shirt.

"Were you going to steal that shirt?" Handle taps his fingertips together.

I shake my head.

"Were you going to purchase it?"

My head movement continues.

"Why did your friend try and take it?"

I shrug. I really don't have any idea. She'd convinced me she had good intentions. I'd believed her when she said the whole situation with Milton's would be taken care of. She'd said 'buy' to me, though I wouldn't have let her do that either because of the price.

"How long have you known her?" he asks.

"All my life." That fact burns more than anything. I don't

think I really know Cam at all anymore. Maybe all the extra commentary about how much better she is than me has been a sign she didn't like me anymore and just didn't know how to tell me.

Mom leans forward, determination in the set of her shoulders. "You can't hold her."

He touches the screen, and it goes black. "I—"

"She's never been in trouble before."

"I—"

"I'll take this to the cour—"

"Ma'am." Handle's voice is low and deep.

Mom jerks back a little.

"I don't intend to keep her. We believe this video clearly shows the situation, and we've taken the only other party in question into custody."

Air gushes from Mom and me. At the same time, my heart beats faster at the idea that Cam is going through the same thing as I am.

"Then we're done here?" Mom asks.

Yes, yes, yes, we are. Thank goodness. I slide to the end of my seat, preparing to rise.

The officer nods as his door opens, yet again, and another guy in uniform crooks a finger at him. Handle rises and heads over where he has some sort of whispery conversation I'd have to really focus on to even catch snippets of words.

Rather than pry, I sit with my hands in my lap, Mom at my shoulder. At least I've got her support.

Handle turns toward us and takes the two miniature steps to get in front of me. His massive finger points down toward my chest.

Mom swats at his hand. "How unprofessional! I'll—"

"The necklace," he says as his cheeks flush, and Mom's turn

bright red. "Where did you get that?"

I reach up, touching my only birthday present. "Um . . . my friends gave it to me."

"May I see it?"

Mom nudges my shoulder, my only indicator that I should comply. Hands behind my neck, I work to get the latch apart, but of course, I can't. "Mom? Can you—"

She flips my hair to the side and unlinks it in two seconds flat. Probably a world record.

"When did you receive this?" Handle asks as Mom passes it to him.

"Last night," I say.

"From your friends?"

I nod.

"Did they mention where they acquired this piece?"

The questions give me that niggle I had the night before. "No, sir."

"I presume, since you mentioned your birthday, that this was a birthday gift?"

"Yes, sir."

With a deep sigh, Handle lays my necklace on his desk. "I'm sorry, Miss Keating, but the computer tagged this as one of the stolen items from a recent break-in."

My hand goes back up to my chest as my heart jumps. "But . . ." I don't even know what to say. My friends would never steal. They probably got it from a store, and it just looks like the stolen one. "But . . ." No way Cam or RK, or any of them, had anything to do with a break-in. No way. They aren't that stupid. They can't be. They wouldn't.

Would they?

Handle walks around his desk and sits in his chair. He taps a few things on his PCD, and with another big blow out of air, turns his unit toward me.

My necklace, my pendant, my gift stares at me from his screen. "Mine isn't real, though." Finally, something eloquent has passed through my lips. "It's just a replica or something." Has to be. Even if they went in together, they wouldn't have bought something more than a single credit from each of them.

Right?

Handle lifts the chair, pops open the heart, pulls out a big magnifying glass and holds the silver jewel under it. A "Mmm", a "huh", and a huff follows. He holds out the glass and the jewel. "Take a look."

"At what?" Mom asks, taking both from Handle before I can.

"There's an etching."

An etching? Wasn't it blank?

"This piece is an antique, from back in the mid nineteen hundreds. It's worth about a million dollars, not as much by the standards then, but you know."

I don't really. I don't understand anything that has happened in the last twenty-four hours. My birthday should have been simple and normal and uneventful.

Mom squints as if she's trying to see what Handle saw.

"What does it say?" he asks.

Her lips squish together. "JFK." Her head pops up. "Kennedy? From … what was that … two hundred years ago?" She switches her glare toward me instead of the officer. "How did you get this?"

Searching for something to focus on, I land on Mom's hand, the chain draped from it. "It was a birthday present."

"And you accepted this? Eri." She says my name as if those three letters are the biggest disappointment in the world.

"It was a gift," I say, as if I'm trying to convince even myself.

"We don't accept gifts like this."

You don't, I want to say. I've never been given something so beautiful before yesterday. I say neither.

The pretty bauble goes back to Handle. "You'll take care of returning this item, then?" Mom asks.

Handle rubs at his chin. "Fortunately for Miss Keating here, surveillance captured the frame sizes of all those who'd entered during the heist. If she had some meat on her bones, she might be under arrest right now, but we know she wasn't there."

Mom releases an audible exhalation. "So that's it, then? You know what happened with the shirt and this."

Handle nods. "We'll make sure this isn't recorded for her registration interview, as well."

"What?" Mom jerks back as if she's been shot.

I'm pretty sure my entire body freezes, teetering on the edge of my chair. He knows about registration? He knows for sure I'm not a fluke? Had I mentioned something? I don't remember saying anything. *Of course he knows.* He's probably been in my file, seen my letter and knows everything about me—all the stuff I haven't told Mom, on top of everything that's happened today.

Handle coughs into his hand. "We'll make sure—"

"I heard you." Mom scoots forward. "But ... her *interview*?" She spins to me. "Erianna?"

Fish-mouth syndrome begins.

"Eri?" Her tone has gone from shocked to sad. To find out I lied, or omitted at least, and here like some criminal, is the worst possible timing. My own heart hurts, and I don't know what to say. Before I can offer even the tiniest of excuses, Mom rises. Her lip quivers as she holds out a hand to Officer Handle. "Thank you for your support and for being kind about the situation."

Knife ... slice heart. Insert deep and twist.

I'm officially the worst daughter ever.

With that, she walks to the door, her back to me, opens and exits.

Scrambling out of my seat, I race after her. "Mom!" She keeps going, down the stark white hallway with the various security posters and rules stuck to the walls. "Mom!"

A door opens just behind her, and Cam steps out, eyes red-rimmed, her Dad's hand on her elbow. He glares at me as if he's just encountered a bear and growling should make it, meaning me, go away. Before I can even say anything, he jerks her forward, mumbling something I can't hear, but I get the gist.

'Why would you ever get involved with a girl like that?'

After the last twenty four hours, I'm wondering what I've done to be shunned by everyone I know and everyone I love.

Anger makes me clench my fingers into fists.

Cam can diss me, but Mom can't.

I race toward Cam and her dad, nudging them out of the way as I search for Mom. The hallway leads to the first floor and the gazillion people milling about, doing whatever they do in the middle of new-stuff heaven. Normally, Mom walks through the north lot, so I take off, darting around people going the opposite way, chasing after a figure I can't see.

Breaking out through the double doors, I scan the parking area. Transpos back out and in; the tram stops at the farthest point on the edge of the perimeter.

To the left, people.

Right. More people.

Mom, too.

"Mom!" I take off at a run, catching up as she reaches the tram's stop. "Mom!"

She whirls, tears falling. "What do you want, Eri?"

"I—" I suck in air, trying to regulate my breathing from all the running. "I wanted to say I'm sorry. I was going to tell you, I just …"

"Just what? Didn't want me to know? I'm your mother, Erianna."

Head down, I say, "I'm sorry."

"For what?" The way she asks means she's gone back from sad to furious. "For lying to me? For withholding the truth? Did you not think enough of me that you had to hide it?"

My lips part, but admitting she's right is harder than I imagined. I should have told her when I first found out that she and I didn't share a status. Hanging my head again, I kick at the rocks, the cold of the falling night hitting me as my adrenaline wears off. Guilt quickly replaces that. "Yes," I manage after too long.

Mom huffs as another tram bleeps its one-minute warning. "I think you need to think about this a little more. You're an adult now. At least your sister didn't lie to me."

The low blow stings. My fingertips and toes even hurt. Comparing me to Mia seems so wrong, but in a way, I can see Mom's point.

"Someday, you'll appreciate everything I've done for you."

"I do!" I waste no time saying that. "When haven't I?"

Mom burns me with her glare. "The mere fact I had to learn about my daughter's status from a perfect stranger tells me where your priorities are." The tram lines up with the entry door, and Mom spins, enters with the crowd and disappears.

Warm air blasts from the overhead vents in the tram's terminal, but the cold in my body is deep down. Deep within. Deep, *deep* inside.

Mom, obviously, didn't want me to ride with her. I can't quite figure out what I did to her, Cam, to RK, to my so-called-friends to deserve what's happened, and sitting here twiddling my thumbs, tapping my feet and crossing and uncrossing my arms does nothing to enlighten me.

I wait an hour for the next transport.

The tram rumbles underneath me as I take it home, in the dark, alone. At my stop, I get off, alone, and start the walk of shame toward my house when I realize the whole day has passed, and I redirect my course toward Milton's. My night of penance must begin.

Cold bites through my coat sleeves, all warmth gone. Stuffing my hands in my pockets, I rub my fingertip against the note chip I'd found. It probably holds a love note to a girl-friend or a last message to a mother or child.

Guilt wracks me again as I consider all the possibilities—the message that won't be delivered, that someone's probably missing the little piece of metal and plastic, and I had the opportunity to drop it in the lost and found bin on the last tram but didn't do that either.

Something I should probably do for Mom since she'll probably never talk to me again.

"I can't do anything right," I say as I open the door to Milton's.

This doesn't bode well for my interview.

6

As planned, an incessant beeping wakes me at five in the morning on January first. The new year. Not only do I have to get to the tram before the normal morning rush, I'll also have to walk or hitch from the tram to Perry Road, and get in line no later than seven, or be flogged. Probably. Maybe. What do they do at a cattle-call of people to keep them in line?

Overnight, a light dusting of snow fell, covering the sidewalks but not the road, the grass but not the houses. My teeth chatter as I walk to the waiting booth in the dark, and the clatter doesn't stop as I warm up, or when I get on for transport. I take that as a sign I'm not cold on the outside but freezing with anxiety on the inside.

Why shouldn't I be?

Mom walked around crying the whole day yesterday. Or talking to herself about Mia and how at least *Mia* didn't lie about wanting to be a registered citizen. That *Mia* had a plan and stuck to it, and why couldn't I have at least been honest?

No matter how often I tried to answer, she'd stop me with a hand in the air, a glare or some quiet sob.

I gave up after the tenth try.

The tram rumbles forward, vents sending super-heated air in my direction. It does nothing to help. Like me with Mom. If I had another three to four days, she might come around.

While she said I should be more like Mia, she also gave Mia the silent treatment for a week. I think she's forgotten that, with all her talk of how *great* Mia had been.

After giving up on Mom's about-face, I decided to try and get answers from Cam. She didn't respond to any of my text messages, and audio went straight to her box. Two security people came by to talk with me more about the necklace, asking me all sorts of questions about my friends. I had no choice but to describe each and every one of them, provide their names and addresses and anything else I knew. The intricacy of their questioning made me think, deep down, that they'd really done it—stolen the pendant—even as my head told me 'no way'.

I itched all over for two hours after that meeting, as if my body tried to tell me I'd done something wrong. Had I? When I stand in front of the panel, should I introduce myself as Tattletale-Terrible-Daughter Keating?

Staring out into the dark morning covered in glistening white from street lamps, with my head against the window pane, I realize today is supposed to be my life changing moment. Yet, if I could go back two days and pretend none of it happened, if I could go back and tell Cam and my mom, and not accept the gift, I'd do it.

"You look like you could use a friend," a male voice says. There are at least twenty other seats still available since it's only six in the morning, and of all places, he plops by me.

I pick at my fingernail, hugging my overnight bag a little tighter. "Um ... I'm actually not really very good company these days. You might not want to chance it." An inhale brings in a comforting scent—one that's familiar, but I can't place from where.

"I doubt that. I'm Zane." His hand appears in my line of vision.

It would be one hundred percent rude not to at least acknowledge him. Lifting my head, I find a boy about my age, maybe a little older. He has sparkling blue eyes beneath the straight, black wisps falling over his crown. A light smattering of freckles pattern a straight nose, and his smile is as wide as the Pacific.

"Erianna. But most people call me Eri."

"Sounds windy."

I can't help the laugh. "Very funny. Haven't heard that one since ..." I stop myself. My dad used to call me windy—before I begged him to stop. If only my mom had used 'Anna' for my nickname instead, I'd have been a normal kid instead of fodder for the name callers. "Let's just leave the breeze out of it."

"Long as you're not gassy, we're good."

Commence mortification. "Um ..."

"I'm kidding. Though if you are—"

My head pops up, and my eyes widen. I'm drawn into Zane's gaze.

He waves two hands in front of his face. "Sorry." His cheeks flush pink. "Sometimes, when I'm nervous, I say things I shouldn't. Really. No offense."

"None taken." Forcing my heart to calm takes a little longer than it should. "It's not like I didn't warn you I'm bad company."

He nudges my elbow. "Nah. Don't see that."

The tram jiggles as it slows, and the overhead speaker calls out stop number thirteen.

"This is me," I say.

"Me, too." Zane stands from our seat and steps back a foot, motioning me in front of him. "Ladies first."

I pull my coat tight, expecting the bite of the morning cold will penetrate its thin fabric when I step off. Stuffing my hands between my jacket and bag, I try to keep warm, but the cold seeps in and more than just my hands go frigid in a second.

Zane points down the road.

I narrow my eyes at him and stop. He doesn't have a bag or suitcase, or anything. "Do you live on Perry Road?"

"What?" he asks.

"Um ... you don't look like you'd be going to the houses. You know ... the selection service day is today."

He waves his hands up and down his body. "Wrong outfit?" The grin stays in place.

On a gasp, I realize my faux pas. "No." I wave my hands in front of me. "I just meant ... I mean ... I ... no, you just ... you don't ... I didn't think you were eighteen."

He holds his hands up in front of his face, his lips forming a circle. "Oh, no! Did I miss it a few years ago?"

Cocking my head, I frown. Someone can forget?

"I'm kidding, Eri, really. I promise I'm in the right place, at the right time."

I expel the breath I've held. "Sorry. I'm a little nervous, too."

Zane laughs as he starts forward again. "Come on. We'll walk together toward the beginning of our future."

Maybe selection day won't be so bad, after all.

During a pre-Winter Solstice sale at the stores, lines can wrap around and around a building, people joining them hours, and even days, before the release of the latest gadget.

The vehicles on Perry Road are like those people. They're everywhere. In line. Backed up past the tram station. Two lines go in. One just as long, also with stopped cars, heading out on the other side.

My double layer of socks does little to keep the chill from

my toes as I try to estimate the incomings. "Are all these people dropping off their kids?" I ask.

Not that Mom would have dropped me off, given how mad she'd been. She didn't even get up with me. Didn't offer to take the tram with me so I could boldly tell her 'no, no, Mom, I'm a big girl'. She just ignored me. Like she did Mia, but at least her hatred of her oldest daughter ended *before* the big day.

"Lots of people here, huh?" Zane says as he and I traipse our way between all sorts of transpos.

If I had to guess, I'd have said hundreds lined up in each queue on the right side of the road, inching forward every so often, and those on the left had families and kids getting out, voices raising, steam from their parted lips filling the air. In between, empty private trams roared their way through, I assume dropping off big groups from surrounding educenters or other places. I could have walked to my level three educenter and caught the transpo there but figured seven blocks north to go three times the distance south with a bunch of people who don't care about me didn't have much point.

"Uh, yeah. Lots of people." *Too many.*

"I'm kinda glad we walked. That way we don't have to do the whole tears and crying and stuff with our parents." His breath coats the air in translucent white.

"Sure, sure." Not that I didn't experience the tears in a totally different way.

"You see that purple dinosaur?"

I stop, turn and furrow my brow. "What?"

"You seem distracted. Just thought I'd see if I could get your attention." He wags a finger at me like that should make me laugh, or something.

"Like I said on the tram, I'm not good company just now."

"Nervous?" He starts walking again, and I follow.

"Yes." That's not a lie.

With every step closer to the houses, I'm slowing. Even as transpos pass and we dart in and out between personal ones, I hear the sorrow and excitement—like we're all going to summer camp and not learning about our entire future—and my nerves get even more tingly.

Zane brushes a shoulder against mine. "It's not a big deal, you know."

I stop. "Not a big deal? Are you kidding?" My voice ratchets up a notch, and the family to my right turns toward me. "This is like the whole rest of my life. This is the moment I can be—" *someone else* "—I can change what I have and get a better life."

He shrugs. "No, it's not. It's just selection. That's all. The rest of your life is up to you, and what you do with what they assign to you."

"You sound like my mom." At least, when she made a similar statement to Mia. "I really think it'd be better if I went on my own. It was nice to meet you Zane."

He doesn't try to stop me when I trudge on alone.

The road leading to the houses isn't smooth like most paths. With all the ruts and potholes, I'm sure it needs to be repaved, and wonder, given how important the once-a-year trek is, why S-D eleven hasn't acquired the funds to fix it, or why the people that live on the road don't submit a request for it to be done.

A blare from my right jostles me from my thoughts. I jump to the left and slam into someone's PTS, only to have its siren blare as if I'd tried to break in. Pushing off, I step, my foot going deep into one of the holes I'd just been thinking about, water filling up around my foot. I yank, trying to get it out.

What in the world?

My heel catches and scrapes at my skin. Pushing back down, I try a second time and pain reaches into my toes.

Oh, my. I'm stuck. Emotion builds up in my throat, but I swallow hard. I put on a little makeup before I left—leftovers from Mia. Ruining it with stupid tears would make the day even worse.

I jiggle my foot as Zane stops at my side and begins to lower. "I'm okay." I wave him onward, though my voice breaks as I speak, and he stands again. "Really. I got this. Just wasn't paying attention." His feet don't move, but I don't want him to see me fighting with a stupid shoe in a stupid hole in the stupid ground.

Why today?

People walk and roll by as I struggle with my shoe. It's no use, though. My foot isn't coming out with the covering still on, and the cold has seeped into my pants, up to mid-calf. If I don't do something soon, I'll probably end up frozen to the ground.

"Eri—"

"No. I got this." I need to deal with this myself. I'm on my own now. I have to be able to handle myself.

"Fine. Okay." His departure tears at me, as if I've lost my best friend, but I force back the threatening tears.

Do not cry. Do not cry. Do not cry!

I drop my bag, dig in with trembling hands, untie my shoes, and slip out my soaking wet foot. Reaching back in, I grab my shoe and after a few twists manage to extricate it from the hole. Not only are my pants went, but my coat sleeves are too, as is my bag that I set on the ground, and my hands are going numb.

As I stand, a loud horn blasts in front of me, and as I tilt up, the lights from the moving tram blind me, just before it hits me full force.

"Higher, Daddy, higher!"

The swing sends me soaring into the air, my feet rising higher and higher, trying my best to touch the clouds.

"Higher, Daddy!"

I giggle as pressure from behind propels me forward, upward, closer to my goal, to the ceiling of clouds.

"Higher!"

Back and forth I go, until the ropes holding my swing wiggle, and I grip them, hoping I won't fall off, that they'll hold me, that I won't go all the way over.

As if he could read my fear, big hands grip me from behind and slow my descent. "That was a little too high, I think." His deep voice booms through the warm, humid summer air.

I scramble out of the seat and into his arms until wrapped in his embrace and the safety of being understood.

"Have I ever told you ..." He rubs my back as my trembles subside. "... how brave you are, my little Windy girl?"

"I love you, Daddy." My arms go around his neck. "Will you always save me?"

"Of course I will. I'll always be here for you, and I'll always save you."

I breathe in the fresh, clean scent of my dad. It's a smell I'll never forget, and I must be in heaven if I'm smelling it now.

7

"Eri! Erianna."

My dad's scent surrounds me. It's a fragrance I haven't smelled in so long my memories have faded, but whatever has happened, it's surrounding me again, keeping me warm and holding me close. I want to remain in it, but the pounding in my skull takes away from my moment of calm, from my memory.

"Eri. It's me, Zane."

The back of my head beats in rhythm with my heart.

I blink, bringing his face into view. "Zane?" More blinks leave me confused, but at the same time, I'm comforted by Zane's presence. Smiling up at him, I say, "What are you doing here?"

His lips curve. "You mean on Perry Road at six thirty in the morning? Or somewhere else?"

"Perry Road?" My momentary shock at the vivid memory of my dad fades. I lift up and grasp the back of my head. "What happened?"

Zane leans against the wheel of a vehicle, his arms around his knees. "You were about to get hit by a PTS, so I pushed you between two of these parked ones, and you kinda hit your head on the way down."

"I did? The tram didn't hit me?"

He shakes his head. "No. That was me. I'm not very good at being Superman, I don't think." He points down the road, where more personal and private transpos barrel on by as if nothing happened. "Can't get off the ground but can definitely hit it."

I rub more at my hair and find it matted with bits of gravel and probably mud. Not only does my head hurt, my heart does, too. Life, since I turned eighteen, has sucked and only gotten worse on a minute by minute basis.

As if the lever breaks, I burst into sobs.

"Awe, man. Girl tears." Zane moves closer to me.

I push him away, but he doesn't go, just tugs me in. This boy, this guy, this person who I met less than an hour before, comforts me, and I let him. All the day's worries, and built up tension and heartache weighing on me, pours out through my tears onto his shoulder.

He's warm, and his arms wrapping around me hold tight. "Let it out, Eri."

I can't—won't— and force myself quiet, pushing away. "I'm sorry, Zane."

"It's okay. I have two older sisters, and they never used me for a punching bag. They actually seem to think I'm really good to talk to. All the time. All night long. Every day. *All* day long."

The laugh bubbles up. "Guess I should thank your sisters for teaching you to be so nice." A sigh leaves as I hiccup another sob. "Do you know where my shoe is?"

He turns his head as I search the lightening dark.

"Uh … yeah." One finger angles toward the middle of the road. "Guess it flew out there when I took you down." He scrambles up. "I'll get it." He's gone and back in two seconds with my muddy, obviously rolled over shoe in hand. "It's not very pretty, but …"

Brushing it doesn't do a bit of good, but I take it as I have no other option. "Thanks." With my wet, heavy shoe back on my foot, I force myself not to cringe at what I must look like. To think Cam said I needed to wear the shirt she wanted to steal, I'm thankful I didn't get to keep it. It wouldn't have made it to the interview anyway.

"Do you have some extra clothes?" Zane asks.

"Only a shirt and ... you know ... clean underwear. But these are my only shoes."

"Oh, well, hey. You look fine." He holds out a hand and draws me to my feet. "Besides, when we get inside, we get uniforms."

"Really?" Brushing off my black pants, I try to get the spots of mud that dot my lower legs. That does no good. "I give up."

"Give up what?"

"What do you think? Everything. I'm going to walk in there and be told I'm a vagrant and the best job I'll have in my life is as a burger flipper. No, I take that back—"

"Good—"

"Not good. I take that back because burger flipper is too high a job. I'll be the trash girl."

"Give yourself a little more credit, Eri. It's not all about what they see."

"Who are you to say, Zane? I got a foot stuck in the one pothole with water in it, almost got hit, apparently passed out, have mud on me, mud in my hair, and I'm a freaky mess. That's not what the selection committee wants to see."

"Interviews are the last day. They got a lot of prep work to do first. You know, like making a pizza. Can't deliver it to eat if you haven't cut the toppings, prepped the crust, decorated it, warmed—"

Holding up my hands, I say, "I get it." Doesn't mean I'm

happy about walking into whatever happens next, looking like I do. "What house are you in?"

"Red," he says.

"Me, too."

"Are you really that worried about what you look like?"

I give him my best glare. "Yes. You're obviously not, though. Why is that?"

"Because in the red house, they aren't there to take you as you are. They're there to make you what you want to be."

Shaking my head, I say, "You've got that wrong. You first have to prove to them that you can be something, and then they make you what *they* want."

"I think you'll be a little surprised." His head bobs up and down. "So, maybe it's a mix of both."

"How would you know all this?"

"Both my sisters were red house candidates, Eri. Now it's my turn."

I start off, knowing I have little time to complete the rest of my walk. Oddly, my head no longer pounds, and the cold no longer stings. Figuring I've gone completely numb or frostbite has kicked in, I carry on, determined to prove myself wrong. Zane walks at my right side, separating me from moving traffic.

After a minute, I ask, "Why can't they just send us all to one house? Why can't we all be equal like we're supposed to be? Why do we have to be tested and considered and interviewed and—"

"Whoa there." Zane stops me with both hands up. "Those are all questions you should ask them."

Right. Ask them. This is about asking me stuff and picking out who's trash I'll be cleaning up for the rest of my life. "Sorry again." I wave him off and turn. "Thanks for saving me from the tram and for the shoulder. I'm just going to ... I need ...

I gotta go." With that, I spin and start a hobbling sprint-and-limp, speeding up as I get closer to my destination.

I need to get to my assigned house. That's my new goal. Get it over with. Find out my fate. Forget the opportunity to be something I'll never be. Whatever they have for me, I'll just take it instead of fighting with fate.

◦━━◆━━◦

"Red house candidates, please make your way to the right." A man's voice through the loudspeaker repeats the command as I mix in with a growing, noisy crowd. "White house candidate, please make your way to the left."

Voices rise and fall, asking what they should do, where they should go and saying goodbye to loved ones as if they'll never come back, and as if they haven't heard the man calling out what to do the whole time.

"Black house candidates, down the middle."

People move about, but don't really go anywhere. It's like they're stuck in position, like fish in a can waiting for someone to pick one, tear open their heart and use it only to throw it away in the end.

Why am I so negative? Palm to forehead, I try to stop my thoughts from spiralling down into an abyss of depression. It could happen; I've seen Mom suffer when a student doesn't pay or uses a dummy and she's already paid the house bill. *I will not do this. I will not do this. This is a good thing. You want change. You need to be better than who you were.*

I just wish I had Cam with me, like we'd always planned—even with everything that's happened. At least I'd have my best friend. That thought, of course, forces me to search for her, as if I'll find her in all the bodies. I have no idea how many people mill about, bumping into shoulders and knocking into suitcases. At a guess, a thousand, but that could include parents. Parents who care enough to walk their kids to their destiny.

Don't go there, Eri. Really, don't.

"Single file lines. Single file lines," the voice booms. "Three lines. Red to the right. White to the left. Black in the center." Over and over, it's repeated.

Rather than wait, rather than let myself get swept away by emotions and cold and fear, I make my way closer to the red house, jostling for space, sneaking through small gaps as people squish together in a hug. My smallness makes this a lot easier than I expected. When I finally reach the front, I stand at a single-story building painted a deep, bold red.

They said 'red house', and they meant it. Unlike most of my friends and classmates, I'd never ventured down Perry Road before. Most said mysterious lights would come out of the dark, if anyone managed to get close enough to the three houses. Spooky is what I call it, so I've never had the interest to sneak past the people who live in the other houses at the start of the road to try and see what might exist at its end.

"At this time, parents and guardians must exit the area," the voice calls out.

A collective moan blows through the crowd. All around me, people chatter, but this time, I know they've heard the directions as they start to break away.

"Ready for this?" a girl asks from my left.

"Yeah, sure." I don't turn toward her, my gaze drawn instead to the two windows. There aren't any coverings but there's no movement inside, either. I'd swear the house stands empty, but, then again, what do I know?

"Parents and guardians must exit the area," the guy repeats for the fourth or fifth time.

"I'm a little freaked," the girls says.

"Mmm-hmm." I'm vowing, in my head, not to get involved with anyone. To just do what I'm asked, get through my week and try to get a job that's not a reflection of my muddy clothes and hair, my frost-bitten fingers or my frozen foot. Maybe someone inside will see through all that, like Zane said. *Yeah, right.*

"My name's Hadley," the girl says.

Politeness forces me to turn. I give her a little nod and say, "I'm Er—Erianna, but everyone calls me Anna." I have no idea why I've just changed my name, but deep down inside, it fits. It works. What do I have to lose by pretending I'm not some girl who lives in a shack on the edge of town, whose mom is a fluke who can't buy clothes except once every couple years, and who hasn't had a decent haircut in forever? No one here knows me. All my friends went to a different house. I'm just me. Erianna Price Keating. I asked for a change, and I'm going to make it for myself. I'm Anna from now on.

Hadley holds out her hand. "Nice to meet you, Anna. Most people call me Hades, but I much prefer Hadley." Her lips curve, and I detect a bit of self-deprecation in her tone.

A smile emerges on my face despite my previous glowering. "Nice to meet you, too." Everything inside me brightens as if I've been given a shot of happiness. I'm Anna now. I'm better than the mud, and if a girl named Hadley can laugh at being called Hades, I can, too.

Her head tilts right and left, and I realize I'm thinking way too long. Shaking her hand, I point with my other toward the house. "Is that smaller than you imagined?"

"I don't know what I pictured, exactly, but kinda. My brother was a red house candidate, and when he came home, he told me about it. But I thought it was bigger."

"Did he say what happens next? Like the details." Wouldn't

I like to know? The outline in my invitation listed the seven days: medical, psychological, physical wellbeing, evaluation, assignment, mentoring, conclusion. It didn't, however, go into detail on each one.

Her lips purse. "A little. I mean, he kinda walked through the process." She bites at the side. "I'm still just really nervous."

I can see that, but I don't want to tell her. Not about that, or the hole in the side of her blue and purple crocheted hat that had to be made by a super old lady. If Mom didn't have one of my great-grandma's old ones, I wouldn't have known what to call it since handmade yarns are as extinct as dinosaurs.

"So, you're here by yourself?" she asks as I try not to stare at her jacket—another obvious hand-me-down with fraying seams.

Straightening my shoulders and forcing confidence to the surface, I say, "Yeah. My sister came through a couple years ago, but she left, and I kinda ticked off my mom, so she didn't come."

Hadley reaches out and touches my forearm. "I'm sorry." Her simple statement, the understanding and offer of support in that one move, makes me want to like her. "My mom's a nurse, and she had to work, so I took the tram in."

"From where?"

"Southwest. You know, out by the airpark." The worst, poorest part of district eleven, according to Mom. Worse than where we live. Mom says that area is where the registration people send the undesirables—people they don't want to even live in society but can't send them anywhere else. Every district has one, or two, areas like that. I've never met anyone from there before, and Hadley seems nice enough. Makes me wonder what anyone would do to be assigned there. Makes me wonder if that'll happen to me.

After far too long, I say, "I'm familiar with the area, but um … only by reputation." Just last summer, Mom had to stop tutoring kids from that section because they all paid with dummy credits.

Hadley squishes her lips together, and her head bobs as if she understands. She turns back toward the house.

"I'm sorry," I say. "Didn't mean to offend you. It's my only perspective. I don't …" *get out much.* "I live here in the north, about ten minutes from the big store, but my mom's a fluke, so—"

"It's okay." She turns back to me. "I understand." Her tone is so soft it makes me want to comfort her, yet I have no idea why. Her life might have sucked, but she could be the next leader of our country, for all I know. She just seems sad. Scared.

Like me, only worse.

That's what it is. I see me in her. The me that's clawing at me from the inside out, to be meek, to step aside, to let everyone else do their thing first. I don't want that, though. I want to be like Cam, even though she hates me. I want her confidence and her excitement.

My need may seem sudden, but the last two days have shown me, have told me, have made me tired of being the girl who takes the blame, makes up for everyone and has to walk in mud puddles to get places.

I want more than what Mom has given me. My entire body trembles. Having that thought, while standing in front of the entry to my future, has to be a good sign.

Or is it a bad one?

"Ladies and gentlemen …" the announcer voice has changed from male to female. "At this time, all those older than nineteen must have exited the premises." A hush falls over our side, while traces of chatter continue from somewhere father away.

"Group leaders will pass through each line. Please have your identification with you as well as your NARCA letter. Once we confirm your address and identity, we'll move to the next step."

I'd folded my details up in the top pocket of my bag and retrieve them as she talks. Hadley does the same. From the red house, two people dressed in black clothes exit, with what look like rocket launchers slung over their shoulder. They head straight toward Hadley and me but keep going.

Given we stand right at the front, I expect to be dealt with first, but they keep walking, down the line, pulling people from it and making a second row. Chatter starts up again as kids are pushed and pulled, jostled and moved about, and what had been one row becomes three. Me. Some super tall guy on my right. Zane on my left.

He smiles at me as if I should have known he'd been born to lead. *Probably a level one edu line leader, too,*

"There will be no talking!" The woman's voice is stern. "It is imperative, at this point, that all conversations cease."

I glance back at Hadley behind me, but neither of us says a word. At the same time, we lean forward, watching the guard-like people move down the row and push people into the new second and a third rows before disappearing into a sea of people.

Wow, that's a lot of people. How are we all going to fit in that house?

"Please keep your identification materials in hand at all times," the speaker repeats.

Another set of three people, dressed in white this time, exit the red house and head straight for me, tall-guy and Zane.

"Name, identification and documentation," the one in front of me says as the other two position themselves in front of way-too-tall guy and Zane dressed in his deep brown jacket and jeans.

"Erianna Price Keating." I hand the one my credentials and, two seconds later, a blue light illuminates my papers from a hand-held wand.

"Zane Alexander Warren."

"Jel Guyen Overfelt."

The guys or girls—I can't tell—move on to Hadley and repeat.

"Hadley Symone Parker."

"Michael Todd Jerome."

"Markita Renee Hightower."

With so many people in line, this process is going to take forever, and as the wind picks up, I'm waiting for the moment I officially turn into a Popsicle. I'd like to ask Hadley if she knows why they do the whole registration outside. Why can't we go in and get warm? I swear Cam said registration happened *in* the houses, not just *at* the houses. If only Mia had been around to share. Rather than voice my question and get yelled at, I keep silent.

After another creak and groan from the red house, three more people come out, followed by a second set of three and a third group, too. They're dressed in, of all colors, red.

The first set passes me but stop two people behind.

The second pass, too, but stop at Hadley.

The third two flank me, Zane and Jel.

"Walk forward to the door, please." A nudge to my shoulder pushes me toward the house, and the guy or girl in red slips in behind me as if I'm supposed to know what to do other than just walk.

I start to turn, to see if Zane's coming, but am given a poke to the shoulder blades. *Not supposed to even look at people?*

Rather than fight it, I march toward the entrance, wishing

with my whole heart that Mom could have prepared me better for this adventure.

8

Zane walks through the doors first, his red-guy moving away. Mine nudges me again, and I slip through the opening into a completely empty room that seems to span the entire inside of the red house. There are no other doors, no back windows, and no light fills in from the front two. No furniture, no pictures on the wall. Nothing, except three rows of lights illuminating an empty gray-ish room.

The tall guy enters and stands with Zane and me, also without his tagalong. The three of us wait. I, for one, am completely lost. I think to say, "What do we do?" and I want to ask it, when the crackle of a speaker breaks the silence.

"Welcome, candidates," a voice says through the air. "Please move to the front, in rows of three, and do not pass the red line on the floor."

It takes no time for me to spot that red line at the far wall. The three of us walk toward it and take spots between the boundaries of other red lines—all on the floor.

The door opens and closes behind me again, letting in a little more light and three more candidates, including Hadley.

"Welcome, candidates," the voice says again. "Please move to the front, in rows of three and do not pass the red line on the floor."

Hadley stands behind me, as the door opens and closes again

and three more come in. "What do we do?" she whispers.

I shrug because I really don't know. There's absolutely nothing in this room. How can it be registration?

"Welcome, candidates," the voice goes on.

It repeats the same verse another ten times, until thirty of us stand in the room, in three lines, and the doorway through which we walked in doesn't open again.

Around me, everyone is silent, but we're all turning our heads as if taking in the room, trying to understand and wondering what in the world is going to happen.

Zane's smile never fades. Jel hugs his backpack. Hadley keeps tapping me on the shoulder, and around us, people mumble and grumble, yet nothing else happens.

"This is crazy," some boy behind me says. "They're just going to stick us in a room?"

"What do we do?" a girl asks.

"I'm getting out of here," yet another boy says, and several grunt their agreement, resulting in shuffling and short exclamations from others filling the room.

"Welcome, candidates," the voice starts again, but the door hasn't opened. "Please move to the front, in rows of three, and do not pass the red line on the floor."

"We've already heard that," someone says, yelling from the back right.

"Let us out!" another says.

"Welcome, candidates," the voice says for the gazillionth time.

Even I'm getting irritated, twisting toward Hadley and Zane, searching for something to clue me in. As I turn back, the floor drops, my stomach with it. A few screams bounce off the minimalistic room.

We stop just as fast as we started. Hands go out, holding on to each other since we have nothing else to grab. It happens again as cries and tears and grunts fill the space. On the third fall, everyone bends their knees as if prepared this time, and the wall in front of me, no more than three inches in beyond of the red line where I stand, changes from a solid white to a shadowy color and grows darker and more black as if it's changing. Somehow.

Craning around, I find we're all standing again. A slight bump has us all gasping, but now I think I know that we're moving, and the wall in front of me must not be, even though the scenery switches from black to white again and to a plaster wall like in everyone's living space, to a metal one, to dirt and again to metal. Swallowing pops my ears, but I'd swear the falling sensation has ended. Yet, at the same time, it can't have since the view in front of me is still changing.

Twisting to Zane, I catch his gaze. "Are we on a riser?"

"Yes," Jel says from my right, and I spin toward him. "My brother was a red house candidate last year and told me this is how they transport us to the facility."

So, we're going down. Wonder how far? The visual before me goes from metal to white and from white to bright light, where everyone screams again, and we bounce up an inch.

A few girls yell out; guys moan.

We all squat as if waiting to fall again. Or rise. Or do something that bounces us all over the place. Couldn't they have at least given us something to hang on to?

"Welcome, candidates—" This time, the voice is male. "—to the National Archives, Records and Citizen Administration of the American Union. When the door opens to the front, we ask that you remain in three lines, keep all belongings with you and proceed to the seat farthest in the row, filling in each seat and leaving no empty spaces between yourself and your neighbor."

The voice stops, and the wall that had changed so many times raises again into a dimly lit room with auditorium-style seating.

"At this time, you may proceed," the voice says, and the thirty of us begin our walk, Zane behind me and the other guy in front, which means whatever I'm going to see will be blocked by his head.

We walk to the end, as told, and I take the last seat. Hadley sits right next to me. She's shaking, her legs jittery, hands gripping her knees.

"Are you okay?" I ask her.

She faces me. "I get claustrophobic, and I have a fear of heights, and that was a really long fall. If we travelled as fast as I think, we're now between one and two thousand feet beneath the ground—that's like almost a hundred and thirty stories." Her eyes are wide, and her lip trembles.

"I think we're on a solid surface now, though, and we didn't go high, just low."

"Yes, but we'll have to go up to get out." She has a point.

"Welcome, candidates."

"Is that all you can say?" someone yells from the far end of the room. His question is a good one.

"At this time, the National Archives, Records and Citizen Administration would like your attention at the front wall." Curtains slide from the middle to the sides. Light blinks once, centering on a small stage, and a man in a suit appears in the middle. Fuzziness suggests he's a hologram—worse, that he's an old-technology one.

He stands, hands clasped, and faces all of us. "Welcome, candidates." The speaker is the same male voice that has been speaking to us since we left ground level. "Today marks the beginning of the rest of your life." That's a slogan we all heard in all levels of educenter. "As an adult in the American Union, it's imperative that you understand our history in order for you to understand your role in our future." Mister Hologram steps to the left, his figure blinking a little.

Hadley leans toward me. "I think this is some old technology."

My lips curve; I like that we think alike.

"Moving from childhood to adulthood brings with it new and significant responsibility. First and foremost, your job is no longer your education, but service to your country. No matter what role you choose—"

"Choose?" Hadley asks.

I'm wondering at that, too, but I want to choose, so I hope there's more input from us than I think there really is.

"—know that your service, your work, your effort is appreciated right up to those who lead our country."

A few snorts go through the room.

The guy walks to the right side of the stage, a funny action to me since, as a hologram, it looks like he's still looking at me. Movement is unnecessary but those who built hologram videos fifty years ago thought it made the speakers look more realistic. Turned out it made them creepy.

With his right hand outstretched, he points to a void and says, "Now let's remember how we got here and what the American Union stands for."

Groans abound as he fades and a picture appears, of our country's flag, with its twenty-eight stars and fifteen red and white stripes. It flaps in an unmoving wind until it, too, disappears, replaced by our country's capital building, a place I meant to visit three years before—like all new final-preparation candidates would if they had money.

If it's a history lesson we're going to get, it's one we've had every year, so it seems stupid to reinforce a message that has never changed, but what do I know? I didn't even know the red house would take me to some underground facility to determine my entire future. I'm guessing what little I learned from Cam and from overheard conversations in educenter is probably all going to be useless gossip.

"Over two hundred years ago, our nation experienced an explosion of growth while, at the same time, reveling in our arts, sciences and music, but lagging behind even some third world countries in our understanding of freedom and in the basic needs of our own." The pictures change as the narrator speaks, each with a date associated with it. From an illustrated image of a white guy holding a black guy in chains dated 1850, to a imagegraph of a white guy walking into one side of a building while the black guy walks into another, dated 1950, to both a white and black guy holding out a plate as people pass by, dated 2000. "Our leaders, with the best of intentions, sought to bring equality to all." Another picture, of a white and black guy holding boxes that look like holiday presents has a date of 2020. "Equality, however, did not mean the same thing to all people." The image morphs into the same white and black guy fighting with a date of 2030. "And the root of all evil was traced back to the financial security of our people." The two guys are back again, but this time, they each hold bills in their hands and smile, though the black guy is wearing a suit with a red tie, and the white guy is wearing a full-body uniform like most teachers. "Therefore, it was determined, that all people should share equally in all our country's resources." The image that comes up is of a group of people at a table, all eating together. It's obvious that it's a setup since the guy at the front of the table is staring straight into the recorder, smiling. That one's dated 2050. "And to do so, all new adults would be evaluated and placed in their proper roles upon the start of the new year once they turn eighteen." The date on this image is 2067, right after what used to be the United States of America became the United States and the American Union—two separate countries.

Someone behind me lets out a soft snore.

Hadley elbows me. "Haven't we heard all this before? Like in second level?"

I nod. The pictures they've used to depict the changes are new, but the story is the same.

"Some, however, did not believe our leaders should have such control." Now, the two guys are fighting again, one with an old-style gun in his hand and one with a big machete-looking thing. 2051 flashes across the screen. "What was once fifty states split into two, with those believing in equality, and the true need to ensure all citizens are properly cared for, remaining in the American Union." A picture of the old fifty states is broken in half across a jagged, horizontal line that bisects the continent. The upper half turns blue while the lower half is shaded a deep red and cartoon blood oozes from it. "The war of the states was a brutal one and, for eight years, it showcased the selfishness of many of our former inhabitants." A picture of a white guy holding a bag away from a pleading woman zips across the screen along with the year 2059. "But our country prevailed, new laws were established and our people now enjoy their lives because all expectations are set upon their eighteenth birthday—a day for all to fully understand their role in our society." A set of smiling boys and girls from at least ten different nationalities fills the space, along with the date of 2068. "Now, as you embark upon your future, know that we'll take care of you until you take your dying breath, as we know you'll fulfil your duty to us in your assigned role. If we all maintain the status quo, our country will succeed, grow and prosper in the world economy."

Without warning, the lights in the entire room brighten, and while I blink to let my eyes adjust, doors open to the left.

"Candidates, please rise and proceed through the open doors. Remain in your lines as you do so."

I have no idea how long the presentation lasted, but the brightness of the light from the doors still blinds me as I stand and, with my bag in hand, walk from history to my future.

Room number two is stark white. No shading. Just plain white.

That includes the suits worn by the people who greet us. Real people this time instead of overhead speakers and holographic imagery—I think, anyway, as the suits pretty much hide what's within.

The one in the middle motions for us to come forward, a gloved hand high in the air. "Females to the right of the red line, males to the left." The high pitch of the voice identifies the speaker as female at least.

I shift to the right, as tall guy and Zane head to the left. Hadley sticks right to me, still blinking, probably from the brightness.

"At this time, physical assessments will be completed," the woman says. "You'll be paired with another—"

Hadley grabs my arm and clings.

"—of your own gender, so modesty is not something to worry about. A physician will explain the procedures, as well as the results. Afterward, you'll be given proper attire and assigned to a pod for the next six days. Each pod has a resident assistant who can answer any questions. Meals are served three times a day in the main dining hall beginning tomorro—"

"We don't get to eat today?" someone yells out.

"Today is a fasting day." She stops for a second as if waiting for someone to question her. "At no time, during this week, will you be allowed out of the facility, above ground or outside. Natural light is brought in from the surface and a courtyard is made available to you for socialization. Any questions?"

A whole bunch of hands go up.

"Good. They'll be answered in due time." The woman steps back.

Another white-suited person holds up a large personal computing device. "If you have a partner, you are welcome to stay with them for the physical assessment, but there is no guarantee you'll be together for your stay. Females, please proceed through the door to the right. Males, proceed through the door to the left."

Yet another door. Yet another set of instructions. Since Mia never came home, I didn't get to ask her about her experience; though, would her experience have been the same, anyway, given she didn't go to the red house? At least I would have something to go on that wasn't a list in a letter. Mom refused to talk about what she went through, and Grandma turned eighteen before the government setup the program. Cam's references all came from her brothers, who made up tons of ridiculous stories everyone knows are lies. In any of our edu-center levels, any time someone had a question, they were told to speak with their parents, as teachers couldn't discuss the topic—it had never been approved in the curriculum.

With Hadley still hanging on to me, we walk over to the door and through it, followed by a bunch of chattering girls behind us.

The new room includes more white-suited people, and a

series of ten doors, five on each side, each with a person and what looks to be a brand new PCD in their hand. The one at the farthest end of the hallway waves, and Hadley and I scoot on down all the way to the open door.

"Good morning, ladies. Please enter, remove all clothing and place them in the bags provided, write your names and living space locations on them, provide a urine sample, dress in one of the gowns and have a seat. You'll have exactly five minutes from the time I close this door to complete the task and be seated.

Hadley and I face each other. I'm sure our expressions are the same.

We're going to have to see each other naked and hear each other pee and we met less than a few hours before.

If I ever wanted to die, that moment has arrived.

9

The door swishes shut and an unheard timer starts. Hadley takes off her hat, red hair falling across her shoulders. Two seconds later, she's removed her jacket, dropped her bag, started on her shoes and stares up at me. "I don't like this any more than you, but I knew it was coming."

"You did?" More and more, I wish Mia had come back and helped me. Shared. Told me stories. Lied. Something to prepare me for getting naked with another girl. I knew medical tests came with registration, but in my head, that meant taking my temperature and reading my blood pressure, making sure I can see and hear, not making me pee in a cup or get naked.

"Even though I don't like heights or confined space, I really don't care about being naked. It's kinda freeing."

The girl who clung to me moments before has become way more confident than me. "Um …"

"I'm not a girl-lover, if that's what you're thinking. I seriously just don't like heights, and yes, even though we went down, it was still a fall, and my brain gets all jiggy. It takes me a while to get over that. I'm sure you have weirdness, too, right?"

"Oh, yeah, sure." Though, I'm not sure what. Maybe my issue is peeing in a cup in a room with another person. I'm quite sure I'm not going to be able to do it.

Hadley's gotten down to her bra and underwear, and I'm still standing in my jacket with my bag tight to my chest.

"You know all this is part of the tests, right?"

I shake my head.

"Everything you do over the next seven days is. It's how they determine what you get to do with your life and at what level you start. They watch and monitor everything." She drops her bra into the bag and doesn't even bother covering up her breasts. I'm guessing she's a C-cup, at least, and I want nothing to do with showing off my triple A's. With her back to me, she says, "They're probably watching right now, even."

I dart around searching for a camera. They wouldn't do that, would they? The eyes exist everywhere in public—that's normal—for our protection and security but not to see how fast we can get undressed and pee in a cup, right?

As I return to Hadley, she's stuffing all her belongings into the plastic bag and attaching it to her personal one. Stark naked, she stands and faces me. Aside from my mom, I've never once seen another woman nude.

"You better hurry," Hadley says.

"How can you be so calm about this?"

She shrugs. "Some things are easier than others. Knowing I was going to have to go down in a giant riser was not easy. I thought I was going to throw up just standing outside with you."

So she knew, and that's why she held on.

"Sorry I used you as a crutch, but I had to find someone to help me until we got down here."

My lips curve just a little at knowing we shared the same thoughts again.

Hadley shrugs. "Knowing I have to get naked in a room with another girl . . . not a big deal. But, I take it, it is for you?"

I nod. It's a huge deal.

"'Kay. Well … since you helped me and didn't even know you were helping, I'll help you. What's the worst part? The getting naked or the being naked?"

"Um …"

"Or the peeing in a cup?"

I point at her. "That. That right there. I can't even pee if someone's on the outside of the door."

Hadley picks up the plastic cup on the small counter. "If you can do this, then, you can do anything, but seriously, you're probably down to a minute and a half left. Start with the basics. Coat first, Anna."

As she says my name, I've forgotten that I told her my new one—the one no one calls me. The one that isn't me, but is me. "Yeah. Coat first. I can do this."

"Yeah, you can, but you probably only have sixty seconds. So face away while I fill this up and, afterward, I'll sing and plug my ears while you do it."

A tiny burst of laughter comes out. Now or never. Now or never.

With that, I strip, stuff everything I have in the bag, and sit on the toilet with a cup under my girl parts as Hadley sings our national anthem, a burst of laughter coming out of me along with a full container of urine.

The door swishes open just as I sit my butt down on the designated seat, paper-like-gown-thing wrapped around me as best I can. I even tried to sit on it so my butt won't freeze on the plastic.

Unlike my method of opening in the back, Hadley's is open in the front, and she's just holding it closed.

The same person who greeted us outside walks in. "Welcome,

ladies."

I'm so glad she didn't call us candidates. Candidates sounds like we have the option to be or not to be adults or the government can decide to unvote us out or something. We all live here. Are born here. Register here. They can't just decide we don't make the cut and get rid of us.

"I'm Doctor Elizabeth Paxton. You can call me Doctor Pax." Bright blue eyes reflect a kindness that matches her voice. "Now, as females, you'll have a full workup which includes drawing blood, genetic testing, a gynecological evaluation, pregnancy test—"

"I am so not pregnant," Hadley says.

"Good, good," Doctor Pax says. "We'll continue with an ultrasound on your ovaries and uterus, full body MRI, DNA sampling, fingerprinting, stress test, echocardiogram, biopsy of breast material from both breasts, one lymph node, and we'll take a stool sample."

"Take?" My cheeks flame at the fact that I asked *and* that it will be done.

"Yes," she says, matter of fact. "Afterward, we'll get you setup in your pod, where you'll move on to a full psychological evaluation."

A glance at Hadley shows me even she's gone a little green.

"Any questions?" the doctor asks.

"Why all that?" I ask, wondering if Hadley already knows.

"How else would we determine if you're healthy and an acceptable specimen for reproduction and adult functions?"

"But ... why does that matter?" Boldness does not become me, but for some reason, I really want to know. "And a biopsy?"

"Again, Miss ..."

"Erianna Keating. I go by Anna." Saying my new name a second time makes it more real and more of what I want—like my future really is a new life without the baggage of the past, what little there is.

"Miss Keating, we are a strong and healthy country because our people produce strong and healthy children. You must know breast cancer is the only disease for which we still haven't found a cure. Thus, if two genetic anomalies were to reproduce, we'd have children who aren't strong and in a world where our safety and security is imperative, it's up to us to be everything our leaders need us to be."

"Oh, okay." I'm not sure I follow completely, but who am I to question their reasons? I can, however, see why Mom hoped I'd be a fluke. Flukes don't go through any of this; they just survive off whatever happens with no say, but none of the responsibility.

"Now that we're clear on that, who'd like to go first?"

Hadley and I face each other, her eyes downcast. I guess all these medical tests might be a little more daunting than she expected.

I turn back to the doctor. "I guess I will."

She spins toward the counter but pats the bed first. "Up here, then. We'll start with the simple stuff first. For example, first day of your last menstrual cycle?"

Oh, goodie.

"Be sure to drink the water provided, take this pill now, and this one in exactly one hour. These will prevent any infection and complete the healing process from any surgical openings, as well as any existing small wounds you may have had upon your bodies." The woman dressed in white places two large and four small cups on the counter in the room she's brought Hadley and me to. "Do not forget to take the second pill in one hour."

She'd been the one to inject the numbing medicine into my arm. She'd been the one to scrape the inside of parts no one's ever touched before, and to press and squeeze all sorts of places I don't want to think about again.

Doctor Pax had only been there to supervise our room, as well as ten others, apparently.

"Someone will be back to get you for psychological testing soon." The woman rifles through a folder in her hands. "You'll also need to keep these on your uniforms from now on." She hands me a small label clip and one to Hadley.

"What is this?" I ask.

"It's your identification number. You'll use this throughout your life. Now just to confirm, press your thumb here . . ." She takes mine and holds it up, hovering her thumb over the black area. "Just press there."

Doing that creates a beep. A second later the numbers F2053425 appear. "This is my ID?"

"Yes. Press it again."

I do and after a quick beep, my name appears.

"You'll need to memorize that number and use it for the rest of the week for all identification, and beyond for all job functions, etcetera. All your current educational and personal records will be associated with it. Details and information from registration will be, too."

Great. Now I'm a number.

She switches to Hadley and has her do the same thing, though Hadley doesn't ask any questions. "Don't forget to take the pill, and clip those to your collars." With that, the door swishes shut just like it had in the medical room.

Hadley and I stand next to each other, neither saying anything. I have no idea what she's thinking, but if it's anything

like me, I'm exhausted, probably going to have horrible nightmares and just want to go home. On top of that, I want my
mom. Eighteen or three, there's something about having Mom
around that seems right.

Rubbing my hand up and down my arm, I stare at the bare-
ness of the walls.

Unlike the white part of the building, our new room had, at
some time, been painted a soft blue with an ugly brown trim.
Much of it remains, but some must have peeled, and someone
just did a patch job. I'm sure it would look somewhat pretty, at
least better, if they painted the whole thing. Even white would
pass—which is fast becoming my least favorite color.

Aside from the four beds inside what can be no more than
an eight by twelve foot room, a small door hides a toilet and
shower, and just outside of that, a tiny counter has a sink and
a mirror. I wouldn't call the room anything more than an over-
sized closet. Even my falling-apart living space, where Mom
and I stay, is better than this.

"Top or bottom, you think?" I ask after an interminable
silence.

Hadley doesn't say anything.

"Top, then." I move forward toward the short ladder, take a
step up and bump my left breast against the rail. It throbs like
nothing I've ever had zing through me. I seethe through the
pain, breathing in air through my teeth as it lessens. They'd
said pill number one would dull all pain, but it must not have
worked on me.

Hadley climbs up, as I stand there with one foot on the
bottom rung. She lies down and covers up her pink jumpsuit
with a white sheet that rustles like paper.

On another deep breath, I finish my climb, careful not to
bump my other side. Breast cancer may be one of the few

cancers scientists can't cure, but they know how to control it. If they're testing for it, why can't they just do blood tests like normal doctors?

Rather than keep thinking about it, I maneuver my way onto the squeaky mattress and lay down in my new pink jump-suit. From what I saw on our walk, girls wear pink and the boys are in blue, each with a different code over their right upper-chest area.

It's like we're tagged for our gender, probably our type and who we are. Like one giant cattle call.

Only one other time have I been rooted from my comfort zone and stuck in a box with a bunch of people I didn't know. My first day at the level one educenter. This time, though, the poking and prodding is done *to* me, and not by me as I indulge my curiosity.

At the moment, I'm not particularly curious about what's coming. My lids want to close, but my mind doesn't want to shut off. I have no idea when they'll come back for us and really don't want to go through more testing without getting some food, but even that, they've denied us. It doesn't bother me as much as it seems to Hadley, whose stomach started grumbling while Doctor Pax did my exam.

So many times, Mom and I have had to hold off a little bit for food. I've learned to deal with it by tightening my ab muscles; that stops the bubbling stomach sounds from giving me away. Did that a lot in educenter to keep my friends from knowing I hadn't eaten, or couldn't even, as they chowed down. Laying there facing the ceiling, which is about three feet from my face, Cam and RK, Jen and the others come to mind. Are they going through a similar experience? Cam would never be able to deal with the pain of the biopsy. I'm sure she'll be freaking out, carrying on and probably curled in a corner in the fetal position.

At a long sigh from Hadley, I shut off my thoughts and turn toward her. "You okay?"

She shakes her head, and the hiccup of air suggests she's holding back tears.

For some reason, not even a single one has fallen from me. "Want to talk about it?"

Hadley flips to her side, her eyes open, wet streaks running down her cheeks. "I didn't know it was going to be like that." Her voice comes out a whisper.

"But I thought—"

She shakes a little. "My sister said they just made her pee in a cup and did the normal breathe in, breathe out stuff. None of the ..." Her voice breaks. One finger extends into the space between us and circles the air.

I take it she means all the stuff they made us go through. "Oh." What else should I say? I didn't know, either, but I guess, for someone walking in expecting one set of activities and being put through so much more, it really could mess with their head. I'm just used to so much disappointment that I guess I've learned to deal with it.

"Why did they do that to us, Anna?" Her eyes plead as if I have the answer.

"Isn't it just part of the processing?"

She wipes her eyes. "Do you really think they need to do a biopsy to determine if we can carry trash? Or extract sheez from us so we can teach kids? This was pure humiliation." She sniffles. "And when I get out of here, I'm telling my mom."

"What can she do?"

Hadley buries her face in her pillow and sobs. "Nothing. Nothing. None of us can. We always have to do what we're told."

Exactly. We do what we're told or the consequences are grave, or so said our teachers, our leaders, even our parents. Except Mom. She always told me to watch out for myself. To ask questions. Mom always said, 'Take control of yourself, your body, your job, and you'll be responsible for and to yourself'. I should have remembered and thought that through.

I beat my fist against my head.

Hadley's pain is visible.

Mine is tucked deep inside, but she's right. I should have asked 'why?' more before I let them do anything to me. Maybe Cam will, and will manage to get out of it.

Should have asked. Should have said something. Guilt weighs on me. Mom also says, 'Hindsight is twenty-twenty, Eri'.

How, though, am I supposed to get a good job, if I don't do what they tell me? People who break the rules, who get in trouble—they have no shot at a decent future. Those are the kids the guys in white suits come and take away in the middle of the day and never return. Those are the families that disappear in the middle of the night never to come back.

I don't want to be like that. I just want to go through registration, get a good job, something I can do well, and go home.

That's all I want, which means, until the week is over, I have to deal with everything they do to me—or I'll risk having nothing, and I don't want to be like Mom. I love her and all, but I want my kids to have more than me, not less.

The door swishes open as I'm pondering, and two other girls come in. Their faces are red, streams of tears still flowing like the rivers that had gone down Hadley's cheeks. Lady-in-white gives them the same spiel she did to us, places another set of cups on the counter, and walks out.

Standing there, as helpless as any of us, I figure someone's got to help them, and I roll over, the pain in my side not as pronounced as before. "Hey," I say.

They both look up, one set of green and one set of blue eyes struggling to stay open behind glassy waves. Girl on the left's hair is a ratty mess of black, as if she tore at it with her fingers. The other has gorgeous blonde waves similar to Cam's—hair I'd love to have been born with. I can only be thankful one part of the medical tests required a complete body-wash-down, so my flat brown is at least clean now.

"Take the bottom beds and try to rest," I say.

Neither girl moves but both shiver. The jumpsuits are pretty thin, more like a body cover than actual clothing.

Rather than wait until they collapse from their own emotions, I climb down, trying hard not to touch my chest in the process, and take each one of them, guiding them to a bed. "I'm Anna," I say as I tuck the first in and pull the super-starched sheet across her body.

"Vica," she says as a new batch of sobs wracks her body

"I'm Brie." The second girl does the same as I guide her to her bed.

Back up on top, I stare at the ceiling.

"That was really nice, Anna," Hadley whispers.

I turn my head toward her. "What? That was just being human."

"Yeah, but you could have just left them. You could have ignored me. You could have just pretended you didn't care, but you didn't. I'm really glad I have you. I couldn't have done this without you."

"Thank you," a soft voice says from below me, followed by another "Thank you," from the other side.

"No problem. We're all in this together."

"Let's just hope it stays that way," Hadley says.

10

"Anna," a voice says. "Anna, wake up."

My shoulder rises and falls.

"Anna, wake up. We have to go."

I roll over, wanting to return to the dream that zaps from my memory the moment I decide I want it to keep going.

"Anna, you have to get up. They're taking us for the psyche testing." Another shove pushes my shoulder up.

Blinking, I realize I'm facing a blue wall, dressed in a pink jumpsuit and laying on a very unsupportive mattress in my closet-room—not in my happy place, wherever that had been in my head.

With a slow roll, I face Hadley. "Did I fall asleep?"

"Yeah."

"Did you?" Lifting up, I drape my feet over the edge of the bed. Vica and Brie stand together next to the bathroom door. Rubbing my eyes, I say, "D'you get any sleep?" Between blinks, they shake their heads. Back to Hadley, she does the same. "Sorry. Guess I'm just really, really tired."

"It's no problem," Vica says. "You didn't snore or anything."

A little burst of laughter leaves me. "Guess I can be happy for that."

"I wish I could have slept," Brie says. "But every time I close my eyes, I—" Her bottom lip trembles. Vica wraps an arm around her. "I can't get any of it out of my head."

"I'm sure that's what they want, too," Hadley says.

I drop to the floor. The four of us stand there, meeting each others' gazes. "Maybe you're right, Hadley," I say. "The next step is psychological testing, right? What if putting us through stuff that's humiliating is part of seeing how much we can take?"

Vica reaches out toward me. "Why would they do that, though? My dad said we'd be evaluated for our strengths and skills, not—" She motions with her hand.

"When did he go through the program?" I ask.

"A long time ago, but—"

"My sister came through last year, and this is not what she described," Hadley says.

"So something changed." Brie rubs a hand up her arm. "Why now?"

While listening, I wipe out the wrinkles in my clothes. "Things can't stay the same forever, can they? Maybe they're trying to impro—"

All the faces go blank.

"Sorry, not improve … I mean, you know, like refine, or something? I mean, if it was different from last year, there has to be a reason, and maybe at the end, we'll get to tell them what was good and bad. Maybe?"

Vica and Hadley narrow their eyes.

Brie touches my shoulder. "Do you really believe that?"

"I don't know. It just sounds like something my mom would think or say, you know?"

Each of them nods a little.

I don't necessarily agree with my mom, but her words do make sense. "So what do you think we'll have to do for this next thing?"

"Maybe we have to tell them what images we see in those black and white inky picture things from back in the nineteen hundreds," Vica says.

Brie giggles. "Ink blots? My dad's a wanna-be psychologist. Those are really cool. Maybe we'll have to answer a bunch of questions about what we think of stuff? Like the old Meyers Briggs test? You know, they still use that."

Hadley crosses her arms over her chest. "Never heard of it. Maybe we'll have to tell them everything our parents taught us so they can see if our moms and dads did everything right." Her lips curve just a little as she faces me. "What do you think, Anna?"

"Um . . . I really have no idea."

Hadley squeezes my shoulder. "That's probably why you aren't affected the same way as we are."

Brie nods. "Yeah. Hadley told us you didn't know much about this when you came in. My brother went through about five years ago. My parents, twenty-five years ago."

"My sister is next, but my best friend went through last year, and she told me all about it," Vica says.

Cam never shared anything, and that makes me wonder if her older brothers, two of them, ever told her anything. If not, if she knew as much as I do, she's got to be freaking out.

"So . . .," Hadley says, "we think you should lead us because you deal with stuff better than us."

"You decided this while I slept?"

The three heads bob.

I'm not a leader. Never have been. "Well . . . I'll do my best to get through whatever and prepare you."

Before I can say another word, all three wrap their arms around me. The hug is one I never expected.

Just as before, so many times, the door swishes open, and a person in a white jumpsuit stands in front of us. "Candidates, please exit the room and make your way to the left." A 'she', by the sound of her voice, points a PCD board toward the left.

With a glance to my roommates, I walk forward and turn but peer back down the hallway.

The space is full of pink bodies standing against the walls, and in the middle, in multiple rows. The person who opened our door walks up to me. "You'll continue on through this hall, following the red line to the next stop."

"Me?" I ask. She wants me to lead the whole group? There have to be a few hundred people in the hallway, if not more.

"You were first outside the house, weren't you?" she asks.

"Um ... well ..."

With a smirk she nods as if I should get moving.

One foot forward, I follow the red line, and turn.

The hallway before me is one long corridor of nothing. No color, no doors, no windows and no people. Lights keep it bright, and at the end, there's another turn, but walking toward it makes me think I'm on my way to my own funeral—as if I'm walking into the light that old Christians used to talk about before religion mostly died out.

Every step draws me closer to the end but brings with it surprise at the fact all this exists down here. Who knew? Not me. That's for sure.

At the bend, I turn and find people dressed in blue coming toward me—the boys.

Getting closer, I realize Zane is leading the same way I am. We stop at a double door.

I could go farther down the hallway, and he could too, but

that would bring his group to our medical facility and who knows where for us.

Zane faces me but says nothing. Hadley is so tight up against me, her movement makes me fidget.

At the rate I'm thinking through my problem—where to go—we'll stand here all day. "What do we do?" I ask Zane in a whisper.

He waves toward the double doors.

"They told you?"

He nods.

"Geez. Okay." There's no button or anything that would show us how to open the panels, so I guess it's just push and go. With a hand to the smooth white surface, I press.

The two doors slide inside the walls, and in front of me is yet another hallway, but this time, it's lit in a deep blue-purple, a calming color like walking through an underwater aquarium might be—if I'd ever gotten to go through one.

I step inside as lights blink on and off like stars in the night sky and waves—or something resembling them—pass overhead.

My steps are slow as I watch, a little mesmerized, a lot curious, my hand touching the surface, making it shimmer.

"This is so ... pretty," I say to no one.

Voices pick up as we progress through. A glance right and Zane walks with me, his gaze meeting mine.

"Isn't this pretty?" The color shimmers as we pass.

He smiles with his lips but not his eyes. The blue of his jumpsuit takes away from the happiness I saw in him when I first met him, to the point I wonder just what torture the medical exam put the boys through.

They're far quieter than any other set of guys I've been around.

We continue on through the cool hallway and into another white one, where a group of white-suited people meet us.

One moves into the middle of the hall and points toward me and Zane. "First door on the right." With a swing of her arm, she motions us left.

As I walk through, she repeats her statement, again and again. Lights brighten the small room, where ten chairs are in ten rows, each with a small desk attached to it, and every one with a number. In muted tones, the same statement is made from within the hallway, I presume funnelling people to other doors.

"Please take the first seat and fill in each of the others," the woman who counted us off says.

I move on to row number one, seat number one. At the front, on a flat metal table, stacks of PCDs, new versions of my old P-Comm, sit on the surface.

As I take my seat and slide the desk around to my front, Zane sits next to me, Hadley by him, and on down until our row is full and, behind us, more and more people take the rest of the seats. Feet shuffle, voices rise, and a woman approaches the front.

"What is this?" I whisper to Zane as if he'd know.

He leans toward me, a fresh clean scent wafting to me. "Testing."

I got that, but I wanted to ask how and what kind, since I expected our second batch of work would be psychological. What can be done without a one-on-one interview? I can't be the only one who's curious and as the volume in the room has grown more and more, I wonder if other people think the same as me.

The doors suck shut behind us, and all sound ceases.

"At this time, you'll complete your psychological evaluation." This is the third or fourth woman who hasn't introduced herself and, while their faces are different, skin tones are different, eye color, too, they're all dressed the same. It's kinda creepy. "I'll come around to validate your identification as I provide you with your examination tablet. Depending on your answers, you may be assigned further assessment, so you should answer all questions as honestly and accurately as possible." The woman comes toward me, a stack of ten screens in her hand along with a smaller version on top. "Your test should take no longer than four hours—"

A collective groan billows through the room. I can't say I disagree with the feeling.

"—which is enough time for one hour per section. You'll start with a clinical interview, intellectual function assessment, personality evaluation, and, throughout this, your behavior will be assessed."

The groaners stop. No doubt, the idea the testing began as we walked through the halls hits them—as Hadley suggested back when we had to pee in front of each other.

At my desk, the lady hands me a bundle. "Take one and pass it down please."

I follow her direction exactly, setting a screen before me. It's as blank and black as my ID on my collar.

"And, you'll conclude with a depression inventory. Left hand, please," she says to me.

Hand out, she takes my thumb and presses to the smaller screen. It beeps and produces my number as the one on my collar also beeps, and her gaze travels toward it. "You may begin." She moves on to Zane as my screen comes to life.

The first question reads, 'How do you handle difficult people?', with answers of 'Depends on the personality', 'Ask how I can help', 'Ignore them and walk away' and 'Smile and hope they solve the solution themselves'.

I choose the second answer and move on to number two of sixty, the timer at the top counting down my four hour window.

Fifty-two minutes later, the screen transitions to the Intelligence Quotient portion.

Here, the first question is 'Which one of these five is the least like the other four?' with answers: 'Dog', 'Mouse', 'Cat', 'Human', and 'Elephant'.

I pick the fourth answer and keep going to question two of forty.

Sixty-three minutes later, the screen pops up for a personality assessment, and Zane's stomach grumbles next to me. He slaps a hand to his mid-section, and it stops.

I haven't eaten since I woke up, and I have no idea what time it is, but nerves must be keeping my body from needing food. Actually, since I arrived, I haven't seen a single clock, or anyone eating any food, but no one's been overly grumpy about it, either.

Being shuffled from one place to the next, drugged for the medical procedures, and napping for what couldn't have been more than ten minutes, has made the day go by, but I don't know by how much, so maybe that's helping me not be bothered. Could also be the last eighteen years of not having food all the time.

As Zane presses into his stomach again, I wish I could find a vitamin bar, or something, for him, but of course I have nothing except my pink clothes and my number on.

The timer catches my eye, and I realize I've lost ten minutes focusing on Zane. Getting back to my questions, I see the number of questions is six hundred.

Oh, boy.

I have less than two hours left and a gazillion questions.

Submitting the next two, I read faster, trying to get through them versus thinking about them. After thirty-three questions, they turn to true-false, which goes way, *way* faster.

As the timer counts down to just eighteen minutes, the program switches again.

The first reads, *Select the color of the hallway prior to reaching this room.*

The color of the hallway?

I don't understand.

My options are blue, purple, red and green, but the last hallway I walked through couldn't have been called anything but white. The walls, doors—even the people—they'd all been white.

Lifting my head, my brow furrowed, I search for someone else doing the same—someone else confused by the question.

Reading it again, I still find it asking the same.

The color of the hallway.

What does that mean?

And what does it mean that the color I saw isn't an option?

Frustration burns through me as the timer continues to countdown to just fifteen minutes.

Anxiety jumps in to mix with my concern, and I begin to tap my toes inside my shoes.

Zane coughs next to me.

The hall was white!

I can't put an answer down because it wouldn't be true. I can't click to skip forward because that's not an option. I just don't know what to do.

Another cough comes from Zane along with what I'd swear is a word.

Using my eyes only, I dart them in his direction. His finger taps on the desk surface once until two fingers rub up against each other.

Back to my screen, I stare at the question and answers. It seems so simple, yet I can't lie; I can't make something up.

The hallway was white!

Now the time says eight minutes are left and, until I get to a second question in a section, I have no idea how many questions I have to complete. For all I know, I have two hundred to finish and barely over seven minutes left.

Another throat clearing from Zane echoes through the near-silent room, and along with it, I'd swear he says *shimmer*.

His fingers slide along the desk, and he wiggles them.

Shimmer?

The aquarium hallway?

The aquarium hallway.

Blue or purple?

Blue or purple?

I check purple.

The screen goes blank for a second until a swirling silver stream circles in the middle. A little shake does nothing but it keeps going, just like the rebooting of a PCD.

Oh, boy. I broke it.

Tilting up, my gaze meets the lady at the table, and I raise a tentative hand. She shakes her head, and I drop it again.

The screen keeps spinning.

In eighteen years, I've never been so nervous about a test and never broken the equipment. Of course, it *would* happen while I'm in the biggest, most important test of my life.

At this rate, I won't even qualify for garbage patrol.

A simple test. Four hours to complete, and I can't do that. I'll end up a fluke like Mom just because of incompetence.

I drop my head to my desk.

Lying on my desk, watching the screen that refuses to change, I'm sure my time is up, and I've ruined all chances of a decent future.

Beside me, Zane finishes and drops his head into his hands, elbows on his desktop. Down the line, each person finishes, one after the other after the other, in line with the amount of time it took our facilitator-woman to get to them with her wand-thing.

After what seems like ages, my screen goes blank.

I lift up, waiting for someone to come and take away my broken system.

Instead, the screen blinks white, letters and numbers scroll through, and a list materializes.

At the top, the letter-number combinations S, S1, S4, S5, 5f, Hy1, Hy5, Pd5, Pa3, Si2, ANX, FAM, LSE2, and Re show up along with a blinking 'transferring' beneath them.

Our room monitor stands. "If your screen says 'complete', you may return to your rooming facility, and have no more testing for the evening," she says. "Please be prepared to begin your day tomorrow at oh-six-hundred. Pre-set alarms will wake you at that time, and breakfast will be served until oh-seven-hundred, upon which time you'll receive your itinerary for the day. Those of you with any other status will need to remain

here for a schedule of evaluations to begin immediately. Leave
the device on the desk and exit through the back door."

My screen still says 'transferring', which leads me to believe
I'll be here for a really long time.

Zane's screen is black again, and he rises, like most of the
room, except Hadley and Vica. They sit in their seats, too. Brie
leaves, as does the super-tall boy from outside.

Despite the huge number of people going through registration in the red house—at least twenty-five hundred if my
estimate is accurate—the organization keeps it free of chaos.
The calmness, the sereneness, of the whole situation just seems
abnormal. From what I've seen in educenter, people don't like
being confined unless they know they're getting something
out of it.

Of course, they'll all get good jobs and I won't, but is that
motivation enough not to gripe and complain the whole day?

Cam, Jen and RK once complained when we had to stay
fifty-six minutes for a fifty-five minute class. One minute and
they'd slap their books closed, huff and puff and roll their eyes.
If any of their lunch time had to be used for educenter activities, they went to the administrator and filed a formal complaint. Cam did it three times before the end of term.

"F2053425, you may depart."

A whole day without food, humiliating tests and four hours
on seated with a broken PCD would make any of my friends
crazy. Not me, I'm used to waiting, but if Cam's group is going
through the same, she'll be pitching a fit.

Yet, no one here is. This is weird—or maybe my friends are
just drama royalty. I could believe either after what they put
me through this week.

"F2053425, you may depart."

Of course, having to wait again will give me way too much

time to think about this. Wait. Wait. Wait. The story of my life.

"F2053425, you may depart." The room lady says from right up close.

I tilt up to her, my attention taken from my inner thoughts. "What?" I glance down at my screen. It still says 'transferring'. "But—"

She takes it and presses a button. The screen blinks to complete. "You are free to depart."

I glance toward Vica and Hadley; their expressions are flat and unemotional.

"You are free to depart, F2053425."

A rocket-flare of anger rises within me, and I turn toward the woman in the white suit. "My name is Anna." The whole use of a number to define me seems wrong—as much as Cam pulling me through security lines with a stolen shirt.

Hadley's lips quirk up for a brief moment.

With a nod her way, I scoot out from the desk and head toward the back door. It opens as I reach it, and I step out to find only one person in the entire mega-hallway. "Zane?"

He juts his chin my way. "It's about time." He starts down the hallway toward where I'd come from before the massive-long test.

I don't really want to talk to him. What I want is to go back to my little room, to climb up onto my little bed and sleep. Or to find Brie, to wait for Vica and Hadley—to find out what all those letters meant, why my screen didn't work, what happened with me. Not talk to the boy who saved me from a tram hours before.

That's unacceptable, Erianna. You owe him more of a thanks.
"How are you, Eri?"

"Anna."

Lines form in his forehead. "What?"

"I've decided ... to ... go by Anna."

"But on the bus—"

Stopping him with my hands in the air, I say, "I know, but ... this is ... you know, my future, and I want to be Anna."

He steps toward me. "You want to be someone else, or you want to be you but better?"

"Uh ..."

"Nevermind." One hand reaches out toward me as if he wants to shake. "Since we're on the introduction portion of our day, my name is Zane, though most people call me ... Zane."

I can't help the smile. "Erianna Keating but I go by Anna."

"It's nice to meet you." He edges closer.

"It's nice to ... meet you, too." I slide my palm against his, and he squeezes, shaking a little.

Without letting go he says, "Will you come with me?"

"Come with ... you?" There's no one else to go with, since the hallway is still empty.

"Yeah. With me. I'd like to show you something."

"Show me ... what?"

He closes his lids and sighs. When he meets my gaze again, he says, "If I tell you, showing you would be pointless."

With my arms crossed over my chest, I lean into the wall. "You're awfully pushy."

His lips curve. "I get that a lot. Come on."

<hr />

Zane leads me back through the main hallway and turns right into what I called the aquarium. As we step inside, the walls shimmer and turn a deeper purple than they were even before. Like before, though, I run my hands along the surface. It's smooth, almost satiny slick, and has a little give. I want to pull it down, wrap it around myself like a blanket, and curl up on the floor.

"What is this?" I ask.

He chuckles. "This, *Anna*, is a mood hall."

"A what?" Fingertips to the wall, I keep running them against it, the softness brushing my skin.

"You were stuck on a question during the test, weren't you?"

Without looking at him, I say, "Yeah."

"In the part of the survey that gauges your depression level."

"Oh." Again, I don't turn to him, fascinated by the space above and around me. The color shifts a little from a deep purple to a lighter one and back.

"What color do you see?"

"Huh? Purple of course."

A soft laugh leaves him. "Not red? Pink? Green? Yellow?"

"Of course not."

His hand around my arm stops me. "Anna."

Staring up at him, his eyes are serious. "What?"

"This is a *mood* room. What you see is recorded in the test and matched against waves that transmit through the pin on your collar."

"Okay. That's kinda neat." I believe what I've said, but his fierce expression suggests I shouldn't.

As if a light switch changes, he smiles. "Right. It's neat."

"You have any idea what purple means?"

His gaze never leaves mine. "It's spiritual. Did the color change, at all?"

With a shrug, I say, "A little blue, but really mostly purple."

He steps in closer. "Blues are born survivors, Anna." A foot more and he stands right at my toes, our gazes locked on each other. "A soul who's in balance, a mind that is strong, nerves that are controlled. Purple is what they—I mean, purple is ... it's goo—cool."

I break the stare-down and return to my admiration of the walls. Never would I have described myself as in balance. Nothing's been 'in balance' in my life ever. "So it's not wrong, or anything? They aren't going to put me through more testing."

"That I can't tell you, but yeah ... it's not wrong. None of the colors are wrong."

"Oh." I don't know why I assumed a color would be a positive or a negative, it just seemed appropriate. "So, how do you know about this thing?" Holding out my arms, I walk through the area encompassing the space.

"I—uh—I've seen one before. Just thought you might not have since ... you know."

With a nod, I say, "Yeah, didn't have a clue we could do this kind of stuff."

Two girls break into our private discussion as they pass by us. Nothing changes that I notice, but they slow in the middle, chins lifting for a moment, before they both continue on quicker than when they first entered.

Back to him, I ask, "So, what did you want to show me?"

He leans against the wall, ankles crossed, arms, too. "Just this. I thought you might want to know more about it."

"Cool. Thanks."

The grumbling I heard in the room echoes around us.

"You hungry?" I ask him.

His lips purse. "I can deal."

"I have a couple of vitamin bars in my bag in my room if you want to come back with me."

He cocks his head. "You want to give me your snacks?"

With a light shrug, I say, "I've gone a couple days before without eating much, and honestly, I don't feel hungry."

"That would be the pill."

"What?"

He'd turned as he spoke, but I'd swear he said a pill made me not hungry.

Zane faces away, rubbing at the side of his head.

"Did you say a pill made me not hungry?"

He squishes up his nose and scratches a finger along the side.

"Zane?" I stride forward and stand right in front of him. "Did you say a pill made me not hungry?"

He answers with one quick nod but still doesn't look at me.

"What pill?"

His eyes close a second. "Blue one? The second after the medical?"

"But—" I pull myself away and pace.

I fell asleep and forgot to take that one. Is that why no one's been aggressive or complaining? Did they drug us all? Makes sense given how many people they have to pump through and all the procedures they put the girls through. I can only imagine what they did to the boys, but at the same time, I don't want to know.

"How do you know that's what it was?" I ask, not sure I understand my own question.

"Wouldn't you rather know what else it does?"

"Um ... do I? Does it matter? They gave it to everyone, so it must have been ... all right, right?"

Zane jumps forward, takes both my hands and holds them up. "If they tied you all up and threw you over a cliff would that be 'all right'?" His tone is full of strife or, as my Grandma used to say, 'spit and fire'.

"Well, no, but I mean, they know what they're doing, so I have to trust—"

"You have to question." He lets go and storms back to the wall as Hadley and Vica walk through the opening.

"Anna!" Hadley comes forward and takes my hand. "You won't believe this!" Her face is full of excitement. Vica's, too.

"What?" I ask.

"My scores came up marked for analytical excellence, so, tomorrow morning, I get to meet with the head of litigation. I'm going into law!"

"Wow. I didn't know they could figure stuff out that fast. That's awesome."

She reaches in and hugs me. "I wouldn't have gotten through this day without you, though. I want you to know that."

Patting her back, I glance toward Zane.

He glares at me.

"We better get back and get some sleep," I say after a minute, still staring at Zane. "We don't want to mess up the early wake-up thing, or whatever's coming tomorrow."

With Hadley and Vica next to me, we start through the rest of the hallway.

I give Zane on more look, trying to understand his expression, but I can't. He'd been kind to me the few times I've seen him but the expression right before the girls showed up contradicted what I thought about him.

As we pass through the end of the hall, Zane's head is shaking as if I've done something to disappoint him. An action I've seen way too often in my life—from Cam.

The blare of an alarm precedes a speaker saying, "All candidates should rise and journey to the main dining hall. Activities commence at oh-seven-hundred in your assigned facility. Designations are marked in your corridor reception office."

This repeats three or maybe four times as I blink open my eyes, not sure if I'm ready to start my day, or not.

After the one before, the one I've now classified as the longest day of my life, made worse because I don't wear a timepiece and there isn't a single timer anywhere that I can find, I can't imagine what they'll put us through. More than that, can it be worse than before? Is that even possible?

Hadley and Vica rise, but Brie's already standing at the mirror applying a coat of lipsheen.

"Morning," she says. "I'm an early riser. Got an internal alarm clock that never shuts off."

"I call toilet first," Vica says and races the three steps into the smallest bathroom on planet earth.

Hadley rolls over and meets my gaze. "You don't think they're going to do more of that ... stuff today do you?" she asks.

"No idea." I'd rise, but I know I'll have to pee as soon as I do. "You ready for your meeting thing?"

She nods. "It's kinda cool knowing which way you might

go, you know?"

I would if that happened to me. Instead, I had a screen of numbers, my soul is balanced, and Zane thinks the people in the facility are drugging us. My lack of deep sleep isn't due to the thin mattress or paper blankets. It's because I couldn't get what he said in the 'aquarium' hallway out of my head. I realize a lot of the people here know more about this place than me because they have brothers and sisters who've gone through it, but his expression seemed off. The question is, why? Another question is, why do I care?

"How about you, today, Anna?" Bria asks. "You doing okay?"

"Yeah. Why do you ask?"

She shrugs. "You just seemed a little upset with that guy in the hall."

This is the stuff I would have spent hours poring over and considering with Cam, once upon a time. "I wasn't. He was just showing me the hallway."

Vica exists the bathroom, and Hadley jumps down, running for it. "That place is freaky. My cousin told me about it. Said you're supposed to think happy thoughts, only, when you go through."

Of course they knew about it. Everyone knows everything, except me.

"What color was it for you?" I ask.

"Red for me," Brie says.

"Kinda teal, greenish, whatever," Vica says. "How 'bout you?"

"Purpley."

The toilet flushes, and Hadley reappears. "Purple's supposed to be the color they want."

"What?" The three of us ask together, as I drop to the cold, slick tile floor and shuffle to the bathroom.

"Yeah," Vica says. "They say purple is the color most people don't get very much, like only in spikes. They're always looking for that in personality profiles, or something." She takes Brie's place in front of the mirror.

"Totally did not know that," Brie says. "Guess someone's gonna want to talk with Anna."

◦——◆——◦

I step out of my door at six-thirty, according to the old timepiece Vica brought, knowing, unlike the rest of us, that our PCDs wouldn't work, and walk into chaos that never happened the day before.

People are everywhere, spilling from rooms, loud, obnoxious voices calling out to one another. Since the eleventh district has its center at Perry Road, it doesn't surprise me to see a few faces I recognize. Our area alone has fourteen level three educenters, though, so I have no idea who ninety-nine point nine percent of the people are.

They aren't kids I spent a lot of time with but are familiar just the same. Seeing them makes me wonder what caused them to be assigned to the red house—me, too, for that matter. It also brings me back to Cam and the others. What are they doing? What's she thinking about? Does she miss me?

Cut it out, Eri, she doesn't care about you.

People file on through and head left, so I presume the cafeteria is that way and turn in that direction. Vica and Brie have already gone off, but I lean against the wall, waiting for Hadley. She wanted to put on a touch of makeup—something I didn't bring.

Standing and watching people is a fascinating sport. Some go up the hall, some back down, some into doors and more out. Despite all of us wearing the same thing, except for color, we're all different. Walks, talks, expressions, tones. All different.

There aren't any signs anywhere, which seems really weird, given the number of people in one place. It's like we're in a mouse's maze, and only the smartest and strongest will find their way to the cheese.

Of course I haven't found the cheese, so that must mean I'm not in the winner category, despite my purple vision.

Hadley joins me a few minutes later. No sooner does she stand next to me, that her eyes go wide and her finger extends. "Oh, my Oz!" Her excitement is palpable. "Jeremy!" Hadley's off and running down the hall as a guy in blue stops and turns, his arms go wide, and she jumps into them.

"Breakfast burrito?" a voice says next to me.

I turn to find Zane stuffing his face. He waves a hand in my direction, one with what I presume to be the mentioned breakfast.

"You brought me food?"

"Thought you might want some."

Pointing down the hall, I say, "I do, but I thought—no, yes. Thank you."

He extends the foil-wrapped food my way.

"Why did you bring this to me?"

"Aren't you hungry?"

"Actually ... yeah." Unwrapping the silver lining releases heavenly scents. My stomach grumbles as if just waiting to indulge in the excess in my hand. My first bite makes it growl, this time, with pleasure. "You didn't have to do this," I mumble through another bite.

Zane takes one last chomp and crumples the wrapper.

"All candidates should proceed to their assigned locations at this time," a voice says from above.

Like the signage, I have no idea where the speakers are.

I point down toward where a big group gathers and start walking. "I need to find my assignment."

Zane stays with me as I traipse my way over. The group swells as more people try to get in front of the one and only screen.

"I'm never going to see where to go at this rate." I try to squeeze through, but there's no room, even less when more people file in. Everyone is, of course, waiting until the last minute to get their assignment details.

This is what I expected with all these people around.

A long beep sounds overhead, and we all lift up as if we're puppets on a string. "All candidates must proceed to their assigned locations at this time," the speaker says.

Half the bunch scatters as I sneak up closer. Every time someone gets near, it pops up a number I presume is theirs and another series of characters beneath it. I guess that's where they need to go.

Twenty people later, I step forward, my F2053425 blinks on screen along with FOB600. One big question remains. Where is that?

Stepping back and bumping into others, muttering apologies, I eventually get back to where Zane's standing, leaning against the wall, his arms crossed. He seems to like that position.

"Get your location?" he asks.

"Yeah, but I have no idea where it is."

"Just follow the mice, Anna."

I jerk back. "Follow the mice?"

One eyebrow lifts on his face. "Isn't that what we all are? Just mice in a maze? Or sheep. Whichever."

"Well ... you'd think they could at least give us direction."

"Why would they do that?" He asks the question as if he's

serious.

Plenty of people have messed with me by trying to be serious on stupid questions, and I get caught up in them thinking they're really serious only to be laughed at. Zane's been nice to me, though, even if I have no idea why he keeps showing up.

I try for a smile, gauging whether he's playing me or actually being serious. "Okay, listen. I gotta go find this place." Stepping away, I turn and follow the group, remembering I haven't thanked my new friend for breakfast and spin back.

My face slams into Zane's chest. His arms wrap around me, keeping me from collapsing to the ground. As my head throbs and I blink open my eyes, I tilt up to him. Ours lips are a breath apart, the intensity of his blue eyes burning into my soul. Neither of us says a word, our gazes don't separate, our chests move in sync with each inhale and exhale.

After what seems like hours, but is probably only seconds, he says, "You should watch where you're going," and relaxes his hold.

I pull away, but the warmth that encompassed the front of my body from being up against him disappears, and the replacing cold makes me shiver. "Uh … sorry about that. I-I just wanted to say thank you. For breakfast. Thank you for breakfast." Heat seeps into my cheeks.

Zane never glances away, not even when he says, "No problem. Get going, mousey." His lips curve.

Rather than let him seem my cheeks get pinker, I zip around, and race after the people that are far down the hall. I refuse to turn back or to slow, figuring if I can catch up someone else will show me where to go.

As I head left, following the crowd in a new direction from any other I've gone, a series of doors with bright letters overhead calls me forward. There's SSM100, FOB100, SSL200 and on and on, but not mine. Continuing farther, I turn right, down another hallway with more doors and one or two people slipping through open spaces. Above the letters read RM300, EMR400 and at the very, very end is FOB600.

Talk about a ridiculous maze. How is anyone supposed to find their location without signs and when there's no order to the room numbers at all?

I dart down to the door as the blare of the alarm sounds and says, "At this time, all candidates must be in their assigned location," and stop before I ram into the person just inside.

"Take a seat. Right or left, it doesn't matter," a male voice says from somewhere I can't see ahead of me.

The room is another auditorium style space like the psychology testing facility. Rows upon rows of people sit, a mix of blue and pink, and in the front, someone in a red suit jacket with blue pants stands at a podium.

I scoot into the back row, a place I'd never choose if I didn't have to, and sit next to a guy in blue, seven seats from the end.

Two seconds later, Zane walks in and takes the seat next to me.

I glare at him. "If you were coming here, why didn't you just say so and help me find it?"

"Like I said, it's a maze for a reason."

With an irritated huff, I focus on the person in front, but in my periphery, more candidates enter and fill up the last seats. As soon as the final spot is taken, the door swishes shut.

"Welcome, candidates," the guy up front says, wasting no time in getting started. "Today marks a tremendous transition from life as a child to life as an adult in the American Union. It is today that we will provide your assignments—"

Already? How can they choose so fast? Aren't we supposed to be here a whole week?

"—as well as begin your transition to that role. From this moment until the end of the week, you will train in your role such that, at the closure of your time, you will have a plan to complete your studies, if applicable, have had some experience in your profession, as well as be introduced to your mentor." The dude returns to a desk and slides back a curtain, revealing a table full of boxes about the size of the new PCDs. He selects one and holds it up. "These devices will be yours to keep, and will work within the confines of this facility, unlike the junk you brought in with you."

Even if our stuff is junk, does he have to diss it?

The man opens a box and pulls out one of the units, moving toward the center of the room again. I really wish they'd identify themselves, give us their name, or something. Surely adults don't go by their numbers, right? I never called my educators Miss ABCDEFG, but Miss Tucker or Miss Layton, or whomever.

"Now," he says, pulling me from my thoughts, "we'll pass these out shortly. To activate yours, you'll connect your lapel pills to the input, here. Afterward ..."

He goes on and on describing the process. It would seem smarter to give us the equipment and explain while we're working on it, versus giving us all the details and expecting us to remember.

Yet, no one complains. No one gripes or whines. They all just stare ahead as if enraptured by the speaker. A glance toward Zane, and he faces me, his eyebrows up just a little, as if expecting me to ask a question. Looking away and turning toward the other guy next to me, I find him facing forward, giving me no consideration at all.

Back to Zane, his gaze is still on me.

I return to the guy at the front, wondering why no one's

raising their hand, or as Mom says, 'raising commotion'. If this were a level three educenter, at least one person, of the two hundred people in the room, would do something.

From the side of the curtain, four people appear. Each takes a stack of boxes and walks into the single aisle toward the back. One stands at our row and begins to pass the boxes down. The others do the same around us.

Once a box is in my hands, trepidation takes over. After I open it, after I attach my lapel piece to it, after I connect and it shows me my future, I'll know just what the American Union expects of me for the rest of my life.

This is the moment I've waited for, hoped and worried about.

Wanted.

All I have to do is open the box and take a few steps.

That's it.

I don't know if I can do it.

"You going to open that?" Zane whispers next to me.

The white box sits in my lap, not a single identifying mark upon it. Every time I touch it, tingling encompasses my fingers as if just that little bit of contact has an effect.

"You know, if you don't open it, they're going to come over here and ask you why, right?"

Will they? Probably. With so many people in the room, it'll be a while. Hopefully.

"You know how to open a box?" Zane asks.

"Yes."

Around me, people are carefully slipping the ends out, as if they can't wait but have the patience of a snail, knowing it'll get to its destination at some point in the future.

"Do your hands still work?"

"Of course."

Smooth, black PCDs slide from within all sorts of boxes around me, including Zane's. The slick front is shiny and un-scratched. I should be dying to open something brand new, since I've never, not once, had a piece of equipment like it. My excitement should be billowing from me at all the possibilities that are about to come alive.

Of course, no one else is ripping up their prizes like holiday presents or jumping up and down with excitement.

"What's going on, Anna?"

Telling a virtual stranger that I'm terrified of finding out what my new PCD is going to tell me seems scarier than learning the truth itself. "Nothing." I take a deep breath. "Just waiting for everyone to get theirs, you know, in case there's more instruction." It's a lie. He probably knows that, too. Sliding my finger beneath the top fold opens it wide, and I spin it around, letting the PCD rest on my palm.

My face reflects in the black surface, stringy hair falling around me, and the gauntness of my face suggests I need to eat a whole lot more than I have been.

Zane's finger appears in my line of sight. He taps the top, and the screen brightens.

Words appear indicating I should connect my lapel pin to it.

My hands shake as I disconnect it from my jumpsuit and attach it to the device.

A white swirl begins on the screen, moving from the outer edges to the center, disappearing and restarting. Once. Twice. Three times. A list of codes, like the ones that showed up after my test the night before blinks onto the screen for a second.

Zane sucks in air next to me. I twist toward him, but he's focused on his PCD, or whatever.

On my screen, the codes go away, and the swirly spinner returns, along with a "Please wait" and a counting down timer of sixty seconds.

A sigh escapes me.

If anyone else has had the same experience as me, they don't show it. Not a sound has come out of any of them.

After what seems like way more than a minute passes, the screen blinks once. My heart races, fingers tingle again, as what looks like a progress report from level three edu appears.

Candidate Report for F2053425, also known as Erianna Price

Keating.
Yup, that's me.
Beneath my name is says 'Factors'.
Superlative Self-Presentation
Beliefs in Human Goodness
Patience/Denial of Irritability
Denial of Moral Flaws
Femininity
Denial of Social Anxiety
Inhibition of Aggression
Self-Alienation
Naiveté
Emotional Alienation
Anxiety
Low Self-Esteem
Family Problems
Social Responsibility
I'm not sure I agree with emotional alienation, but the rest
do seem to fit me. Below that is another category called profes-
sion, and under it, the numbers 1, 2 and 3.
The first profession has 'Life Coach' next to it.
For that matter, so do the second and the third, as if I might
have had other options, though for some reason, I don't. My
option is Life Coach or Life Coach or Life Coach.
I'm going to be a life coach. How did they get that as my
career with one day of testing? They're going to pick me for
life coach when my mom's a fluke, and my friends abandoned
me, and I have nothing good to offer unless someone needs
to know how to live on nothing, not care what people think
about them, or how to repair super old household appliances.
This can't be right.
Worse, it's like I should have had some choices but don't,

since there are places for three. Maybe I'm wrong about that. Maybe choice is all in my head.

Scanning further, I find more codes listed under 'Activity': S1, W2, NOB, D16, H11, 2Y, but those have no definition or description.

Going down more, three names show up at the bottom of the page under the heading 'Responsible'. The first is Cooper A. Markstum. The second is Dannielle R. Pitts. The third is Egan Hakan Mann.

None of the names are familiar, and I have no idea what 'Responsible' means. Are they responsible for me, or, as a life coach, will I be responsible for them?

I can't help people with their lives. I haven't even lived enough to know how.

What are they thinking?

"Anna, relax." Zane's voice hits me right before his hand covers mine. "If you grip that any tighter, you're going to break it."

Letting go takes effort, but I drop the PCD onto its box and turn toward Zane.

"Awe, sheez, girl. It's going to be okay." He reaches over and rubs a hand across my cheek.

I should bat him away, but the touch is so nice I want it to stay. I want him, or someone, to take me away and hide me. Life coach? I'm a problem-riddled teenager at the beginning of my life, not a life problem solver.

"All candidates, please rise," the guy at the front says.

Zane drops his hands from my face and stands with his box.

On shaky legs, I do the same, as does the rest of the room.

"Place your right hand over your heart and repeat after me."

A round of throat clearing rolls through the room.

"I do solemnly swear ..."

The whole room repeats, voices filling the space.

"... that I will faithfully execute my role and profession ..."

What had begun as murmurs grows stronger. A glance at Zane suggests he's repeating the words, but I'd swear I don't hear anything coming out of his mouth as I finish saying them.

"... and will to the best of my ability ..."

Everyone says it.

"... uphold, preserve, protect and defend the laws and ways of the American Union."

Despite my earlier anxiety, a little giddy bubble rises. I'm an adult. It's official. I have a job, whether I like it or not, and that means credits. Actual credits that I can earn, that I can use to get stuff and food and whatever Mom and I might need. It's all for real.

"As such," the guys says, "you are formally a member of the American Union's workforce." His voice is as monotone as anyone could be.

A smile breaks out, and I jig a little.

My hands involuntarily move toward a clap, but no one else makes a sound, or even so much as moves, so I stop.

"At this time, you may exit this room and proceed to the rooms with the designation from the Activity section of your reports," the dude at the front says. "Room names will match those listed. You should have six, total. You will complete the first two today, upon which time you will proceed to final orientation and your quarters for the remainder of your stay. Congratulations."

No one exclaims.

No one shows any emotion.

There's no cap throwing like at final completion ceremonies. No celebration, at all.

In the hallway, people file out of rooms, heading back the way that brought us in. I stop and lean against the concrete wall, hold my brand-spankin' new PCD against my chest, and close my eyes.

A hovering presence forces them open. "What's wrong?" Zane asks.

I stare at him, into trusting eyes, into a sincere face, wanting to tell someone—to ask them, rather—why people aren't acting normal. Why aren't they excited about becoming an adult, getting their own places, having independence and getting to move on? Maybe that's just me, though—the girl who wants change so badly that she's excited about anything different than before.

Even as I look at Zane, I know I can't ask. The question is one built on some inner anxiety about not being like them, having emotions or something that others don't. If I'm so different, why am I going to be a life coach? How will I even relate?

"Anna?"

Shaking my head, I say, "It's nothing. Just ... you know, a lot to take in, and all. I'm just tired, I think."

"You sure?"

I nod. "I better get back ... you know, and find my way around to the next room."

"S1, right?"

"Yeah. You going there?"

He chuckles. "No. Trust me, that's not for me. S is for salon. No, thank you." He shakes his head and the mass of flopping overhang flickers.

I want to chuckle, but my brow furrows. "How do you know that?"

His eyes widen for a second. "Previous family ... you know,

that went through."

"Oh, yeah, sorry." A hand over my forehead cools my embarrassment. "I forget who knows what around here, you know? It's all so new to me. What are the others for? D? H? Two Y? Nob? Why can't it be simpler?"

His face turns serious complete with slight frown. "Knob?"

"N-O-B, sorry."

His eyes darken. "You have N-O-B on your list?"

"Yeah. Why?"

He spins away and runs a hand through his hair, flipping it all over the place. "You can't go there."

I jerk back and my head bumps the wall. The zing rattles my skull even as an immediate anger takes hold of me. "I have to go there. It's on my list." Rubbing the back of my head, I say, "And who are you to tell me what I can't do?"

He stalks back up to me and stands at my face, as close as we were before. "You don't want to, and ... just skip it."

I blink about a hundred times. "Skip it? Are you kidding? You can't skip stuff during registration. I'm a candidate. I don't want to be a nobody or—"

"A fluke?" He changes direction and walks away. I swear I hear him say, "I can't do this," but when he comes back, his face is the picture of kindness. "Sorry, Anna. Listen ... my family's been through a lot, and I've been around them all to hear ... stuff. But you need to listen to me. Do not go to the N-O-B."

"Give me one good reason." Shaking my head, I say, "Not just good, Zane ... but something so out of this world I wouldn't even want to be down here."

He raises a hand to the wall above me and gets within a millimeter of my nose. "I'll give you three. One: this place isn't what you think. Two: The life you think you're going to lead isn't what they're telling you now. Three: N-O-B is a new program, Anna. Like most of what's gone on so far. It's sterilization. You've been designated as a woman to sterilize."

He's joking. Has to be. "That's just a cruel joke, Zane." I slip out from under his arm and march away. To think I trusted him. How stupid am I? No one sterilizes women. That's against the law. It's just not right, either, which is why it's a law. *I'm a idiot.*

Several steps later, I'm spun back with a hand to my bicep. Zane glares down at me. "You're special, An—"

"Oh, don't give me that crap. I'm a girl just like every other girl. I'm eighteen just like everyone here. I'm being given a future to serve our country in the old 'one person makes a difference' philosophy." Heaving a breath, I carry on. "And I didn't ask for your help. Actually, I'm pretty sure I told you I wasn't good company and you should cut your losses. Or something." I wave a hand at him, trying to calm myself as I talk. Ranting has never been my 'thing'—more Cam's. Seems she had some influence on me over the years. "Thanks for breakfast, and all. Thanks for being nice to me on the bus. I don't know what you're looking for here ... with me. Why you've latched on, but I think you need to find a guy instead of me. I'm really sorry."

Turning away, I try to keep my steps light as my chest heaves. Zane's been so nice, but so have other people. It's time for me to stop associating with people who don't share my same values—whatever they are. Like Cam. If I ever see her again, I should say goodbye. I should. Really.

"I gave you breakfast so you could think," Zane says from behind me.

Craning my neck around, I face him halfway. "I said thank you for breakfast. You need me to pay you back? I don't have any credits, yet."

We stand at least fifteen feet apart in an empty hallway.

He holds up both hands, palms out. "Truce for a second, Anna. And no, no payback. I gave you breakfast so you could think." His repetition of the previous words don't change my confusion. Zane takes a couple steps toward me. "I figured it would be the end of the week before I had to tell you."

Tell me what?

Closer still, he stops again. "Did you take your pill from the procedure?"

I hadn't. After I'd fallen asleep, I didn't have time when they came to get us and didn't want to be late, so since it only had healing properties, I knew, eventually, I'd actually heal. Besides, Grandma always said, 'time heals all wounds' and would kiss my boo-boos as she applied a cartoon bandage.

Zane takes another couple steps. "Did you take it, Anna?"

"What does this have to do with anything?"

"Please. Just answer me."

With a little headshake, I stare down at the ground.

"And you got flustered during the psychological testing."

He'd seen that? He had. I knew it. Fire burns in my cheeks.

"Because you're not a zombie. Haven't you noticed everyone else is?"

My mouth opens, jaw dropping. "You ... think that, too?"

He reaches me again, our toes touching.

"They want ... no they *need* everyone to follow orders. This is the red house, Anna. It's meant to brainwash you into subservience. They have to make sure, when you walk out of here, that you believe only what they tell you." His voice is close and soft.

I tilt up, unsure what to say, if anything.

"You don't have to believe me if you don't want to. But you should. You should trust me."

"Why?" I finally manage. "What do you care about one girl

from District Eleven who hasn't had what most citizens have had? Why not tell this to someone else, like Hadley or Vica or Brie or ... or ... someone else?"

"Because you're Erianna Price Keating."

"So *what!* Why does that matter so much to you? I'm just like everyone else. I'm just a girl, just getting her job. Just ... me."

Why did this guy have to get on the bus with me yesterday? Why did he have to save me from being run over? Why does he keep showing up? Why is he telling me all this stuff?

Zane tilts my head up with a finger under my chin. "You're Mia Keating's sister, Anna. And—"

He knows my sister?

"Mia sent me. To—"

My sister sent him?

"—watch over you."

Why didn't she come and watch over me?

"To save you from what's coming."

"All candidates should now report to their first of six orientation classes," the speaker says through the ceiling somewhere.

My hands shake, and a tingling runs through my legs to the point I'd swear they're asleep, but since I'm still standing, they can't be.

I pull away from Zane. Nothing about what he's said makes sense. Why would my sister send someone to take care of me? Why would she send Zane? He's just another eighteen year old like me. He has to be if he's a candidate.

What if he's not?

No, that can't be right.

"I gotta go." I spin and walk away for what seems like the tenth time since the guy introduced himself to me the first time.

"I won't be far," Zane says to my back.

Great, now he's a stalker.

Following the hallway toward my room, I search for someone, anyone who isn't Zane, to help me find S1. At the corner of the main hall of rooms, a woman in a white jumpsuit stands with a PCD in her hand.

I race up to her. "I'm sorry, but I was … late … and I don't know where S1 is."

She points with the tablet's pen down the only other hallway

I haven't entered yet. It's a duplicate of the hall with my room on it, but in a direction I just haven't gone. I think. My bearings and left, rights, easts and wests are getting all off.

A few people exit doors as I start my trek down. At the end, the hall goes from white to a pretty beige with pictures lining the space. It's a totally different look to the clinical nature of where I've been, and wearing a jumpsuit seems silly and out of place. Doors line this path, too, labelled A1, A2, A3, etcetera on one side, and B1, B2, B3 and on and on down the other.

I pass them all and, at the end, reach E. A squinting glance ahead finds more people entering and exiting. Taking a wild guess, I go right. Stop a few feet down and go left instead.

M, N and O greet me as I come to another turn and find P, Q, R and if I narrow my eyes harder, I swear I see S.

Picking up speed, since the speaker has announced three times that candidates must be in their locations, S labels come into view, and I dart into S1.

The door swishes shut behind me.

A woman in a pink frock, jeans and cloggy shoes stands right in front of me in a small anteroom. "I'm guessing you're F2053425," she says.

Immediate irritation at the use of my number consumes me. "My name is Anna."

"We all have names, darling. Don't mean anyone cares what they are during registration." She ticks something off her PCD.

My heart flip-flops; she could be writing down my attitude issue and that could leave me stuck in some awful version of the job they've assigned me.

"Come with me, please."

I follow her into a room with at least five rows of chairs in front of mirrors, and a bunch of accessories that look more suited to Cam's room than mine. Each chair holds a girl in pink. Behind her, a woman messes with the subject's hair and chats, though the ones in the seats don't seem to be talking back.

"Now, Miss *Anna*," the lady says with a little bow of her head, "you're scheduled for a complete reproduction—"

What?

"—from head to toe, including wardrobe. Sit right here."

"What do you mean reproduction?"

The lady, with her green eyes and deep dark hair, scrunches her eyebrows together. "Overhaul. Do over. Makeover."

"But why?"

She chuckles. "Oh, boy, we got one who's asking questions, ya'll. What should we do with her?"

A few raised voices fill the space, but I can't tell what they've said. I take a step back. What are they going to do to me?

"I'm just teasin' girl. Most who come through registration are so freaked and exhausted from all the activities, they get to us and just want to relax. You can, you know. You'll be with me until me until the end of day, today. I handle both the S-one and S-two levels as well as the W-one and W-two levels."

As I'm led by the lady, around me, girls are getting up and following their person.

"You know, people at the three and four level won't be seen for two days, and level five gets a cursory upgrade, seeing as they're usually the fittest and the brightest."

So I'm not fit and not bright, and I need to be. My shoulders slump.

"Now sit here, and let me take a look at you."

I climb into the seat and it raises as she stands behind me. "Ma'am?"

Her eyes go wide. "Oh, gracious me, don't call me ma'am. I'm only twenty-four, you know."

I don't, of course.

Her hand lands on my head. "Geez. Six years older than you. Got picked to volunteer for this, since I got mad skills." The grin she gives me is part-smirk, and I'm wondering just what 'mad' implies. "So I'll get you right as rain." She picks up her PCD. "Now ... says here, you'll be a life coach, and you need to dress appropriately for home visits and working with children. Man, I feel for you. I'm an adults-only stylist, and I gotta say, I'm grateful for picking the long straw."

"The long straw?"

"Yeah, when I came through I had three choices. Kids, adults or just women. I chose adults figuring it would give me the best mix of people to work with." She drops the PCD and runs her hands through my hair. "You got super fine hair. When was the last time you had a professional haircut?"

I shake my head. Mom never has enough credits for a professional cut, and luckily, she doesn't force me to go to the super cheap places, either. If my hair grows too long, Mom takes care of it. Mia hacked at it once, but only that one time since she cut one side four inches shorter than the other and shaved off part of what hung in the front. My third, level one educenter imagegraph is easily the worst shot of me—ever.

"Um, excuse me?" I ask.

"What, sugar?" She taps on the device as she answers.

"Would you mind telling me your name?"

She belts out a laugh. "I'm Marlena." The PCD is set to the side, on the counter in front of me. "I'm from the southernmost border of the country, right where the Great Wall is. Heck, Mama says if you drive down registration row in my district, it cuts right through the wall—if you can see it still. All overgrown beyond the three houses there. Kinda weird that they make all the southern registration buildings right on the border. I mean, do they want us to try and see what's on the other side?" Throughout her introduction, she massages my head or does something with my hair.

The chatter in the room is minimal, but I tune it out, letting her run her fingers through. Despite my earlier misgivings, Marlena's hands relax me, and the muscles in my shoulders loosen, along with my forehead.

"Now here's what I'm thinkin' ... and you tell me if you like it. You're gonna be workin' with people, you know?"

I don't really know what I'll be doing, but I nod, going along with her.

"So you need to look normal, not too uppity, but not poor, either. You look too rich, people like me won't believe what you tell them. You look too poor, rich people won't listen."

"Is that what I'm supposed to do? Tell people what to do?" I ask to the mirror, our gazes meeting.

"Something like that. I mean you gotta show people how to live when they run outta credits, and how to be patient when they want to move up a level. Like me ... I started off in a salon with just the dudes with shaved heads, but over six years, I've learned how to do stuff, and now I can cut all kinds of hair, and I got licenses for a bunch of new services to make sure you look good as well. Now, I got my application in to have my own place to teach others, too. See? Progress. But that takes time. My life coach helped me to do that, and I got more credits added to my weekly pay because of it." Her expression changes a little as a slight frown creeps in. "Though last week, my deposit was missed." A second later, the deep lines etching her brow smooth away, and her face is the picture of happy again. "Anyway ... what I'm thinking is, if we take some weight off this limpness, add some layers and whispies, the body will come out naturally. Right now, you just got too much hair for how teeny you are. S'why it falls flat over your shoulders and back. We gotta pluck a little, enhance a few places, and I'll show you how to maintain it at home. That's really important, but you gotta remember to see a pro at least every three to four months. Especially for the color. I think we should go a little darker."

"Darker?" My hair's already brown. Ugly brown. Long, plain brown, but brown is dark. Isn't that enough?

"Give you a little bit of that Snow White look, but for the modern age. You have the pale skin and even the bright lips. You just need to go a little darker in your frame and enhance with some colors. Guys love that."

"I didn't think I was here for guys, but for a job."

"Oh, honey, you always gotta think about the men. Helps, too, when you're trying to go to the next level in your career. Gettin' rid of some of this length will make you look eighteen instead of fourteen, too. Then you can show a little lip and put on a little pout. Might not win, but it sure helps."

"But ... that's not how it works." Does it? "You earn your way up the ladder." No way I'm using my body to earn credits. That would be as bad as a fluke's life—or worse. I'd rather be a fluke.

Marlena nods. "If you want to move a little faster, there's ways to do that, too. If you want to, of course. Legs open really does it."

My shock comes out in a shiver. She's seriously got to be kidding.

"Though, that's probably why we got so many extra mouths to feed. You know, I heard ..." She lowers right to my ear. "... and you can't repeat this, but one of my customers is a lady that goes up to District one for those leadership meetings—"

One of our leaders or someone else?

"—and she said something about cutting down on the professional mothers this time around. Guess we're all going to have to work for a living, instead. Not that I want kids, yet."

Cutting down on mothers. This can't be related to what Zane said, can it?

"So, anyway …" She stands again. "You've got pretty skin under the skinny. Need to add some meat to your bones. Guys don't like nothin' to hold on to. I could give you some boost for them boobs, too."

I raise both hands. "I thought you said hair."

"Oh, honey …" Her lips build into a wide grin. "Like I said, I have a few more certifications. And … I'm your body consultant. It's not just the hair, but I got authorized treatments for everything to make you look just like you need to."

"But wouldn't me being who I am be best for my job?" Then again, I did say I wanted change.

"Girl, we got a lot to chat about if that's what you think's coming for you."

⊙━━⊷⊶○

Marlena is a talker. A nonstop talker. I don't think I've ever met someone who can just go on and on and on, sharing stuff I'm sure she shouldn't. Even the other workers around her don't talk as much, but as she's doing whatever she needs to do—based on the list of stuff I've agreed to—the others are yelling out their encouragement of whatever she says from one end of the row to the other. Clearly, this group listens to her. She ought to be a life coach, not just a body makeover consultant, or whatever.

For at least two hours, I've faced her and had no opportunity to see exactly what she's done. I agreed to hair and makeup, but none of the body sculpting. Why anyone would want a chest enhancement is beyond me—even for free, and even if it supposedly doesn't hurt.

"Okay, now, let's go back to wardrobe. I think I've got the perfect suitcase for you."

When she crooks a finger at me, like so many have already with their person, I get up from the chair and follow her, glancing over my shoulder and trying to catch a glance in the mirrors, but they've gone dark. It seems Marlena doesn't want me to see me, and neither does anyone else.

The room she brings me to requires a walk up four flights of stairs. By the last step, the muscles in my legs burn and my balance is wobbly.

Chatter abounds as she pushes through a set of double doors into a massive warehouse of color on racks two levels high.

"Come on, sugar," she says in her genuine accent I've stopped thinking as country and more 'just Marlena'.

The enormity of the room overwhelms my senses and makes me stop. Even our cafetorium in my level three educenter wasn't as big. Not only that, but people are everywhere, moving about, forward, back, left and right like a factory. Empty racks attached to some contraption move off through a door, disappearing as a new ones returns.

"Social worker people are over in section G-one-hundred," Marlena says.

If I don't stay by her, I'll get lost, so I traipse on through, a few faces turning my way, a few glances given, but we continue past all the letters and reach the 'G' section. Here, the colors are more muted.

"Of course, you're so tiny, we might have to go back to the kid section, but let's see what they got. Oh!" She stops and turns toward me, withdrawing a measuring string out of her pocket. "Need your numbers." Around my waist it goes, and a beep follows. She holds up her PCD and taps on it. "I'm just going to fudge a little here. You know you can't get more than ten percent larger from this measurement or you can be dropped a level, but you need to eat, so we're just ... going ... to do a little ... adjustment." She taps and clicks as she talks. "There. Now arms." Moving around my body, she runs the strip and, with each beep, does some of her own 'minor adjusting', as she calls it. "Good. So we're at twenty-four inches which is the smallest of the adult sizes, so let's see what we have."

Onward down the row, we come to the last rack. It seems to me that everything I've had to do has been at the end of a hallway, the end of a rack, the last of the group. I start to wonder just how I get to be so lucky?

"Here we are." She pulls off a group of clothes hanging from the very last spot and lays them on the table. "These will be good enough colors for you, too. Could use some more, but, well, that's what we got."

With the cover off, Marlena holds up a pink and a blue shirt, each with V-necks, two pairs of jeans, a navy suit jacket with a skirt and a white blouse for underneath. "This is for your big meetings with the big bosses and the interviews for your level of entry," she says. After that, she shows me a plain black dress that will have to be hemmed. "You'll be working with the military, too, and sometimes they have these events where everyone has to dress up. So, just in case, you know?"

I don't, but I'm enthralled by the clothes and try to tamp down my smile. In eighteen years, I don't remember ever getting anything like the stuff in front of me. They may be simple and even a little bland, but they're new and clean.

Marlena holds up a pair of black flats and a pair of running shoes with a black streak down the side. "These are last year's models, and ..." She leans in close. "... I heard they had to buy them from the U.S. because China refused to send us anymore. But, hell, they're new, so what do we care, right?"

Cam would throw a massive fit, but I'm in love.

As Marlena puts those clothes down, she holds sweatpants and a sweatshirt in deep gray with a slash of pink through them. "Gotta keep up the exercise." Those go back into the bag, and she brings out white underwear and a bra that I know won't fit. "Okay, girl, so you either gotta take my breast enhancer, or we gotta find you something from the starter series. This one—" She fiddles with the tag. "—is at least two sizes too big, but I can adjust that for you."

She'd mentioned, before, about enhancing, but didn't say exactly how it's done.

"And now you've gone all worried on me. Listen … enhancing is nothing. One dose of a tranq, I inject the material right inside, and voila! Done. Doesn't even hurt. Had it done myself." She tilts down as if looking at her own breasts.

The idea of having a bigger chest isn't one I've had on my list of to-dos. Ever. The old Eri cared a little, especially when compared to Cam or in the girls dressing room. Being nearly flat-chested, I could probably get away with not wearing a bra, at all, but then, what would women think that I work with? Would they think I'm a boy with long hair?

"Takes like ten minutes, too. Seriously, if you want to fit into this …" She wiggles the pink lace. "… now is the time. It's why you're in level one and not somewhere else. It's the one time you don't have to save up your credits."'"

… anyone who's going to the red house goes there for a reason, and not one you or I—or anyone else here—should get involved with. RK's words echo through my head. I went to the red house for a reason.

"You want to look good, don't you?"

I changed my name for a reason. I want more than just being me.

"Tons of girls your age are doing it."

"It really doesn't hurt?" I can't believe I've asked.

Marlena claps her hand. "Not a bit. Seriously, it's the best body sculpting any woman could ask for. And when it's free as in F-R-E-E, you ought to take advantage."

That's when my mother's words hit me: 'You get what you pay for'. Is it really true?

15

Even the idea of having Marlena dose me up, and have anyone stick another needle into the middle of my boob, should
have made me run away far and fast, but for some reason, I've
put my trust in her. Just not enough trust to actually have it
done.

"You're serious about not wanting the enhancement?" she
asks for the umpteenth time.

"I am."

She nods, sucking her bottom lip. "Okay, so ... um ... can
I trust you?"

Why is she asking me? I'm *her* pincushion for the day. "I
guess that depends."

She motions with her hand for me to follow, and I do, like
a trained pet. An internal tremble makes me hope she's not
taking me for the procedure anyway, and when she opens the
door to a room with a slick metal table, I step back.

Marlena holds a finger to her lips and jerks her head to come
in all the way.

I shake mine.

Her hand waves in front of me. "Not for that. Just come on."

I force myself to walk in all the way.

She shuts the door and turns her PCD to me, displaying a
series of gorgeous miniature artwork pieces on the screen. "So,

um, it's probably good that you didn't do the enhancement, 'cause, well ... I just got licensed, and you'da been my first. But ..." One finger points to the ceiling. "... I've been working on a little something, and it's going to take me years to actually get permits for it."

Her cryptic speak and our private room are building up an inner anxiety that's making me want to fidget. Holding it back so I don't freak her, or myself, out is getting harder with my tensing muscles and itchiness.

She aims her finger toward her PCD. "These are removable tattoos. They ... um ... they go on permanent, like your eye liner—that's where I got the idea. And, they don't come off unless you use a special cleanser I made. I was hoping, maybe, a few candidates might want to try it this year. Would you?"

Blinking commences. Here, I'd thought she be drugging me into upgrading body parts and she wants to offer me a product she designed. "How do you apply it?"

Her grin reaches her eyes. "The same as the liner and mascara I already put on you. It's the same ingredients and method, but I add a little color and lay out the design by hand and then, voila!" She beams like a seven year old who's just won the art contest.

"Does it hurt?"

"Did that gorgeous, deep blue under your eyes hurt?" she asks.

I shake my head. It didn't hurt a bit.

She comes close to me and leans forward. "It's the chicken and the egg, as my grandma says. I can't get this approved without subjects, but I can't get subjects unless I do a career change application." With a flourishing roll of her eyes, she says, "And we all know that won't happen until after I die."

"Why does it take so long?"

Pulling back, she says, "There are two million new job applicants in this class, you know. They all have to work. Competing with that many new people every year makes it impossible, since the selection committee is already—" She stops and puts a hand to her mouth. "I'm sorry, Anna. I'm not supposed to be a downer, I just wanted to try something new—"

"I'll do it." For her.

"You will?" Her eyes go wide and she wraps her arms around my shoulders.

"Don't give up on your dreams. Okay? You make people feel better about themselves by helping them look better. I could learn a lot just from that."

"Are you sure? Do you think?"

What do I really know? "Yeah. Probably."

She sniffles and wipes her hand under her nose, emotion laying all out there on the surface. "So what design do you like best?"

I study the variety of unicorns, birds, words, and whatnot. "No idea."

"Will you let me pick based on what I learned about you today?"

Let her pick? I consider for a moment. What would it hurt? I can always take it off, so no harm to me. Maybe that's what a good life coach does? "Yes. Let's do it." My quick nod follows involuntarily.

She claps and turns to the table. "Yes! I have the best idea."

Fifteen minutes later, at a ding, Marlena pops up from her PCD. "That's the timer. Let me just take off the cover and show you. Want to see?"

I totally do.

She lifts up a hand-held mirror from the counter and digs in a drawer, pulling out a second. "You ready?" she asks from behind me.

I close my eyes. "Yes."

Her fingers rub along my shoulder where she worked for all of ten minutes. "Normally the big reveal is in the full-body mirror, but I know you'll want to see your face and hair, too. So ... when we go back out, fake it, okay?"

A little bubble of laughter bursts from me, and I hold the mirror in front of me.

Dark hair, more a deep chestnut than brown, with soft golden brown highlights, frames my face. It's way shorter than I expected it would be, above my shoulders, some pieces barely reaching below my ears. Turning right and left, my hair moves a little, and tucking it behind my ear gives me an altogether different look. *Wow.*

"Do you like it?" Marlena asks.

I can't contain the smile that flits onto my face. I never thought I'd say shorter is better than longer, but I love it. "Yeah," I say on a hushed whisper. "It's so different. So ... new. So ..."

"Trendy. And current. And really makes that transition you need."

Nodding, I study the brown-blue colors lining the top and bottom of my lids, the way a black coating on my lashes makes them extend out at least an inch, and my grin gets bigger. Added to that, there's a definite blush to my cheeks and a bit of color to my lips.

I point at reflection in the mirror. I'm different.

"You're so pretty, Anna."

Yeah. That. I'm pretty. Never before have I really thought that, but I am, and I can see it.

"And you have a good soul."

"What do you mean?"

"You let me do an undocumented procedure on you. You trusted me with something that I asked of you. Anyone else would have gone to my supervisor and told them how horrible I am and made me go back to sweeping hair off the floor and having to work my way back up. But you ... you gave me confidence."

A woman with her energy telling me I gave her confidence is like my mom agreeing going to registration is good. I never expected it would happen. Not in a million years.

"That's why you have a good soul. Ready to see the back?"

I so am. If my face and hair is anything like what she designed on my shoulder, I'll be grinning for days. "Show me." Marlena holds up the back mirror, and I move mine around until I can see the reflection. "It's a butterfly."

"It's the symbol of freedom and pureness. Like you." She removes her jacket and pulls down her collar. On it is a similar butterfly, but with yellow wings instead of the pink she gave me.

"You're an amazing artist."

She shrugs. "That's what I wanted to be, but my choices all came down to hair, so I do what I can. Thank you for letting me have this."

It's her I should be thanking. Everything inside me tingles and there's this fullness within me that can only be explained by having spent so many hours with this woman. Mom always says, 'Downers bring you down, Eri', and I think she's right. More than that, I think smilers bring me up.

"And these ..." Marlena shakes a bag one of the other hair people had brought to the door before she started on my tattoo. "This is some lingerie. Jemini had to go scrounge for the smaller stuff, but I think you did the right thing by staying you." Her smile brings out my own again. "I figure you deserve it. You have no idea how many girls say yes to the augmentation. You get big props from me for being true to yourself."

RK said that going to the red house meant I'd change. He had no idea by how much. As I walk down the hall dressed in my pink T-shirt and jeans with my flats on, my hair, which I can no longer feel on my head, and my bag of new clothes on my arm, the stares I get aren't the usual 'get away from her' faces. They seem interested. Curious. Yet, none of them know me—or few do.

So far, registration has been weird, but I have to say the weeks of worry over getting away from all the people in my educenter and whether I'd get an invitation, and what house I'd go to, have all disappeared. Even yesterday is in the past.

With a smile, I follow the directions Marlena gave me to my new quarters. I've been told to go there, hang my clothes, say hello to a new set of roommates, and prepare for dinner—that the location of my dining hall will be sent to my PCD by eighteen-hundred hours. On top of that, now that I've had all the physical assessments, I get to start my life and focus on learning what it will take to be a life coach. Marlena even said she'd make great notes in my file to help me get the best level I can.

"Anna!" A voice calls as I pass a hallway. "Anna, wait."

I stop and turn.

Hadley rushes forward in a three-piece suit. "Oh, my Oz, I thought that was you! You look ... wow!"

The blush, the heat, just as it always has creeps up. I guess I'm not changed as much as I think I am. "Um ..."

"What did you get?" she asks. "Career, I mean."

"Life coach. You?" As if I don't already know.

"Attorney." She jumps a little. The suit suits her and the profession. "They called me flawlessly logical and objective. They even want to put me on international relations, like right now-now. You know, like fighting about the border with the U.S. and Canada, maybe. Or stuff like that."

"That's a lot of work, right?"

"Yeah, but I have the Attorney General as a mentor and six years of apprenticeship planned. I mean, oh, my Oz, Anna, how great is this? Can you believe it? I mean, I'm the girl from the dumps, and they picked me!"

They, whoever they are, since they never give us their names, have changed her.

My lips curve, and I move in to give her a hug, but can't with my hands full. "That seriously rocks, Hadley. I mean it."

"So you know what's going on tonight?" Her eyes shine with brightness.

"Not really. Just got out of my ..." I don't know what to call it exactly. Body image do-over?

"I'll be eating with all the other to-be-attorneys!" She claps a giddy clap, and I'm so glad to see emotion. It makes me wonder if Zane fed her some lunch or if she skipped. Since I stayed with Marlena all day, I didn't get lunch, but breakfast still lays thick enough in my stomach.

It also makes me think that the zombie reference he'd brought up had just been a story like the whole reproduction thing. I'm such an idiot. If I believe that kind of junk, how am I going to help people who will probably lie to me? Maybe Marlena lied about the tattoo thing. She probably sells them on the street. *Geez, I'm such an idiot.*

"Did you find your room, yet?" Hadley breaks me from my

thoughts.

"No, just searching for it now and—"

"Hadley!" someone calls

Her head swivels in that direction—Jeremy, if I remember from morning. He waves and comes forward, his lips split in a super-wide grin. He looks way, way better in the snug jeans and black T-shirt than he did in the blue jumpsuit.

Hadley turns to me, an unsaid plea of 'I don't want to leave you, but this is true love' on her face.

"I gotta find my room," I say to let her off any obligatory friend connection.

"So I'll see you later?" she asks.

"Totally." I give her one forceful nod, and she skips away, jumping into his arms. For a girl on the brink of throwing up a day ago, she seems positively radiant.

A smile builds on my face for her. From that little shy and claustrophobic girl to a lawyer. Talk about change. I'm quite liking the effect of the red house.

I carry on, scanning the room numbers as I go, searching for MF3521.

"Anna." My name comes from inside one of the rooms I've just passed.

Backing up, I find Vica lazing on the bottom bunk of a room about the size of our old one. "Hey!" I walk to the frame. "How are you?"

"I'm fine." She says it without much emotion—more like the other people.

"Everything okay?"

She nods. "Yeah. Just tired. Been a long day."

"Yeah, me, too."

"You look different," she says.

"I feel different."

"Is that good?" she asks.

"It is, I think. So, what will you be doing when we leave here?"

She slides out from the bed and saunters to me. "You won't believe this." Even though she asks in a way that makes me think she's not happy, she smiles. "I'm going to be a fulltime mom."

"You are? I mean ... you are! That's ... great, right?"

Her eyes are downcast for a moment before her gaze comes back up to mine, and her grin shows itself. "Actually ... yeah. I ... didn't want anyone to think I was weird, but being a mom's really all I've ever wanted to be."

I drape my bag over my arm and bring her in for a hug. "I'm so glad you got what you wanted. That's the best feeling ever, isn't it?"

"It is, but there's a problem." Her shoulder droops more like when she first called my name.

"What? Tell me. Maybe I can help?" That would be my job, I think.

"Well ... in order to be a mom, I have to get married and get pregnant in no less than two years or agree to take an unwanted baby from the current general population, or be impregnated for scientific purposes, or be reassigned. All in two years, Anna. I don't even have a boyfriend, and I don't want to choose wrong, but—"

"But you want to be a mom, and if you can't, that would really suck."

She gives me three quick nods. "What am I going to do?"

"Well ..." I'm not sure how to answer her, or if I should. Hadley may be off and running with her law stuff, but I've only heard about my new job. It seems, though, that I might already be doing it. *Wonder if I'm being watched and tested al-*

ready. Would they do that? "So . . ."

Vica wraps her arms around me. "You're so awesome, Anna. Really. Let's not lose touch when we leave."

I haven't done anything to help her, yet she's telling me I'm good? As she returns to her bed, I back out with a promise to check in later. Two turns later, my name rings out again. I spin back and find Brie walking toward me, dressed in jeans and a red T-Shirt. Her blonde hair is up in a bun; her eyes glisten with tears.

I half-jog, half-walk toward her. "What's wrong?" Stopping before her, I take her in my arms. "Tell me."

"They want me to be a mortician, Anna. They want me to work with dead people!" She sobs on my shoulder, her entire body shaking. "I can't work with dead people. How am I going to live? How will I survive? I can't do it."

"Shh." Soothing her brings her from hiccupping sobs to a light sniffle. "Maybe there's a process to appeal?"

"You think?" She pulls away and swipes a hand under her nose. "You think there's a way to get something better? How can they think that about me?" Her moment of consideration falls to a deep frown and tortured voice again, and her hands grip my shoulders. "How can they think I'd want to work with dead people? Why, Anna? What did I answer in that stupid questionnaire? What did I answer that would make them think I want to even touch dead people?"

I purse my lips. "No idea."

"And all three of my options were the same, Anna." Fresh tears fall in streams down her cheeks. "All three!"

Craning my head around, I search for a room, a place we can go so we can talk, not to mention put down the stuff in my arms that's weighing me down.

Brie backs up to the wall, crossing her arms over her chest.

"I even got that stupid … chest … enhancement. Who's going to care that I can wear a C-cup now? Not dead people." Her eyes close as she sucks in air. "I'm never going to find a real boyfriend or a husband, if I spend all day long with dead people!" Her tone ratchets up.

"I'm really sorry, Brie."

She waves me away. "It's so not your fault, either. I can't believe I've slobbered all over you, and told you about this—" Her finger points to her chest. "—and that I haven't even asked you about you."

"It's okay," I say.

"You look … different."

The shrug happens without me thinking about it. "Um … thank you."

"Your hair is … really, really cute." An impish smile creases her face but doesn't last.

"Hey, you know what? I saw Hadley a little bit ago, and she's going to be an attorney. Maybe you can ask her what you can do?"

"You think?"

"It can't hurt, right?"

Brie squeezes in for another hug. "What would I do without you?" Before I can respond in any way, she say, "Thanks, Anna," and gives me a wave as she heads left, walking backward the way I'd come before. "You'll catch me before we leave, right?"

"Sure." I wave with my hand still full of my clothes and gadgets.

Back to searching for my room, the letters change from M and F to MF and the numbers increment until I stand in front of 3521 with its door open, and one and only one person standing in between two beds.

"Oh, no, no, this isn't right."

1 6

"Mia?"

She jumps past me and presses a button, forcing the door shut. As soon as it closes, she turns to me and wraps her arms around me. Her hands run up and down my arms, to my cheeks, back down my side and up to my face again. "Oz, Eri, you're so pretty."

I narrow my eyes at her. "What are you doing here, and why are you in my room?"

"I'll explain in a minute. Look at you. Wow."

I would look at myself, have wanted to since I had to fake surprise at the big reveal, where everyone showed off one outfit, talked about their new physical features and what the salon room meant to them for their new roles.

"Marlena really brought you out of ... you."

Given I spent a full thirty seconds up in front of at least fifty girls and fifty stylists, my time to admire myself stayed very limited.

A shiver zings up my spine. "Is Mom okay?" Mia's presence has to mean something is wrong.

"I'm not here about her."

Moving to the bar next to a door I figure leads to a bathroom, I hang the bag of clothes Marlena gave me, buying me time to accept the fact my sister has just shown up out of nowhere. "What are you doing here?" I face her—a girl I haven't seen in over four years—a girl who could have told me about this place and saved me from two days of anxiety and worry, but didn't.

She raises her hands, the action flashing white shirt cuffs beneath the sleeves of her black suit jacket. It dawns on me that she's dressed a lot like Hadley. "You're probably a little bitter, what with me leaving and all, but I had to go."

I don't comment, but cross my arms over my chest. I want to be excited that she's here, but caution and concern and plain-old-mad take over.

"I wanted to tell you right when you turned eighteen, and I was going to catch you at the commerce center—"

"That *was* you!" My finger points. "I knew it."

"I'm sorry." Her green eyes plead with me to accept her apology, but I'll need more to understand. "This wasn't something I could tell you before, and that was a really awkward moment, what with your friend there, too. Then, when Zane told me how reluctant you were to believe him, I knew I had to see you."

"Reluctant? That's what he said? He's basically been stalking me, Mia. Like everywhere I go, he's there. And he's saying really weird stuff."

"He's warning you. It's supposed to be sweet."

I blink. "Sweet? He's … nice, yeah, but as you should know—" *or would if you were around* "—I'm not used to that much attention. And then, like out of the blue, he goes and tells me I'm not supposed to go to some of the stuff I'm registered for while I'm here. Stuff I *have* to do. How would you feel about all that, since you were so desperate to go through this yourself?"

She paces past me. "No, no, you're right." There's not more

than twelve or fifteen feet in the room, but I'd use it, too, if she hadn't beat me to it. "This probably wasn't the best plan. And I hoped Mom would tell you the truth, but—"

"Mom knows where you are?"

Mia stops in front of me. "Yes, of course."

I stagger backward and hit the wall. "Mom—kno—Mom …" I can't catch my breath, and heave air, forcing it out and bringing it in. Back to the wall, I slide to the floor. "Mom … Mom knows?"

Mia comes and kneels in front of me. "I'm sorry, Eri—"

"Anna. I go by Anna, now."

"Okay." Her hand lands on my knee. "I didn't know Mom kept what I'm doing from you, but, Er—Anna, I need you to know now."

"Wha-what? What do you need me to know?"

"Things have changed in the A.U. It's bad, Eri—"

"Anna."

She closes her eyes. "Anna. I'm sorry." Tilting back up, she meets my gaze. "Listen. Don't worry about Mom. She probably did what she thought was best."

"What was *best*?" I can't believe those words even left Mia's lips. "Holy cow, Mia. Mom's done what was best forever, but this is not 'the best'. Making me believe you're never coming back, acting mad at you because you're gone? I've spent the last two years *not* asking about you because, every time I did, Mom cries. These are not good things—not for 'the best'."

"You're right. You're right. I know." A nod comes with her acknowledgement. "Mom made her own decision, I guess. Call it what you will. But I'm here … not for the reasons you think."

"Why? Tell me why you're here."

She shakes her head. "I can't, Er—Anna. Not right now. It's not safe. I'm here to just ask you to trust Zane."

"Zane?"

"Yes, Zane. I need you to trust him. To listen to him."

"*Zane?*"

"Yes, Anna. *Zane.*"

"But he's just like me. Why do I have to listen to him? Why not you? Why not someone sane? Why can—"

She stops me with a finger to my lips. "He'll explain, but Anna, please. Things aren't good in our country. We're on the verge of huge change, and it's not going to go over well."

"But—"

"I'm trying to keep you safe, and Zane's promised to help me."

"Is he even eighteen?" I wondered that on the bus, since he seemed older.

"Yeah, he is. He's going through all this the same as you, but with a few extra responsibilities and a little bit of insight many others don't have."

"If all you wanted was someone for me to believe, why didn't you pick a girl? Why not ... Cam or ... one of my roommates, or someone I already know?"

"Because they're all newbies like you. Zane ... he's different. Yes, he's eighteen, and he's the only one in *this* area that I could get into *this* registration, but he's also got the background I needed. And *I* trust him."

"But *why*? Tell me Mia. *Why* should I do something that's not on the agenda? All I wanted was to come in here, get a job—a good one, if I could—and get to work."

She grabs both my biceps and holds me still. "That's the problem, right there." A head shake follows. "A hundred years of no one questioning our leaders, following their orders, and them making really bad decisions. This latest is the icing on the cake, and it has to stop."

"What is the latest?" I grab her hand. "*Please*, Mia. I'm not a child." Though, the more I beg for answers, the more it seems I'm whining. "I'm eighteen, like you just said. I'm starting my new life in five days. If I don't know what's coming, how am I supposed to prepare? How am I supposed to know what to do? How to help people in my new job?"

She sighs, deep and long. "Anna." Her head hangs. "The country's out of credit—"

"That's not—"

"Shush." Mia tilts up. "The American Union *is* out of ccred-its. Has been for two or three decades. But now ... China's not willing to invest anymore. The United States voted against additional funding and won't send any more either. Everyone we've ever borrowed from has said change or be done. Change or be lost. Change or be overtaken."

Tears well in my eyes. "That can't—"

"It is." She holds my hands up between us. "The news isn't being shared. Hasn't been for thirty years. And now, what they're doing is ... it's just plain wrong."

"*What*? What are they doing?" I hear my frustration in my voice, getting higher and faster with each repeated question.

"Example number one. Have you noticed how there's abso-lutely no babies born to anyone under eighteen?"

"Of course there aren't. We're too young. You have to have a job and—"

Mia rolls her eyes. "Hell. I never thought a daughter of Jack Keating would be so naive."

I pull away from her, and my head hits the wall again. Rubbing, as I ponder, I realize one of the items in my report had been naiveté. Of course, if she'd been around, I might 'get' more of what's going on. Maybe if Mom shared anything, I might, too.

"You do know what sex is, right?"

"Oh, my … yes, Mia. I'm not stupid."

"Good. Phew. At least Mom didn't try to hold that back." She smiles, but I don't return the gesture. "So you know under-agers can't get jobs, and with educenter programs ending at, like, three o'clock, what do you think they do more and more?"

I know exactly how she wants me to answer. Cam didn't go have sex in the afternoon just because. Jen, RK and everyone else didn't either. Her question is just downright mean, and inside, I have this desire to protect my entire generation's repu-tation. "We're not a whole generation of sex-crazed people."

"Well, *you* might not be, but most are. Anyway … twenty or twenty five years ago, every kid was temporarily sterilized at birth. Until they went through registration. The first day used to be checking those levels and determining who would make good mothers. Now, it's a whole, full genetic work up to determine if you're worth being allowed to procreate, or if you need to be kept shuttered."

I can't believe she's saying this.

"And then, on the last day, they either let you go do what-ever you were going to do, or some get that whole professional mother thing." She steps closer to me. "But … now? Now, they're either taking away the right to bear children or giving it to you. Period."

"Why?" My question comes out soft, one I didn't meant to ask.

"Because there are too many people being born, and not enough dying, and all in a country with no credits. So …" She takes a deep breath. "That's only example number one. Population control. Do you understand now?"

Zane said something similar, but I thought he'd made up a lie to shock me, or something. This time, I say nothing.

"Alright, you need more. Example number two. This year's candidate pool is a lot different than in years' past." She lets free another long breath of air. "White house candidates are being shipped away. Out. Over the border. Out of the country."

My eyes go wide. *Cam.* She's going away? No. "*No!* My friend, she's—"

"Forget about her. Listen—"

Panic consumes me. "I can't forget about her! Like I couldn't forget about you, even when you weren't there. I can't—"

"Erianna, get yourself together." Her fingers wrap around my biceps. "There're over two million people reaching adulthood. There *aren't* two million jobs. There aren't even one million. There aren't a hundred thousand or even fifty thousand. On top of that, there's no credits for all those adults to do nothing either. There are no more houses and no funding to build new ones."

"But ... they can't send Cam—"

"I said forget her, Erianna." Mia's tone is insistent.

"No." I bark my answer at her. "I will not forget my friend. I will not sit here and know that she can be shipped off to somewhere other than her home, just because. Why wasn't this in the media? Why haven't they told people?"

Mia laughs, full and hearty, and maybe a bit psychotic. "Oh, my dear, dear naive sister. Who controls the airwaves?"

"But—"

"And the radio. Channels? Everything that is shared with the general public is controlled. Why in the world do you think there hasn't been massive rioting? They keep it all tucked away, brushed under a rug. It's way safer for our so-called leaders to keep power that way."

"They gave me a job." My statement comes out quiet, like before Mia incited an inner riot within me.

"Yes, because for the first time ever, the red house candidates are the ones they want to keep, *if* they can keep you in line. You're the ones who can live on next to nothing. You're the ones who don't need ten rooms in one house for a family. You're part of the bottom feeders—the ones no one has cared about before. They need you to survive. To start over. To teach the next generation how to live off nothing and not to question everyone in power."

"Why is that bad?"

"Are you not listening to me? To do this, they are taking away all your freedoms, your true independence, your essence, Erianna." She huffs a breath before mumbling something that sounds like, "Hell, Dad was right." Her gaze meets mine again. "I've changed your schedule so you will not go to your last day's event. It's illegal to take your reproduction rights away, and yet it's one more thing being done without authorization."

"They can't—"

"Yes, *they* can." Mia leans her forehead against mine. "They have unlimited power and authority to do what they need to keep the country going, and they don't have to care how they do it."

"How do you know all this?" My voice comes out a whisper.

She tilts back but only by a couple inches. "I really, *really* can't tell you that. But do you believe me?"

When she told me it would be safe to jump off the trampoline and into the little pool Mom made for us, I did. When she said monsters wouldn't come out of our closet if we slept with the little light on, I believed her.

After too long, I nod.

A small smile remains as Mia withdraws her PCD and flips it toward her. "Sheez. I gotta go." Her palm to my cheek, she says, "You didn't see me. You don't know who I am, if you see me in the halls. If I need you, I'll find you. If you need something, ask Zane." Standing, she holds out a hand.

I take it and rise with her.

"I'm going to take care of you Er-Anna." One finger wags toward me. "See? I'll get it soon. Do not go to your last location. Zane'll tell you how to reach me when the week is over."

"So, between now and then, what do I do?"

"Listen. Learn. Process. No matter what, anything they tell you, read between the lines. Don't take any pills, or eat anything Zane doesn't give you. That'll keep your mind open and not zombified like everyone else here."

"Zombified?"

"Oh, baby sister ... stop letting others tell you what to do." She leans in and gives me a tight squeeze.

"Then, why should I let you tell me?"

The grin that appears is genuine and reaches her eyes. "You shouldn't. But would I ever steer my baby sister into something that would hurt her on purpose?"

A memory of being told to add the red strawberry sauce to my ice cream, which turned out to be hot sauce, hits me. "Yes, actually, you would."

"Hot sauce?" Mia asks.

I can't believe she remembers. "Yes. How—"

She taps her temple. "I'm the big sister. You just remember that." She heads toward the door. "Listen to Zane, Er-Anna. Trust me." The door swishes open and closes again.

What she told me is surreal. Unreal. I can't believe it, yet I believe her.

With Mia gone, the room is mine, yet I have no idea who my roommate will be or why she hasn't shown up. I drop to one of the beds and ponder over all that Mia told me. At some point, I'll have to go find Zane, though with the way he seems to find me all the time, I could probably just stand outside my door and he'll appear. Probably with some sort of food in his hand.

Worry courses through me for Cam and Jen and the other of my friends. Mia didn't mention the black house, but most of them were assigned to the white house. Does that mean they all live in another country now? Already? Can they come back? What about their families? How will they survive, if they're shipped off somewhere else? And where?

"This can't be right. Can't be." I pound my fists against the mattress. I'd fall to it and cry, if I thought I'd have time before the official dinnertime. Of course, without Zane, I guess I won't be eating anytime soon. He got that right, too. "Zombies. They've created a bunch of brain-washed zombies … or will have, by the end of the week." How could I not have known? How did I get suckered in like everyone else?

Mom wanted me to be a fluke. Since she knows about Mia, maybe she knows this would happen and that being a fluke would be better. Did she? Would it? Should I have listened to her the whole time?

Probably.

"Why is this happening?"

The door swishes open. "Why is what happening?" Zane asks from the empty frame.

I point at him. "How did you—only someone with access—no, no." I stand and back away, my finger still extended.

Dressed in all black—black slacks, black shiny shoes and a black shirt under a black jacket that extends to his thighs—he stands facing me, his hair no longer covering his forehead, but styled and cut.

"How did you get in here?"

A smile forms on his face. "I'm sure you can figure that out."

Just like he did in the hallways before, he leans into the frame, arms crossed over his chest.

"You can't be my roommate. You're a—a—a—"

"A what, Anna?" The grin doesn't leave his face.

"You're a boy!"

One hand extends low and grabs at his crotch. I wish I didn't look, but I couldn't help myself. "Seems so." A laugh follows. "Come on, Anna. You've probably had boy-girl sleepovers, and stuff, right?"

I force myself not to shake my head. Admitting I had the strictest childhood isn't going to help the fact I'm definitely naive.

"No answer? Okay ... well, consider this a sleepover. You have a bed, and so do I."

"But that's not ... allowed ... right?"

"Are you kidding? Half the girls here have requested to be with one of the guys. Getting switched to staying with you took less effort than getting that breakfast burrito here for you." He walks in the rest of the way. "And see?" One hand reaches for the closet door. "My stuff's already here."

"But—"

"I don't bite, Anna. I'm just here to learn details, to be with you for your sister's sake, and at the end, go back to helping find a solution for the bigger problems."

"But—"

He chuckles again and holds out a hand toward me. "C'mon, Anna. Dinner. Let's go."

"But where?"

"That's for me to know." He extends a hand out to me. "And me to show you."

I take it, but he doesn't bring me in closer or pull us out the door. After a second or two, he still doesn't move. "Is something wrong?"

"Um ... I need a minute."

I try to see past him in case he's heard something I haven't. "Is everything okay?"

"Anna?"

"What?" I meet his gaze again.

"You look ... um ... you look amazing."

Glancing down at myself, I realize I've forgotten he saw me before my new look. My cheeks flush again. "It's just ... I mean, I'm not—"

He stops me with a tug forward. "I'm going to have to stay closer, I think."

"Why?"

"To keep the rest of the guys from you." His entire mannerism has changed since we separated that morning—from when we had our ugly jumpsuits on.

"No one's going to come near me." I'm still just me—the girl who doesn't make waves.

His head does a slow back and forth movement. "No, Anna. You have no idea what your day has done."

"Oh, okay."

Zane blinks a few times. "Now ... dinner? I have a special place just for us."

"A-alone?" I'm not sure I can handle being along with this guy. He's not the same one I met on the bus. That guy was a little frumpy, a bit geeky and nervous. The one in front me is super confident and, holy moly, he's hot.

"Yes, alone. I figure it's safer, since I know you'll have questions you want to ask me. Right?"

"Yeah, um ... right. Maybe ..." I firm my spine. "Yes. I do have questions. Yes, I want to ask them." My words come out as if I have to convince myself.

"Great, then come with me, and I'll tell you everything I know."

17

Zane guides me down more unmarked hallways to a door that says 'Do not Enter'.

"We can't go in there," I say.

He twists back to me. "Yes, we can."

"But it says—"

"Anna, come on. Trust me."

Everyone keeps telling me to trust them, to just do what is told of me, but that's also what Mia told me not to do. Confusion reigns in my head. Has for days—since RK did his vanishing act, and Cam used a dummy credit, and all but made me shoplift in Rise21. Since then, my sister mysteriously reappeared, and I'm standing in front of a door that clearly says not to enter with a guy only Cam should get to hang out with. Maybe if I hadn't changed my name, none of this would have happened.

Zane snaps in front of my face. "Wake up, Anna. We're going through." He pushes on the panel with his hand.

"Wait."

"No." His body moves forward.

"Please." I know I sound like some wimpy girl, but I can't help it. "Have you been this way before?"

Zane faces me completely. "Yes. This door is a stairwell that will take us to the surface."

"But they said we couldn't go—"

The muscles in his jaw clench and release. "Did your sister tell you to trust me or not?"

"Yes, but we have to go to dinner, right? Won't people miss us? Won't that be suspicious?" That excuse is all I can come up with on such quick notice.

"Once the day's activities are done, you're free. No need to be a zombie. It's actually how it works. All day, you get brainwashed. All night, you're free, seemingly, to think like you want. The idea is that by the end of the week, you will think like them, and they don't have to worry about pumping you full of drugs to keep your mind foggy."

"But—"

"No one cares what you do unless you're in your class. Trust me, Anna. Through here is a little bit of freedom, some food, and answers. Isn't that what you want?"

Answers, yes. Food, probably. Freedom—well, I never thought I didn't have it.

"Okay, but do you promise we're not going to get in trouble?"

"I promise."

⁜

At the tenth extended-length stairwell, Zane doesn't even seem winded, but I'm huffing and puffing like some out-of-shape Sumo wrestler.

As I take the last step up, he turns to me and says, "Down is way easier, but not nearly as fun when you reach the destination."

I hold onto the rail and take deep breaths. "I can't—" Air escapes, and I fuel up again, sucking in more. "I can't do more stairs." Plopping down on the top step, my legs can't be any more gelatin than if they were the actual food. I'm sure they aren't going to work, especially if Hadley's calculation is right on how far we went down. My ears have popped several times already.

"One more flight, and we'll be at the top of this level. Then we take the service risers to the surface."

With my free hand, I wave at him. "Go without me. Save yourself."

Zane's laughter makes me smile. His shoes slide across the tile, and as I try to get my heart to slow its pace, he sits next to me.

That doesn't help the slowing of my heart. In fact, I'm pretty sure it skips a beat or two as he presses close to me.

"How much do you weigh, Anna? Ninety pounds?"

My eyebrows shoot up. "More than that, but why do you need to know?"

"How about I carry you?" His suggestion is insane, but the request comes with a straight face.

"No. No way."

"Piggy back."

I'm waiting for the punch line.

"Oh, come on. If you weigh a hundred pounds wet, I'd be surprised. I can easily carry you up a flight of stairs."

"Not a chance."

Mia once carried me across our tiny yard and dropped me when she got too tired. My butt hit the only slab of concrete in our mostly-rock sidewalk, and to this day, my tailbone goes numb if I sit too long.

"There's no food here, and no answers, either."

Dropping my head to my palms, I say, "I get that. Promise it's just one more leve?"

"Promise."

With a heave, I press to a stand, overtaxed muscles screaming at me to sit again. One step up and I crumple forward.
Before I can get my hands to the ground, Zane lifts me into
his and starts moving at a speed far faster than we'd been going when I walked.

The bumping and jostling against his chest is bad, but his
scent, a mix of soap and something else I can't even describe,
makes my position far worse. I'd like to hang on and just smell
him for a while, but that would be totally awkward.

He makes it up the last flight without speaking another word
and relaxes his hold until my feet touch the ground with a soft
thump. Before us are three risers, each numbered and each with
a key code for activation.

"Please tell me you have a number for that so I don't have
to walk all the way back down."

Zane pats his jacket, stuffing his hand inside and bringing
it out empty. "Oh, sheez."

My eyes go wide.

His smile makes me want to shake him. "Just kidding. I
don't have it written down, of course."

Of course he doesn't.

Numbers accepted, we board riser number three. Zane
stands in the middle; I take the far right side. The space is
nothing like going down in the red house. It's metal, sure, but
it's tiny—made for five or six people at most, not the thirty or
more of us who stood together before.

"What do they—" I start but Zane stops me with a finger to
his lips. He could have told me not to talk before we boarded.

My ears pop a few more times until an interior ding signals,
and Zane motions me forward as the doors open.

Darkness greets me. With one step, the entire area illuminates, and walls of glass surround us.

Zane takes my hand and ushers me out, dragging me along with him, even though my legs haven't fully recovered, and each step tells my brain I need to stop and sit and never walk again.

We stay close to the glass, edging our way around to a set of doors with another keypad.

Through that, Zane brings me outside.

Into the middle of a skyscraper-filled world.

Buildings climb high into the sky. People traipse along the sidewalks and trams shoot on through the roads. Streetlamps show off a gritty, dirty, unkept area, and the smell reminds me of rotting trash with an overlay of fake flowers.

Zane tugs me to the left, crossing the street, and to another building with yet another keypad.

Once inside, the lights brighten, and I'm surrounded in lush reds and blues, leather divans and fake plants, along with a nice fresh scent like someone just cleaned wood floors.

"This is really pretty. Where are we?"

"This is the downtown district."

"*The* downtown district? As in—"

"Yeah. Haven't you been? Even on an educational field trip?"

I shake my head as he leads me to another set of risers. "I've never been downtown."

We board riser number one and head up five floors. As the doors open, all the ugly blandness of the registration room is swept away in a sea of green plants, blue walls, dark wood floors and light streaming everywhere. Floor to ceiling windows call to me, and I make my way toward them, careful not to touch the glass. Surrounding us are more buildings, lights on various floors, dotting the horizon and every inch of space.

"It's so pretty." Nothing like my district or my rundown shack of a living space, or even Cam's multi-level building I'd always thought to be the biggest personal place out there because of how many people live in it.

Zane stands next to me as I gawk. "You've really never been here?"

"No. I've seen pictures, yeah, but not real life." I imagine it's like being underwater and all the little twinkly lights are fish. Some move; I assume those are trams or personal transports. Others don't—stationary like the sun. "Where are we exactly?"

Zane tucks his hands into his pockets, but has yet to take off his jacket. "This is Mia's, Anna."

I spin, interest and awe filling me. My sister has fifth floor housing in the downtown district, no more than fifteen minutes from where I live. She could have visited in the last four years. She could have come by. I could have come here. A few tram rides for me and we could have been together. I didn't have to miss out on four years of time.

A spark of anger ignites within me. Mom kept us apart. She lied to me. I'll bet anything she knows where Mia lives and didn't tell me on purpose. All the tears and drama when I mentioned my sister's name. For what? She has a good job, an awesome place and is doing what she's supposed to do for our country. That's what we're here for.

Zane walks into the space and around a wall, disappearing from view. "She's not here much, which is why she gave me access for this week." His voice floats from the other side.

Following the sound, I find the living area we entered through opens to a small kitchen with a dining table and another door.

"Back there is the bedroom and bathroom. You can get to it from the living room, too."

My sister's living quarters aren't big. Probably no bigger than the space mom and I live in, but it's refined. Clean. It smells fresh, and I'm sure all her appliances work. "Can I see the rest?"

At Zane's definitive nod, I open the door to a short hallway with two other doors. The first is my sister's bedroom painted a soft mauve with a big bed. Nothing is out of order. She lived like that at home, too—all her clothes lined up, papers and desk organized. No clutter. The clutter-girl is me, and even I'm not that bad.

Closing her bedroom door, I move to the other, and it opens to a small but nice bathroom with an actual tub. *A tub!* What I wouldn't do to lay in one of those and soak.

I sigh as my own bathroom pops into mind; Mom and I just have a shower stall.

Back to Mia's room, the walls are painted a soft yellow, accented with blues, and there's a marble countertop without a scratch in it. Ours is plastic, and whoever had our place before us burnt little holes into it.

A pang of jealousy tightens my chest. I could have lived here for the last four years. Mia could have brought me up from below the poverty line. She could have helped Mom. She could have gotten me into downtown schools and let me eat every day.

Family can do that. Strangers can't, but Mia's my sister. Why didn't she give me this life? ... *the red house candidates are the ones they want to keep, if they can keep you in line. You're the ones who can live on next to nothing* ... Her words haunt me. Did she leave me there so I'd learn how to survive on nothing? Is that why mom is so mad at her? She follows the rules? Rules Mom hates and thus why she never applied for her documentation?

"Anna?" Zane's voice brings me out of my growing insanity and all the what-ifs dancing around in my head like concrete butterflies slamming against the edges, wanting to get out but having no idea how.

"Coming." I close the door and follow the hallway to the end. It opens to the living room. Geometrically, the space is a square but the design has a flow, a feel to it that tells me my sister is doing well in our country.

Our country's out of money. Right. She's a liar, like everyone else.

A few bangs sound in the kitchen, and I make my way there, only to find Zane at the cooking slab with a couple pots on top.

"What're you doing?" I ask.

His grin is sincere. "This is how I make sure not to eat their food. I have to come up those steps whenever I want to eat—one, two, three times a day, make something, and go back down."

"You can cook?"

He cocks his head. "Is that wrong?"

Flaming cheeks give away my embarrassment. "I didn't mean it like that. I just . . . none of my friends can cook—or, at least, I've never seen them in a kitchen other than to eat."

He brings out lettuce and spices, some sort of pink package, and sets it on the table and hands me a glass of clear liquid. "It's just water. Mia's kind of a health freak, so there's nothing with sugar in this entire place."

Zane seems to know more about my sister than I do. That's both cool and bothersome at the same time. I slide a butt cheek onto the stool on the opposite side of the counter—a wood-grain marble if the texture under my fingertips is right.

"When did you meet my sister?"

"When I was six." He works, answering me without looking up. Watching him brings my inner turmoil down to a low boil.

"Six?" My glass clinks against the surface a little too hard.

"Yeah. She came to our house with—" He stops, worry glossing over his otherwise happy face.

"With who?"

"Uh . . ." Head tilted down toward his cutting board, he says, "With a group of people who'd come to talk to my uncle. He lived with my family at the time."

"Oh. Okay." Why would that make him falter? Did mom go to that meeting? What about Dad? I lift up. What about me? Had I met Zane before and not even known it? "Anyone else there that I might know?" I'm curious more about me than anything.

He stops and lifts his chin. "No idea. Bunch of adults. And Mia. So, anyway . . . I thought someone brought me a babysitter since both my sisters wanted nothing to do with me, and I tried to get her to stay and play, but she wouldn't. She sat in the room with the adults and refused to have anything to do with me." My sister butting into an adults-only conversation sounds like her. He chuckles a little and throws a bunch of green stuff and what looks like chicken into a pot. "I'm going to let that simmer for a while."

"What are you making?"

"Chicken soup. Most of it's done, but I wanted to add some fresh ingredients and more chicken. It just needs to simmer for about thirty minutes." He turns to the fridge and comes back with a plate of cheese and little breads.

"You didn't make that, too, did you?"

"I did." His grin is devious.

I pick up one and bite into it. The taste is heavenly on my tongue, so fresh and with some herb I'm not familiar with.

"You taste the basil?"

I wouldn't know what to call it, since the only spice Mom can afford is salt, and my expertise in the kitchen extends only into products that can be made with lettuce. Rather than offend him, I offer a few *Mmms* to show how much I like it.

"I learned how to grow basil in my mom's backyard. She

wasn't licensed to sell the herbs, but we could have them."

"Where are your parents now? And your sisters."

His lips seal, and he spins to the bowl, stirring a little without speaking.

Dropping my hands to the counter, I don't pick up any more food. It seems rude, since I've obviously said something that bothered him.

Over five minutes pass before he faces me again. "My sisters immigrated to the United States. My parents died three years ago."

I hold back the gasp, and the questions about what happened. Not only with his parents, but his sisters. I'm guessing they left because their parents died and they had no other ties here, but what about Zane? Why leave a fifteen year old alone?

"You remember that big tram accident in the upper northern district eight? Where the operator freaked out and went off course?"

With nothing but an old P-Comm, I didn't get much video, and no wall unit at home meant none of the news stations, either. I have a vague recollection about some incident, but honestly don't remember it.

Zane stirs the pot, eyes downcast. "Mom and Dad were visiting up near that district. They were on a fourth honeymoon. It was gross when they told me when I was fourteen that they were going and why, but now, I get it." He chuckles a little. "The operator slammed into the rock wall between the AU and Canada, going three times the speed limit. They didn't even know what hit 'em. Dude killed twenty-eight people."

I reach out, but don't touch him, wanting to but unsure that I should. Tears burn the back of my eyes, but he's not crying, so I don't want to do that, either. "I'm so sorry, Zane. I understand only a little of what you lost, since my dad died when I was four. I don't remember much of him except a few pictures my mom has. And his smell. I don't know why, but I have that stuck in my head."

His features quirk for a second but harden again.

Wanting to bring the smile back to him, I decide changing the subject is a necessity. "So ... did you get your assignment ... I mean, you know, for your job?"

He nods once.

"Care to share?"

"Does it matter what I got, if I'm not going to keep it?" His tone is clipped and irritated.

I scratch at the back of my neck, rubbing to loosen the muscles tightening there and wishing we could reverse time by six or seven minutes, before I asked about his parents, before I asked about the job. Cam once told me I always knew what to say and when, but with Zane, I seem to step into mud holes even when there aren't any.

A beeping starts behind Zane along with the rolling of boiling liquid. He doesn't move.

The spill-over sizzles against the stove, so I slip from my chair and go to it, lowering the temperature and stirring. Freshness invades my nostrils. I want to ladle a cup into a bowl and dive in right there. The grumbling of my stomach suggests now would be a great time to eat, but I don't want to mess that up, either.

At a shuffle behind me, I spin, only to have Zane's hands land on my waist, his body against mine, gaze intense.

I look away, staring at the floor. Glancing up, I find him still staring and turn away again.

He says nothing, but I don't want him to let go, so I don't try to make him release me. "Do you know why the tram operator freaked out?" His hold tightens.

I give a little wobble of my head, keeping my gaze everywhere but on his.

"Because his daughter, who waited for a transplant for two years, got bumped while in surgery for Osso's step-daughter."

Lifting up, I stare straight into Zane's eyes. "Osso? Our current Chief Executive Officer? That's not possible. It's done by whose turn it is. No one gets—"

"Bought or born, Anna. The leaders of this country aren't elected like they used to be hundreds of years ago. We don't get to pick and choose them."

"Sure we do, there's an election every—"

"When was the last time the incumbent lost?"

"Well ..." I think back but can't remember a change in leadership. The last time, in fact, when Osso went up from Executive Officer to Chief, no one opposed him.

"None of them have ever wanted for anything, and since the laws and rules don't change, their roles get to be just as cushy as they can get, and people who want to impress them do *anything* they want." Zane hasn't released his hold, his fingers tight around me.

"Okay, but then, the doctors and people who jumped the line should have been brought to the Medical Jury."

He huffs a laugh. "The same jury appointed by our CEO? Are you kidding?"

"But the rule is equality."

"Like equality in jobs? Pay? Life?"

I tug from his hold. "Not everyone can be CEO. Not everyone is smart enough or motivated enough. Levels of jobs are different, and pay grades go with what you're capable of. That's why we're tested, to find out what we're good at, to be given a good job, to know where we should start and be able to grow as we learn more."

"Then why isn't your mother, who speaks thirteen different languages and tutors kids around the world, one of the top ranked teachers? Why isn't she way up the food chain?"

Circling my finger on the countertop, I say, "She's a fluke. She doesn't get those—"

"She's not a fluke."

My head pops up. "Of course she is. Why else would I live in a dump with no money or food? Mia has it all, why wouldn't we?"

18

No way did Zane just tell me my mom's not a fluke.

"She's not a fluke, Anna." He stops and closes his eyes. Opening them, he says, "Never mind. But listen—"

"No, no." My fingers dig into his chest. "You tell me right now why you think my Mom's not a fluke. You don't even know her."

"You asked the better question. Why would you live in a house with no money or food?" His head shakes back and forth.

The visceral sound that leaves my lips is a growl mixed with a cry wrapped in eighteen years of frustration. "Why do people do that to me? Make a statement and not follow through."

He holds his palms out to me. "I'm sorry. I shouldn't have said anything. Really. My bad."

Walking away from him, I clench my fists. I want to beat them against something, but instead, I plop on the seat at the counter and drop my head into my hands.

"They want me to be a chef," Zane says after an interminable silence.

"Good. That fits." At least everyone knows what a chef does.

"I don't want to be a chef; don't you see?"

I don't.

"This country went down a path of destruction a long time

ago, when it adopted the new constitution. When it started making all the decisions for all the people, instead of giving us the free will that our God above intended."

God? I frown. God exists only in the minds of zealots. *Why's he bringing God into being a chef?* Is Zane one of *them?* No one believes in that. Well, no one I know.

"Free will is something we don't have any more, here," Zane says.

This is all getting way too weird.

"The rules Osso and his family have in place are like the old dictatorships where everything they say goes. Studying the old texts and the histories proves just how backward we've gone. How we're repeating what the first forefathers, what George Washington, wanted us not to go through."

First forefathers? Old texts? George Washington? Who is this guy? That's not our country's history. At this point, I just want to get back to my room, sleep and start over tomorrow, but of course I still haven't eaten, and I'll need Zane to take me back.

Stuck. As usual. *Why does this always happen to me?*

"I wanted to study that more. I wanted to be a historian. See?"

It makes no sense. History doesn't repeat. Who goes back to forefathers in a normal conversation? That time means nothing and has no relevance to today. "Historians earn less money than janitors, you know." I can't believe, after all Zane's said, *that's* what comes out of my mouth, but maybe it'll get him off the history rant. Then again, maybe not. I don't even know what historians make.

Zane throws up his hands before running them through his hair. "I don't care about credits, Anna. And they earn less because historians think, and thinking-people scare Osso and his goon-squad in district one." Zane leans forward over the countertop and tucks a hair behind my ear—not a gesture I expected. "That tram operator's daughter died on the operating table because they took lungs meant for her, in the middle of surgery, and gave them to someone else. On the table, Anna. Tell me *that's* fair."

My heart lurches. "It's not, but there had to be a reason. Maybe you just don't ... know ... it." I slow as his eyebrow wings up. "They can't just—"

"Have you read our constitutional documentation lately?" Zane wags a finger at me, going from girl-in-surgery to our abiding laws just like that? "It doesn't say anything about being fair. The people that thought fairness should be implemented are those who didn't work hard enough to get to the top. They thought it was their job to determine what's fair, saying it's not *fair* for a rich person to pay less taxes than a poor one. On the surface, that seems true, but no one would implement equality in taxation. Instead, they said, 'if you're rich, we'll tax you more' and guess what? People decided they didn't want to be classified as rich, and they stopped doing the work to become rich. They quit because our leadership quit them. How's *that* fair?"

Wow. Maybe historians do earn a lot of credits. "That doesn't have anything to do with your parents."

His fist bangs on the counter. "Was it the tram operator's choice to have his daughter die in the O.R. because another person needed the same organs?"

"I'm guessing no ... but—"

"There aren't any buts! Don't you see? It's a philosophy. Some believe equality means everyone should get the same stuff, and everything they have, and do, should be given to them to ensure they can be everything they want to be. Others believe equality means everyone has an equal shot, but what they do with the life God gives them is totally, absolutely and completely up to that individual."

There's that God mention again. I wonder, for a moment, if Zane has ever done any public speaking. He's obviously passionate about this stuff, but telling me isn't going to get him anywhere. Maybe I'm just a practice dummy?

"My parents died because equality, here in the AU, means nothing to the very people who are supposed to enforce it, and knowing those people have a kid who's alive, and knowing they have plenty of credits when there are people on the street eating out of garbage cans, and that tram operators—" Zane throws up his hands and growls, turning as he does.

Whoa.

"I wanted to be a historian because I wanted to study this and understand what happened to get us here. To find a way to fix it. But they want me to be a chef. How's *that* fair?"

His question seems so simple, but the answer can't be. Not with his back to me, shoulders hunched and hand on the lower bar. He almost looks broken—nothing like the guy from a second ago, so confident in whatever he said.

"One person can't fix this," I say with softness.

Zane whirls toward me. "Are you kidding?"

Uh ... no? Do I dare answer?

"Everything in life starts with one person. Christopher Columbus, Martin Luther King, Jr., Rosa Parks ..." He names people I've never heard of. Except for Columbus. We studied him in level one. "Do you know why there are no choices in jobs this year?"

"Huh? No ... why?"

"Because they don't have the money to pay everyone at the level they should be, so they have to control everything. Right down to what job you can have, to keep you on minimal income needs, and control how many people can have babies to keep the future population down."

And ... we're back to Mia's rant.

"If I lived anywhere else—the United States instead of here—I'd have true freedoms. I'd live under the *old* constitution. The one from seventeen-seventy-six."

Whoa. He's forgetting stuff now. "They're like ... violent criminals over there," I say. "With guns. And people die if they can't pay for their medicines and stuff."

Zane chuckles a little. "You're so brainwashed, aren't you?"

If I say 'no', he's going to disagree, so I stay mute. Probably shouldn't have said squat before either. As Mom would remind me, 'getting people riled up is never a good thing if you can get the same information peacefully'.

"The U.S. has the best economy in the entire world. *Entire world*, Anna." Both hands land in front of me as if pleading me to understand, but I just don't. It just ... never affected me. It won't, either. By having no credits, any credits are a boost.

"We take care of our people, here, Zane. They don't ... over there."

He takes me by the biceps. "Listen to yourself. You think someone else should take care of you, run your life, tell you what to do, where to live, *how* to live, even when you don't want to. Do you want to be a life coach, Anna?"

I shrug. Now, we're back to me. *Sheez. Will this never end?* It'd be impolite not to answer, though, so holding back the sigh, I say, "The tests say that's what I'll be good at."

"Fuck the tests, Anna."

The jerk of my shoulders pulls me from Zane's grip.

"Don't you want the chance to run your life the way *you* want? Succeed or not, don't *you* want to choose? Don't you want the opportunity to fail?"

Staring down at the speckled surface, I say, "No one wants to fail."

"No, no one *wants* to fail. But failure makes us stronger. We learn from mistakes. It's a basic psychological premise. Human nature. What Osso and his kin are doing is taking all that out of our hands. If we don't have motivation to achieve greatness, we'll never think we need more and, in not needing more, we'll never grow out of our own shells. They're making us into a country of duplicates. Why don't you get this?" He stalks away from me and spins around.

"I'm sorry I don't understand." Why should I? I like my life. Most of it anyway. Not the no-credits part, but the chance to be independent so I can earn funds and help support Mom. That's what I want. "It's just the way it's always been."

"In seventeen-seventy-five ..."

Oh, sheeez. Another history lesson. Why can't he be like a normal guy?

"... Benjamin Franklin ..."

Who?

"... said, 'They who can give up essential liberty to obtain a little temporary safety deserve neither liberty nor safety.' Don't you see? We gave up control of our lives to the Osso's of the world, and the Osso's of the world have screwed us over. Power breeds corruption and, without limits, chaos. We're moments from chaos, Anna."

Not that I can see.

He smacks his palm against his forehead. "Did you know that over a million people have left the American Union and gone to the United States in the last year?"

"Is that bad?"

Hands back on the counter, he says, "They left because they're like the tram driver. Screwed over in the name of 'fairness'. Of some kind. I've seen the files that document the why on some. Your dad says—"

"My dad ... *says*?" Shock doesn't come close to the internal war going on inside me. Not only has Zane ranted at me for at least an hour about stuff I don't understand, he just talked about my dad in the present tense.

Zane's eyes go wide. "Sheeze." His head droops, and he runs a hand through what hair falls forward. "I can't believe I said that."

"Said ... what?"

He lifts his head, his eyes sad and worried. "Mentioning your dad. It was insensitive."

"But you said it ... like you know him. Now."

After a really long pause, Zane says, "I do, Anna. I do."

A spinning takes over my head until everything goes black.

⚬━━◆━━⚬

"Dammit, Zane. Why'd you tell her about Dad?"

"I already told you. I got going on a rant, and it slipped out. I'm really sorry, Mia."

A light slap to my cheek jostles my head and my brain. I've been listening to them for maybe ten minutes, going back and forth, as open as can be about the fact my dad isn't dead, how Mom made up the story, and if she didn't think dad would eventually come back to her, Mom might have gone with him in the first place.

Keeping my eyes closed longer than necessary is a trick I learned a long time ago when Cam came over for a sleepover. She'd get up early and work on her hair, mumbling to herself about how pretty and nice everyone thought her. I'd listen, thinking if I said those said words to myself in the mirror, maybe I'd be more like her. That reminds me of Cam and the white house candidates, or whatever that group goes by, and whatever their fate might be.

"Anna, come on. You've been out way too long," Mia says.

"Maybe we should get a medic," Zane says.

"No, she'll be fine. She's always taken longer to recover from fainting. She was like this as a kid, too."

I try hard not to smile and let my head loll to the side when she gives me another tap. Life will catch up to me, but that doesn't mean I have to let it do so on its terms. A few more slaps and my hot cheeks are going to be super red.

A groan helps me fake waking up.

"Anna! Anna. It's Mia, can you hear me?"

Yes, of course I can. "Mia?" My voice comes out groggy and unsure.

"Come on, Anna. I'm here." She, or probably Zane, lifts me by my elbows so I'm sitting halfway up.

"What happened?" I ask, rubbing my forehead and knowing full well what happened.

"You passed out cold," Zane says from behind me.

Yeah, because you blurted out the fact that my dad is still alive.

"Up you go, Anna. Lift, Zane." Mia's direction comes right before Zane does exactly as he's told.

Regaining my balance takes a second or two, as I brace a hand against the wall with Zane's arms still holding me at my waist.

Mia walks to a cabinet and opens it. She pulls down a big bottle of Gin and sets it on the side. Ice goes in a glass, and she fills it up with some tonic waters and a lime. "You guys can have water or … whatever, but it's time for a drink for me."

I've never seen her drink. For that matter, I've never seen her do a lot of adult things. The last time I saw her, she walked away from us and me. I wanted to pull her back and make her stay, but Mom held me still.

Mia chugs a few big gulps and drops the glass to the table. "Well, Anna, big news for today. It's not surprising that you collapsed." One hand shakes in Zane's direction. "Of course, none of this was supposed to come out like this. But it's out now." She stalks toward me in prey and predator manner until she's right at my nose. "I told you before that you are to pretend you don't know me, and that's still true. But now I have to make sure you understand the position you've put me in."

Me? "Me?" I managed to eek out the question on a cough. "How did *I* put *you* in a *position*? I didn't ask to come up here. I didn't ask to be told Dad is alive, or that Mom is liar. I didn't want to know my life is a sham. I was perfectly happy before."

"Liar, liar, pants on fire," Mia says. "You weren't happy."

"How do you know? You weren't even there."

She and Zane exchange a glance. "This one is all yours, Mia," he says.

With another gulp, she downs the rest of her drink. "I wasn't for the last four, but I was before. Dad wasn't around, but he was. Mom's just ... well ... Mom does what Mom wants to do." She twirls the glass on the counter. "Dad didn't disappear because he wanted to. He disappeared because he had to." Both hands lift, palm up. "When you were two, some people sent him to the Treason Jury accused of conspiracy. To keep everyone safe, he agreed to move to the district's interior and be monitored for five years."

Treason Jury? What did he do?

"And met my uncle and Dad," Zane says.

Well, that explains how they know each other, then.

"But Mom refused. She didn't want anything to do with taking credits from our government, or being monitored to prove herself. So she stayed behind."

"Why didn't he come back when it was over?" I ask.

"You'll have to ask him."

Closing my eyes is the only solution I have to not slapping my sister.

"Anyway ... none of that is the point," she says.

Except, it matters to me. All of the important stuff keeps getting glossed over.

"Dad, along with a bunch of others, is using a loophole in our country's bylaws that still refers to the old constitution."

Not her, too.

"It said that the people were 'endowed by their Creator with certain unalienable Rights' and should alter or abolish a government that is taking away those rights."

"That's not in our laws," I say. *Is it?* We studied our laws in government class, but it was so boring I had to work just to stay awake.

"It's tucked away, but it's there, and with everything that's going on, some are trying to fix the mess, but it's not going well. Hasn't been for a really long time."

"Because," Zane jumps in, "people don't like change."

Of course they don't.

"Anyway, Mom's been furious with Dad for ages. One of the reasons I wanted to go through registration was so I could understand what our leaders do, and strangely enough, it was Dad who got me in. But I'm in undercover. A little like Zane is."

She's what? "Undercover?"

Mia exchanges glances with Zane. "Yes."

"Am I? Undercover that is." Is it possible to be without knowing it?

They both laugh but squash their emotions a second later. "No," Mia says. "Honestly, you weren't supposed to know anything about this, but some people don't know how to keep their mouths shut. So we'll work around it. But, that said, you *cannot*, now, tell Mom that you're involved with me. You have to pretend you don't know that Dad's alive when you get home. But I will say that you would be a great asset—especially with your life skills leading up to Life Coach. I mean ..." She takes my hands. "We need people who can explain our plan to those affected, and who can get them not to leave, but to overthrow."

I pull away. "Overthrow? Overthrow what?"

Another set of glances are shared.

"Osso. We're going to overthrow the government."

Zane nods. "That's the plan."

"But that's illegal! That's not right. That's ... that's ... insane!"

Mia's gaze never falters. "That's what all brainwashed people think."

Mia shooed us out of her living space, after feeding us both and reminding me to keep my mouth shut. All the while on the riser going down the eleven flight of stairs, my mind whirled with the thought that my sister would be overthrowing the government.

If I actually had a relationship with my dead dad, I'd have to go to him to get him to stop her. Mom won't care enough to do anything since she's still mad at me, let alone Mia, but someone has to stop Mia from getting herself arrested—or worse, deported for treason, like the last few up-risings we studied at educenter.

One time, a group of just five people stormed district one and proclaimed themselves leaders. They were all tried for treason, convicted by the Treason Jury, and were all relocated to facilities for the mentally insane.

Another time, just last year, if I remember correctly, a bigger group—something like a hundred, or more—did something similar, but the cops only caught ten of them and, after weeks of interrogation, they, too, were relocated. Did they get shipped to another country like the white house people? Did they go to some facility? Why can't people just leave well enough alone?

I didn't ask when she planned to take action, but figure something like that will take months or years. I don't want to lose Mia again. I don't want anything to happen to Mom, no matter how mad she is at me. "I don't want anything to happen to me."

"What?" Zane asks as we make our way back down the hallway to our room. He's been walking fast ever since we got off the riser and kept about ten steps ahead of me the whole time.

"Nothing." I didn't realize I spoke out loud. "Why are you walking so fast?"

People stand outside their room doors, some in pajamas, some all dressed up, laughing, crying, emotional. Seems odd to notice, and odd to think I'm grateful they aren't zombie-like.

Zane, though, he continues on and doesn't answer. I keep after him and try to stop my thoughts from jumbling up on each other.

At our room door, his collar activates the door, and I follow him inside.

Our room is a disaster, as if someone came in and rifled through everything. My clothes are on the floor; the mattresses are flipped up; Zane's clothes are strewn everywhere; and while there wasn't much to begin with, both our PCDs lay on the floor, their screens facedown.

I don't know whether to scream or cry. Screaming seems pointless, since there's no threat to me at the moment, but how did they get in here in the first place?

Zane kicks at my only other pair of jeans as he lifts his PCD. "Sheez."

Rather than wait for an answer, I spin and race out of the room, down the hallway toward where I'd seen Hadley a long time ago. Lawyers always seem to know everything; maybe she knows what happened. Down the corridor, people stand and, as I pass another room, I find it, too, has been tossed.

Jel stands outside, arms crossed, a scowl in his features.

I stop in front of him. "Excuse me."

He tilts down to me. "Hey." A small smile graces his face though it's not a friendly gesture.

"Do you know what happened? I was ... um ... in the courtyard ... and just walked back in. I'm Anna, by the way."

"The authorities came down here, going through every room one by one. They say someone is a spy. Can't believe they'd think I am. Seez, what do they think I can spy on when people can see me coming from a mile away?"

"Oh, wow. So they went through all the rooms?"

"Still are. They're on the M hallway, or something, now, and every time they find something, they blast this stupid air horn. We're supposed to stay out of our rooms until given the all clear."

"Okay, thanks."

"No problem. Nice to officially meet you."

With a quick smile as acknowledgement, I turn and find Zane, his gaze directly on me, a firm set to his mouth. Passing him, I return to the door of our room and stand outside the frame.

"Spy?" he asks as he joins me.

"That's what Jel says."

"Same with the room right next door. Should have seen this coming. This year is too precarious for them to think all would be easy."

"I wouldn't know."

"Right. Exactly."

After fifteen minutes of chatter from others, but unsaid words between Zane and me, the speakers crackle. "All candidates may now return to their rooms. Due to program changes, new schedules will be sent to your PCDs in the morning. Lights will dim at exactly oh-one-hundred. No candidates will be allowed in the hallways tonight after oh-one-hundred-fifteen."

Silence hangs over us as people re-enter their rooms, Zane and me included.

I bend over, pick up my clothes and start to re-hang them. Zane bumps up against my butt as he does the same. "Sorry," we both say.

I can't be happy about the arrangement of me sleeping in the same room as him, and the fact Mia put us together makes me clench my fists. She doesn't know me from Crazy Sally.

She *doesn't* know me because everything I've ever known is a lie.

On a huff, I throw my belongings on the bed, sit on it, and drop my head into my hands. The bubble of air-filled tears burns my chest as I try to hold it back. If Cam were here, she'd know what to do. If Mom were, she'd come up with some way to make me stronger. No stuffed animals to cry into. No old ear-buds to stick in my ears and drown out the world with some music. Nothing.

Everything inside me wants to explode, to shatter into a million pieces, and I only have me and all this stuff that's piled on me in the last forty-eight hours to hold onto.

Air wants to expel from my lips, but if I let it, I know what will happen. Watery eyes, puffy nose, pink cheeks, turning me into slobbing, snotty girl.

Not a real girl, though.

I'm a woman made of glass, now. I never should have agreed to everything Marlena did to me. I never should have gone with Zane, even if I didn't know we'd end up in Mia's place. The pieces of my life are no longer together. They're out there, floating, waiting for me to recapture them, but I can't because I have no idea how to put them all back together.

All I want to do is cry.

I can't cry, though, because that's not what weak girls do. My life didn't have 'Awesome' written on it. It had normal there. Plain. Neutral, maybe. Ordinary. I wouldn't have complained if it stayed just like that. I asked for changed, but I didn't want it. Not deep down.

If anyone had asked, I'd have been fine with just a job, living with Mom and going on with life as I know it—knew it.

One hundred percent fine.

Oh, boy. Who am I kidding?

Holding back is no longer an option, and my sob bursts forth.

Wetness leaks onto my hands. My eyes shut tight against the flood, but not all dams are created equal, and mine doesn't do its job.

My mattress depresses, and when Zane's body leans into mine, I jump.

He pats me again as if that's going to fix everything. There's nothing he can do to change what I now know, and his gesture produces another set of blubbery sobs from me. At the rate I'm going, I'll never stop, the room will fill up, and we'll both drown.

His hand doesn't leave my back, only adds a light rub up and down. "I'm really sorry, Anna. I didn't mean to make you cry."

I want my stupid stuffed bunny in my room and my pillow so I can curl up and drain all my tears in them, so I won't have any more to embarrass myself with when I do finally lift up and face Zane. It's bad enough he's here with me, that I don't have a real friend to share with. It's worse that he's not going to leave.

The reminder that Mia stuck us in the same room builds up another tidal wave of emotion.

My mattress rises and dips, and a coolness takes over the side where Zane sat. A tug on my arms accompanies Zane saying, "Come back here, Anna."

I shake my head. If I speak, my words will be a mumbled mess; no point in making me sound stupid, too.

He pulls harder. "Come on."

I let him drag me back, but instead of leaning against the cold wall, I find myself wrapped in his arms, against his chest, and together, we shift to laying on the bed, his arms around me.

From behind me, he says, "Before my sisters moved away, they each sat me down and had a talk. Not a sex talk, a girl talk. Fanny said, 'Zane, baby, if you ever find a girl who's crying and doesn't have a stuffed teddy bear to do it in, be her bear." His arm stays around me, warm and caring. "Cindi made me practice more than I thought I'd ever have to, since she couldn't keep a boyfriend. Never actually thought I'd have to use these mad skills with anyone else, and I don't figure you want to hold me like a real teddy bear, but this worked for her. If you want me to leave, though—"

"No!" I manage between sucking in air and letting more out. "Please … don't … go." My whisper is forced, but I get the words out.

He presses in closer, his warm breath on the back of my neck as he toys with strands of hairs, tickling me with each touch. "I promise to stay as long as you want."

❦

"I'll never leave you, my Windy girl." Daddy pulls my hair into a ponytail at the top of my head. "Do you know how much I love you?"

"Yes, Daddy," I say as I climb onto the swing. Swinging is my favorite at the park. Mia doesn't like to swing, but I do. I like to go high, high, higher. "Higher, Daddy!"

He pushes me once, and my little legs kick out. Another push gets me where I want to be, but I'm too small to stay there.

"Need you, Daddy! Push!"

I need you, Daddy. I've always needed you. Why did you leave me? Why did saving the world matter more than your own family? Why did you not love Mom enough to work through it, or convince her to go with you? Why did you tear our family apart? Why keep Mia but not me? Why let her back in but leave me to find my own way.

"Need you, Daddy! Push!" my little self says.

I need you, Daddy!

"Go higher. Let Mommy see!"

"Erianna, come inside now." My mother's sing-songy voice calls for me as I play in the back yard, in the dirt, with a doll with no head. We're making mud pies together. Or, I am, and she's pretending to eat them without her head.

My mother's feet appear, and I tilt up. "Hi, Mommy." One hand reaches up. "Want one?"

She leans down. "Oh, Eri, look at you." Even though her tone is a complaint, she smiles. "Maybe we need to start some real cooking lessons—now that you're going to level two."

I nod, excited because I want to learn how to cook, like Mom. She cooks for Mia and me all the time and makes the best noodles and sauce of anybody. Even Cam likes Mom's noodles and sauce. She says her mom never makes the simple stuff, and she has to eat gross things with green in them.

"Mia's on her way home from her meeting. You remember that, right?"

"Yes, Mommy."

As she wipes my hands with her apron, she says, "So we're

going to make her favorite dinner."

"Noodles with cheese?"

"Yes. Her very favorite. Your Daddy's favorite, too." A light sniffle draws my attention to my mother's face, but I can't see it. While I know I'm talking to her, she has no face that I can see. "So I want you to come inside and get ready. You're a big girl now that you're nine, so let's make Mia feel special, okay?"

I drop my doll and put my hand against my mom's.

Eighteen-year-old Mia slams the doors to the cupboards, breaking one off the hinges. "I told you, I'm going to get into the registration class, and there's nothing you can do to stop me."

Mom sits on the back of our two-seat divan, her face a picture of seriousness as she worries her hands together. "I'm not stopping you, Mia. I'm not keeping you from greatness. I just want you to consider—"

"Consider this, Mother …" Mia stalks up to Mom. "Dad wants me there."

Mom's face tilts down, but I still see no tears or anything sad from her. "You don't know—"

Mia shakes a finger in front of Mom's face. "I know it for a fact." She storms out the door, slamming it against the frame.

I run to it and stand outside yelling, "Mia! Come back! Come back!"

If she hears me, she doesn't show it. If she cares, she gives no indication. That she's leaving is obvious.

Mom's hands land on my shoulder. "Sometimes, Eri, people leave, and their reasons aren't always the right ones, but we have to support them and trust them and hope they'll find their way home eventually."

"I'll never leave you, Mom," my fourteen year-old self says.

"I know you won't, baby." She rubs my cheek. "Unlike everyone else in this house, you're the only one who doesn't get influenced by everyone around you. You're smart like that."

Even in what I know is a dream, I want the end to change. My heart hurts so much, desperate to see a different outcome. To see my dad stay. To have Mia return. To have Mom understand why I didn't actually want to be a fluke and how all that changed with Mia leaving us.

Dad, though, will leave, no matter how much I beg him not to—even though I never did—in my dreams.

Mia will leave, whether I want her to or not—and I didn't.

Mom wants us all to return home.

Home. Where the heart is. Home. Where I must be, since I'm warm and cozy and curled up on a pillow that smells like my Dad, with a hand rubbing my cheek and the weight of the world off my shoulders.

This is where I want to be.

⌐━╼╾━⌐

"Erianna, wake up!"

The words tear me from my memories; good or bad, I'd found solace in my unconscious mind.

Cold seeps in all around me.

"Anna, hurry, wake up!" Zane's voice calls to me from too far away.

My body rolls back and forth twice.

"Anna! Anna! You gotta get up."

I blink two or three times. Maybe four, five or six.

Zane's face is an inch from mine.

"What's going on? Why are you whisper-yelling?"

"Because," he says. "They've identified a spy."

I'm still dressed from the night before and realize the warmth I'd had in my dream came from Zane. Had to have, since there are no fluffy or soft pillows or blankets on my bed, and unless he got up and made his, he never used it.

"What do you mean?" My mind is still processing as I rub sleep from my eyes.

He's stuffing clothes into a backpack. "Mia got in touch. They figured it out—sorta—and are starting their search. Or will soon. We gotta go."

"What do you mean *we*? I'm not a spy. I don't know anything. Mia told me to promise I'd say that."

Zane stops for a brief second, his eyes so soft but serious. "You don't get it."

Well, of course not.

"They think the spy is you."

I bolt upright. "What? Are you kidding? How?"

He goes back to the packing and stuffing, as if this revelation is no big deal. "Like I said, they think they've figured it out, but they're wrong."

"Obviously. I'll just tell them—"

"And get deported. Or tried for treason. Or set up in front of Osso to be crucified?"

"They can't—"

He stops for a brief second. "We gotta jet. Now."

"Where to?"

"My uncle's place ... or somewhere."

"Why not Mia's?"

"She's on their list, too. I had about ten seconds of airtime with her this morning before she blipped off." He points to my feet. "Those shoes going to do for a while?"

I stare down at my tennis shoes. "I guess." I'd prefer my flats, but something tells me running in them—assuming we have to actually run—isn't going to work well.

"Good. Shoes are hard to pack. Let's go." He grabs my hand

and yanks me from the bed, two bags slung around his shoulder.

"What about our PCDs?" My brand new PCD—the one I just got. I have to take it with me.

"You want them to track every move we make?"

"But ... maybe you're wrong," I say as I pull free and stop again.

"You want to take that chance?"

None of this is real. I'm supposed to be the normal girl who gets a normal job in a normal country, not some fugitive from something I don't even understand.

Zane waves me forward. "If you don't come now, you'll risk everything. Everyone. Your ... sister and hundreds of others, who have worked so hard to bring change and a solution."

"But I'm not a part of this." My plea mustn't be worthy because Zane grabs my wrist and pulls. "And if they know about her and me ..." *What about Mom? What will they tell her? What will I tell her? How can I? What if—*

"You *are* a part of this." Zane breaks me from my thoughts. "You always have been. In a way. You just never knew it."

He has part of that right. I never knew. It's not fair, though, to lump me in with some group I hadn't heard about until last night.

Commotion echoes from down the hall, including the stomping of feet and high voices. They're coming for us, I just know it.

"Now or never, Anna. Seriously." Zane's hand jerks as if he means it.

Everything I've ever known, everything I've ever wanted to be, comes down to one moment. One single decision.

20

I've never run from authorities—no matter what kind they are. If a teacher needed me to stay, I did. If my mom asked me to do something, I did—registration being the exception. I didn't run in the commerce center when Cam pulled her stunt. I didn't leave Mr. Milton without his credits.

Yet, running from an unknown, to an unknown, down a short hallway, around a bend and through two sets of doors leading to a dark room that smells like a trash can, isn't bugging me the way I expect it should.

This almost feels like the right decision.

Zane strides, tugging me along, to a small silver door. He lifts it, and shows off a space no bigger than three feet squared.

"What is this?" I pinch my nose shut at the stench burning my nostrils.

"It's the trash riser."

"And why are we standing in front of it?"

He throws both our backpacks inside. "Because this is how we're going to get out of here undetected."

Backing away, hands up, I say, "Oh, no. I'm not getting in with trash."

"You won't be in with trash."

"Good. Then, how?"

"You'll be in alone."

"In the dark?" I ask too loud.

"Shh." Finger to lips, he motions me closer. "I'd go first, but if I do, I'm not sure you'll go."

He's right. I won't. "No way." There has to be line that I won't cross, and this has to be one of those. "This is insane. Isn't there another door without a camera—not that they aren't going to know we went this way."

Zane gives me that 'are you really so naive?' look that seems to afflict people around me. "No, there's not. And once we get up higher, there are several exits without eyes. They won't know where we've landed to know where we've gone."

"But, once we're on the street—"

He angles his head toward me. "Which would you rather get, Anna? Tortured by our leaders for information they think you have …"

"But that's illeg—"

He raises an eyebrow. "Or out of here before they come for us—"

Aren't they already chasing us?

"—and take a little round trip to avoid being seen for a few hours." The other eyebrow joins the first. "We probably have one or two more minutes, Anna. Seriously. Max."

"But I'm not a spy! I don't know anything about all this stuff. I don't want to overthrow the government. Nothing's wrong with it!" With each statement, my voice ratchets up a decibel.

"That whenever any Form of Government becomes destructive of these ends, it is the Right of the People to alter or to abolish it, and to institute new Government … from where does that come?" Zane asks as if I should know.

His calmness makes me want to wrap my hands around his throat, shake him, and say, 'just tell me what you want me to know already!' Instead, I say, "I have no idea," and run a hand through my hair as I blow out a breath.

"It's part of the Declaration of Independence from seventeen-seventy-six. From the original United State of America. Not the United States. Not the American Union. The original country. It's a part that no longer exists in our country. People can barely disagree now, let alone do something to change what's in place. You want that to keep happening? You want to be sterilized without consent because you're in the registration class of twenty-one thirty-two?"

"I still can't believ—"

"If you go with me, I promise to show you how bad these people are. To prove it to you. But you have to come with me. You have to trust me, Anna. Don't let them brainwash you more."

"I'm not brainwashed." I can't believe he's just said that. Again.

The outer doors bang open.

Zane's head whips toward the sound. "Now, Anna."

My heartbeat picks up speed.

There's a secondary barrier before whomever is out there sees us standing right here.

"Please, Anna," he whispers. "I have to get you to safety. Please."

I glance at the tiny riser, knowing I have seconds or less to make a decision. As my body is lifted from the ground, I yelp, and my head bumps the top as Zane stuffs me inside with a cursory 'sorry!' and shuts the door. "Jump when you see light."

"Or what?" The riser begins to move, going up but with no illumination. I have no idea what's going to happen, where I'm going to land, how to get out.

"You end up . . ." His voice trails off as I go higher.

Now, not only is my heart beating at a frantic pace, I can't breathe as the stench from trash overpowers every ounce of my being, but if I don't jump when I see the light, I'll do, what? Die? End up in a heap? Burn up?

Oh, no ... does this go to an incinerator?

A gag hits me as anxiety fills me. Throwing up when my knees are against my chest and my potential vomit has nowhere to go is not going to be pleasant. I swallow, trying to bank my body's response as well as my growing mental anguish, and breathe through my mouth, but that, too, produces another unpalatable smell that goes straight to my stomach.

My ears pop, and I swallow, not just air, but particles filled with whatever putrid contents had been in the cube before. The cough hits me again as desperation heightens. My hands splay out, pressing against metal, hoping it's been cleaned, wishing I could take my hands back and there not be anything on them.

Not that I can see them, anyway.

Up farther, I travel, alone and stuck in a box, about to puke. Wondering. Waiting.

I have no idea how far I'll have to go, how many gags I'll have to deal with as I travel. Did Zane make it? Did my bag? What will I do if he doesn't show up?

A lurch throws me off balance even though I'm sitting, squeezed into place.

Another jerk bumps my head into the back.

On the third bounce, my black hole of nothing stops.

Oh, my goodness. I'm going to die in here.

My hands search for an outlet, a security latch, a something that will free me.

Why did you shove me in here, Zane?

Silence greets my inner cries.

As they did last night, the tears form again, but I force them to stay away.

"Anna." My name comes from above, far away, echoing and faint.

I must be dreaming. That's it—I never woke up to Zane telling me to wake up. I'm still asleep, and whatever's going on is just some detailed mental play.

Closing my eyes, I say, *Wake up, Anna. Wake up, Anna* to myself, inside my head.

Lids open, I find myself in the same cramped space, breathing in the same nastiness, without Zane and without any light.

To be stuck in a trash riser, who knows where, in the gazillion story building, in the dark—I'm so stupid for following him in the first place.

"Anna, listen to me."

I'd swear Zane's talking to me, but wouldn't he be below me? Why does it sound like he's above?

"Anna, listen. Kick with your feet."

Kick with my feet? Is he insane? I can't kick anything. My knees are in my chest; my head is against the back. There's barely room for me to breath, let alone kick.

"When the light shines, kick hard."

"I can't," I yell back. "No room."

"Push then. Get ready."

'Get ready', he says as if I have any other choice, as if I'm having my nails tended to, or having a cup of tea with Osso's wife.

A sliver of brightness follows around the edges where my feet are wedged.

The light!

"Now!" His voice calls out.

I push, but my legs are just as wimpy as the rest of me. Strong in spirit, my teachers used to say.

"Now, Anna!"

"I'm trying! I can't—it's not—this isn't working."

The light disappears, leaving me in total blackness again. In silence, too.

I wait, straining to hear, cocking an ear upward as if that would help.

Nothing.

"Zane?" I whisper. Not that he can hear me, but I have to say something just to make sure I can hear myself.

The loudest screech of metal against metal scratches at my ears. I cover them, but the sound penetrates. Light fills my cubby hole from a corner that's torn back.

"Now, Anna. Hurry."

Now, Anna. Hurry. Everything is a hurry with this guy. I've never moved so fast in my entire life, and in two days, I do nothing but learn stuff I don't want to know and run from people.

Zane pries as I press with my feet, our dual action peeling the metal away.

The riser lurches.

A clang sounds on the ground.

"Sheez! Kick it."

With the little extra space, I can get my foot through, not that the rest of me will go, but I can't do anything except press on it.

My box falls a little, jostling me.

Zane's hand reaches in. He fumbles above, mumbled incoherent words spilling from his lips. After what seems like only three or four seconds, the entire front face falls off and Zane stands there holding it. "Now, Anna! Climb out."

The riser screeches and falls and inch.

"Now, or you're going back down!"

I scramble as best I can, getting my feet out first and pushing up. Zane drops the metal door that had sealed me in, and takes my hand, pulling me out.

Onto a six inch ledge of metal support.

The riser makes a long, low moan and starts moving, its pace slow but steady, my broken-open box area disappearing from the beam of light Zane holds in his hands.

Below me vast emptiness exists—an echoey, hollow space.

Clinging to him, I stand there, my insides shaking, my outsides ready to burst into a waterfall of tears. I hate heights. Being in a cramped box not seeing heights, I can deal with. Being in a place without walls is something altogether different.

His hands stay around me, but he extinguishes the light. "I know how to get us out from here, but you're going to have to trust me."

He thinks I won't trust him *now?* We're in the middle of a riser shoot. One wrong step and I will fall to my death. I have no choice but to trust him.

Without speaking, I give him a little head bob, hoping he understands that I'll do whatever it takes, whatever he tells me to get out of here.

"I need you to get on your hands and knees and crawl across this beam to the other side. When we're there, we have to climb up about one floor and there's a hatch door. It's for maintenance. If we can get that open, we can get out."

If?

Did he just say if?

I am *going to die.*

"This beam is about eight inches thick, and I think ..." He stops as if listening, but the only sound is him talking and the riser making its way up and down.

My entire body shakes as Zane lowers us together.

"Across the beam. You're between me and the other side and crossing over you is probably not a good idea. So, you go first."

Me? He wants me to go first? But I'm supposed to trust you, Zane!

"Come on, Anna. Now or never."

He's said that so many times, I'm wondering if it's become a habit.

Down on the metal, my hands wrap around the edges, and I hold tight, my knees digging into the rough surface. One leg forward. The other. The first again. The second. Repeat, repeat, repeat, I go with next to no light, since Zane can't shine and crawl at the same time—or not very well.

"We're getting close—"

I bump my head. "I think we're there." The fact I've been able to spit out any words surprises me.

"Good. Now there should be rungs. We need to climb them. Not like a ladder, but a diagonal ladder." He shines the light up and over, illuminating the metal surface and the rungs.

A foot apart.

A foot up and down from each other.

Some horizontal.

Some vertical.

He expects me to climb that? I have no strength.

"I'll be right behind you. I promise to hold on to you."

How can he hold on if he's climbing, too?

Now or never? I'm expecting the words from Zane, but he doesn't say them.

Reaching over, I grab the first rung, and using what little light Zane can shine, find footing on one near my left foot. Right hand. Right foot. Left hand. Left foot. Sometimes searching by waving and hoping I'll get hold of something.

"I'm right behind you, Anna. Right here."

My entire body trembles, not from fear—I've numbed myself from that—from pure physical endurance that I don't have.

Rock climbers would be tired from this exercise.

Right hand.

Right foot.

Repeat.

Repeat.

Repeat.

"Just a few more, Anna."

A few more and then what? Freedom? No. Running from more people. And where is my backpack with my new clothes? The only new clothes I've had that were mine in years. No brand new PCD for me. No new clothes and only the sneakers on my feet.

How did I get involved in this?

Oh, yeah.

Mia.

"Up a few more."

I reach again, but my fingers slip. My scream echoes as I grasp for something, anything, and can't get it. The muscles in my right arm tense, but do no good, and my hold slips, fingers losing what little grip I had.

A hand braces my back. "I got you."

Shaking my head does no good because he probably can't see it. I want to scream at him that this idea is stupid, that we never should have left, that he's wrong and so is Mia. Our leaders don't hurt people for having different views. Our country isn't out of money.

Everyone is wrong.

My body swings up again as Zane pushes from behind and I reach.

Leaning my head against the metal, I give myself a minute to breathe and to get some measure of calm back to myself.

"Just a few more," he says again, as if I don't know that. As if I haven't heard him say that a dozen times. When is a dozen a few?

The light shines up and hits what looks like a door, or what looks like the inside of one—a big metal garbage-like door. It's at least 'a few' more rungs up. "That's where we have to go. Grab that handle and pull. It should open with no problems."

"Sure it will," I manage to say out loud.

Zane chuckles. He actually laughs.

With a roll of my eyes, I pull and push myself up the last three rungs, grab the handle and yank.

It releases just like he said.

Oh, thank heavens.

"Up. Go," he says.

With a surge of adrenaline, I grab and reach and haul myself up the last steps and belly-down, flop onto the floor through the door.

My foot hits something hard as I slide inside, and the light goes out.

A clang resonates through the space, and no other sound returns.

Zane doesn't speak.

I can't see him, either. The only illumination at all is on the other end of whatever short hallway I've entered.

He doesn't appear.

No hands.

No body, like mine.

No light.

"Zane?"

Nothing.

Panic and fear makes my entire body tense.

"Zane?" I ask with more desperation. "Zane!" I want to get close to the edge again, but I can't bring myself to go there, to risk falling in when I can't see the lip.

He wouldn't fall.
I would have heard something.
Right?

"Zane?" I whisper.

A thud sounds on the floor next to me. I grab him by the shoulders and pull, getting him all the way in, shutting the little door and sliding back to the wall.

"What happened?"

"You kicked me. Wifyourfoot." A blocked-sinuses sound mixes with his words.

"I'm so, so sorry. I really, really am."

"I'bsurbibe." Translation: I'll survive.

Thank goodness, too, because I don't know where to go in the pitch black.

⚬━━◆━━⚬

Being able to walk on both feet, not have to use my arms to go from point A to point B, and standing up straight are all blessings I will never take for granted again. Zane slid us against the wall to the end of the short hallway, and around a couple bends to a door with a red light over it.

The full effect of my foot to his nose is a hazy, bloody mess. It has stopped bleeding, but his shirt is covered in splotches, and there's a sickly color fading into his upper left cheek. He doesn't seem to care as he takes my hand as we stand in front of the 'Do not Enter' sign.

"We're going in there, aren't we?" I ask.

Even in the midst of the mess, Zane smiles. "This is our way out."

"Of course it is." Nothing would be complete without breaking more rules.

He pushes a few buttons above the handle, and it swings

down, the door opening to the brightness of morning and a
metal staircase on the side of a building about two stories up
from the ground.

The alley this opens into seems empty as we stand on the
single-person platform together. For an early January morning,
the weather isn't too bad. Goosebumps form on my arms, but
I don't see my breath in the air.

"Down these stairs and ... uh ... a while ... and we'll be set."

"A ... *while*? Aren't they going to be waiting for us around
a corner, or something?"

"No. You gotta trust me, Anna. I know where the eyes are
and how to get around them."

He knows, how? Is that even possible? Pulling myself from
going down the rabbit hole of uncertainty, I point to the ladder
where the rungs stop at least halfway up the first level. "*That*
doesn't go all the way down."

"I'll jump first and catch you," he says.

And I'll break your nose instead of just bloodying it. "Okay." I
don't have another choice, do I?

Zane climbs down and jumps, landing with a light thud. I
follow, and at the last rung, drop until I'm hanging. At least
this way, I get even closer before crashing into him and the
hard surface below me.

"Okay, go," he says.

On his command, I release.

My body slips down, hands come around me, and my feet
land with ease on the ground. Zane spins me around, bringing our lips a breath away from each other. His eyes dip low.
Our chests move in tandem, his arms around me, mine stuck
to my side.

"See?" he asks on a hush.

See what?

"I told you I'd get you out of there." He smiles as his arms slip down, hands connecting with mine. A second later, he pulls away and drags me with him.

My mind whirls, the moment of connection gone. "How did you know about all that?" I ask as I refocus. "Why didn't going all the way to the top, or whatever, work? Why'd you stop it? How did you get above me? Why—"

"All good questions, but right now, we gotta jet, because if anyone sees me looking like this, with a tiny girl like you, they're going to get the wrong idea, fast."

He's got a point. People call security for everything, not that they can get to everyone. Last month, something like fifteen people sued our district because security couldn't get to their location fast enough. I had to wonder at the boldness of the criminals, taking advantage of the poor folks who could only stand there and watch, and right in the middle of the day, too. If only our security could have gotten there sooner. Of course the administration had no comment except to say, "We can't always help in the middle of an attack." Can't argue with that, but security is supposed to arrive to help. That's their job. Otherwise, what would be the point of that role?

"How far do we have to go?" I ask as Zane turns me down a road that leads into a bustling part of the inner district—a different part than I could see at Mia's. Buildings reach into the clouds, one after the other after the other.

"A ... while." He rubs at the side of his nose.

I cringe at the purples and blues already streaking his nose. "What does that mean, exactly? And shouldn't we maybe go to a clinic?"

"Can't."

"But—"

He waves me silent. "I lost my bag on our way up. No credits." His voice comes out muffled.

"I'm really sorry about your nose." Every time I catch a glance, my heart does a flip flop.

"S'okay. It'll heal."

We pass one building. Two. Three. Making our way through people walking with us and against. My shoes rub the back of my heel, and I'm sure a blister is working its way into my skin given the warmth and slight zing that keeps pinging my the skin there. "How much farther?" I bump into someone as I try to rub my foot.

Whatever Zane says is unintelligible over the tram, the people and the general noise of the population.

"Huh?" I ask as we continue down the sidewalk. If my feet didn't hurt, and I weren't on the run, I'd have been more interested in my surroundings. Especially since I've never before to the center of our district, or of any, for that matter.

"We've got about ten miles. Ish. Maybe twenty."

I stop. "What?"

He keeps going.

"Zane? Where are we going?" My feet hurt so much I slip my shoes off. Even the thought of walking that far in brand new shoes makes my muscles cramp.

He spins, exposing the rainbow of color creeping across the other side of his nose.

My hands fly up to my face as I cringe.

Zane turns toward the glass building where we stand. "Oh, wow."

I inch up to his side again. "Yeah."

He taps the side of his nose and seethes. "Ouch."

"Yeah," I say again.

The door to the building opens, and a woman walks out. Her head tilts down and up, facing us. "Here." She walks toward Zane and me and holds out her hand. "Please go to a clinic." She drops a credit into his hand. "And get some shoes." That, she directs to me before returning to the door.

"Guess she saw me staring at my face," Zane says. "But, hey … now we have what we need to get where we need to go."

"And where *is* that exactly?"

21

Zane and I exit the tram right at a building that's three or four stories tall with green reflective surfaces glistening under the late morning sun. He types in a bunch of numbers at the building's door lock, and it opens with a quiet swish to a room of pure beauty, with glass walls, wooden floors, soft lighting and loads of colors, plants and chairs.

"This place is amazing. No way this is a clinic ... unless clinics for everyone but flukes and southern territory dwellers are ... gorgeous?"

Zane chuckles. "No, not a clinic. This is headquarters. Or the CFABG club. Depends on who you are as to what you call it." He carries on, no longer holding my hand, to another set of risers just to the left of the lobby where we entered.

I'm not so keen on getting into yet another metal box, but going up stairs isn't going to work either. "Hey ... Zane?"

"Yeah?"

"Where would the garbage riser have ended up? I didn't hear what you said."

"Oh, it just dumps into a big bin that then gets transported twice a day to the incinerator."

A shiver races up my spine. So I wouldn't have died. At least, not right away. Wanting another topic, I ask, "What's CFABG stand for?" The riser comes down to us from the fifth floor.

"Citizens for a better government. Or, again, depending on who you are and what you know ... Comedy for boys and girls."

"You're kidding, right? Those letter combinations aren't even the same."

He shrugs. "They have open-mic nights every Friday and Saturday."

He has to be joking. Has to.

The doors open to the riser, and Zane nudges me inside. "This one isn't going to hurt or get stuck. I promise."

"Never make promises you don't know you can keep."

He cocks his head. "Are you getting philosophical?"

The doors open again into a room similar to Mia's place, only much, *much* bigger and with a scent that is so real, so familiar, yet so distant—the aftershave my dad wore but I haven't smelled in forever. I take a moment to breathe it in. I wish I knew the name. If I asked Mom, she wouldn't have told me. With her, Dad could only be talked about in the past tense. Asking about a scent he wore would be just plain wrong.

Returning from my visual introspection, my gaze lands on a rug in between two divans, in the middle of the room. I could sleep on it. Probably. That's how soft it looks—like cotton in the sky just waiting for me to drop into it.

Zane moves toward the far right side of the room, and I follow, taking in the portraits on the wall, the art and the technology. Panels of screens and monitors cover one wall in front of a deep black desk. To the other side, a painting of a woman stares at me.

I'd swear I recognize it, though I'm sure I haven't ever seen it before.

Zane drops to a chair at a bar in the kitchen, grabs a towel and wets it, before putting it to his face.

"Here, let me." I take it from him. My foot did the job; the least I can do is help him clean up. Wiping the side of his nose shows off the black and blue forming there. "I think I might have broken it."

He smirks as if it's okay.

It's not, but I won't argue.

As I work to get a bit of dried blood from the side, Zane hisses. I cringe as he closes his eyes. "Is there a clinic we can go to? I really think you need—"

He waves at me as if trying to stop me from making the suggestion he knows is right. "It'll be okay."

"Zane—"

Both hands go up as he opens his eyes again. "I'll be fine."

"But a clinic can—"

"No."

Obviously, I'm going to have no luck convincing him. "So ... um ... I need to wash these clothes." I stare down at my shirt—the first new thing I've had in ages. The fabric soaked up the stench of garbage that, while out in the fresh air, didn't have the pungent smell it does now.

"I can get you a new wardrobe."

"No, no. I'm okay if I can just get these clean." A waft of rancid air tickles my nose, and I pop my head up to get my nostrils away from the stench. "If maybe ... there are some sweats, or something, or even a towel, I can clean my stuff and let it air dry."

"You can wash them here, but the woman across the hall keeps extras for people." Zane holds out a hand. "On top of that, I think she'd love to meet you."

"Me?" Wiping my hands down my legs doesn't do a bit of good. "No way am I meeting someone smelling like this." I may be able to live without much credits, but disgusting aromas need to go away.

"Come on, Anna. Lucie's a clothing designer. Well ... she wants to be. Anyway, she's got clothes. That you need."

"Only wants to be?"

"Yeah. Her boss hasn't been promoted, yet."

My brow furrows as I follow Zane back out the front door. "Why does that matter?"

He zips around, his squished up face suggesting I've just proven I know very little about how the jobs work. "You're really not up with what goes on in the real world, are you?" Zane asks as we pass through the plush carpeted hall toward a bend.

And there it is. My cheeks flame. "No, I'm not. I'm just this helpless, stupid girl, who knows nothing."

Zane stops and backs up a step. "That was sucky of me, Anna. I'm really sorry. Look ... Lucie keeps all her designs and prototypes at home until the moment she gets her shot."

"Why doesn't she share her ideas now? Is she not ... good ... enough?" I cringe even as the words slip past my lips. "Wouldn't that help her get ahead?" Backtracking is good; I'm just thankful I didn't make that comment in front of the lady.

Zane takes my right hand between his palms. The gesture makes me shiver; my dad used to do that whenever he wanted to tell me something important. "I forget sometimes, you know? Not everyone has my uncle, your ... your sister, this place, my background. I just ... I want, no ... I'd really like you to understand what's going on and why being a part of it is going to be so great."

He wants me to be a part of it? I'm still not fully sure what 'it' is, except for what Mia said.

Before I can avoid more conversation, Zane says, "You remember Marlena, right?"

"My salon technician lady? Of course." It's been less than a day since she made the shell of me into something else. I don't think anything happened to the inside of me except to jumble me up worse.

He nods. "Let's say she had a new idea for a haircut. If she brings it up right away, someone else will get the recognition, and the annual promotion and increase in salary, presuming it's all approved and funded—which it won't be right now because of the credits crisis, but that's beside the point. She can't have it because it's not her turn." He does a roll of his shoulders.

I stop, disbelief running through me. "That's *her* idea. She should be able to show people she's got talent and skill, and …" The muscles in his jaw tense. "Sorry. I'm getting this all wrong, aren't I?"

"No …" His failure to finish makes me think he's holding back something.

I'm an idiot. Should have just stayed home with Mom and become a hermit.

Zane leans in a little closer. "When you walk out of registration, you'll be a Life Coach at level X or Y, right?"

"I guess." Of course, now I have no idea what will happen.

"Well … if your boss never goes up a level, because his or her boss doesn't and their boss doesn't, you won't either. Ever. You'll be stuck, and what will happen?"

"I don't know." I really don't, either.

"Would you want to stay in that meaningless job?"

"Of course, if I need to pay for groceries and stuff."

"You say that, but if you can't leave, *ever*, until the person above you is promoted, but you can drop down—lower and lower until you're on subsistence living—"

"Who'd want that?"

"Subsistence living makes more money than most Level one workers, and they don't have to give up one bit of what they had before. So let's say you can keep your assigned living space, transpo, PCDs. No downgrading. All the annual benefits, too. Just less credits. Wouldn't you take it?"

"But everyone has to work, Zane. If you don't, you don't get—"

"Nope."

"But—"

"Nope."

"Stop that! Everyone has to work."

"Not if they can prove hardship, which can be just about anything. Like a hangnail."

I shrug. "But that's ... wrong."

Zane's lips curve. "Not everyone thinks like you. If you don't get what you want, but are entitled to everything even if you can't be promoted, why not just give up?"

"Because it's not right," I say with more insistence.

"It's human nature," he says with a shrug.

"But it's wrong!"

"Good breeds good. Bad breeds bad."

"Zane, quit! It's just plain wrong."

"It's the domino effect."

"The what?" I shake my head. His changing the subject in the middle of a non-argument seems weird.

"Dominos. The game?"

"No idea what you're talking about."

"It's an old game where you take these white marble pieces with up to six little black pock marks on each. They're the numbers one through—okay, never mind. The other thing they can do is a lot more fun than the game. So ..." He holds out his hands, index fingers and thumbs together as if he's holding something. "You line them all up, one by one in a row ..." His hands move as if he's doing just that, lining up invisible something-or-others. "... and then go back to the start and push the first down. That leads to the second falling. Then the third. Then the fourth and on and on until all have fallen. *That* is the domino effect."

"A little hard to picture but sounds cool."

"I'll have to show you sometime. Just don't forget what I just told you." He turns us and drags me the rest of the way through the hallway to another door and knocks.

Footsteps follow until the door opens a crack, and a woman, Marlena's clone, if someone asked me, stands in the frame. "Zane! What a pleasant surprise!" The twang of her accent matches Marlena's, too. "'Cept, what happened to your nose?" She reaches out, but her eyes dart in my direction. "Well, my, my."

I break my gaze from hers and glance at Zane.

"You look like a younger version of Miss Mia herself. Different coloring. Bit of facial structure difference. And teeny tiny. But I see it."

"You know my sister?" *Isn't that obvious?*

"Why of course, I do. Know your daddy, too."

My chest constricts as if someone's thrown a ten-pound lead ball right at it. This is person number three who's said they know my dad. Know, not knew. I want to believe them all, but at the same time, I really, *really* don't.

"So, Lucie," Zane starts, "we need some clothes that don't smell. Got any extras?"

"Oh, baby, yeah. Ya'll come on, now."

I follow, keeping my hand tucked against Zane's curled fingers, my world shattering every step of the way.

⚬══✦══⚬

Color. There are more colors—reds, blues, purples, pinks,

shimmers, sheens, softness—all over Lucie's place. I've never seen so much mixed color. Walls. Chairs. Floors. Fabrics hanging from every available high spot. It's like a manic, psychedelic rainbow painted by a two year old.

"Ya'll like our place?" Lucie asks as we follow her farther inside.

"It's ..." I start.

"Eclectic," Lucie says with a light giggle.

We continue on through, ducking past and pushing material to the side as if wading through waterfalls.

"Sorry 'bout the mess. I got inspired 'bout a week ago and went on a spending spree. Haven't got through all my projects, yet, though." She takes us into a room, still a variety show in the making, but organized by color, on rows and rows of hangers. "You're what? A two?" She moves to the section with mostly reds.

"Um ... or ... smaller," I say.

Lucie pulls out a shirt and puts it back. Another, and back. A third, and back. The fourth is a gorgeous raspberry—essentially the color of the one Cam tried to steal, but prettier—with a shimmer to the fabric. Holding it out to me, she says, "Oh yeah, this one. It's your color."

"It's beautiful, but—"

"Oh, honey, don't say you won't take it. You smell like a garbage dump, and I'm not sure any sort of cleaner will get that out, so ya'll are gonna need to ditch what you got and go with new." She shifts to the right, slides a bundle from a shelf and hands that to me. "And you ..." She points to Zane. "... I know what you need." She moves to the blues and lifts a shirt from it. The color is somewhere between a deep blue and a sky blue with a hint of purple. Or is that green? It's like it changes depending on how the light hits it. "All right, then, ya'll go change. Come into the kitchen when you're done. I'll make us some lunch. Oh, and just drop that stuff in the garbage. I don't know why they insist on dressing you in such drab, plain colors. We're humans, you know, not lab rats."

Zane takes his stuff and walks to the door. "I'll just go change in the bathroom, and you can change in here. Will that work?"

I nod and stand there, holding the new clothes—items that are ten times as beautiful as the brand new stuff I received just the day before. As he leaves, I drop the bundle to a round, bright pink chair and hold up the shirt. Awesome doesn't even begin to describe it. I've just never had anything with so much life to it.

Getting out of my other stuff takes me all of ten seconds, including stripping my underwear and finding more in the bundle—in a color that matches the shirt. "How did she know?" Asking myself seems pointless, but the soft material slides on with such comfort and ease I just want to hug myself inside it.

Once dressed, I slip on my shoes and make my way out, following the sounds of voices to a kitchen. Zane sits with Lucie at a small, round, neon blue table. He, wearing dark blue jeans, black shoes and that gorgeous colored shirt, his blue eyes sparkling like a cloudless sky.

He points me to the third seat, where a plate with a sandwich and a glass of water wait.

One bite in, and Lucie says, "So ... will you be travelling with us to the U.S. next week, Anna?"

I face Zane.

"I haven't told her about the field trip," Zane says.

"Oops." Lucie sips from a frothy pink drink. "Marlena and I are both ready."

"Marlena?" I ask.

"She's my twin sister," Lucie says, confirming what I already suspected from her looks. "She's gotta finish up registration, and then we're in."

"Are you ... coming back?" I ask.

She shrugs. "Depends. We both got dreams and neither of us will be able to make them happen here. Been trying for a visa for over two years. Took your daddy's help for us both to get one. Them idiots in district one kept mixing us up and sending us one with my name and her identification, or the reverse."

My dad.

My *dad* helped her.

The more his name pops up, the more my entire body goes on alert, quivering like a bow pulled taught and ready to shoot.

"Of course, legally, we'll have to come back, and if we do, well, then we'll stay a part of Delta Street."

"Delta Street?" I manage, forcing another bite of food down my throat. "How can you be a part of a street?"

"That's the organization your daddy leads." Her eyebrows lower. "It's where we are right now. On Delta street."

"She didn't even know her dad was alive until yesterday," Zane says.

Lucie's hands go to her lips. "Oh, my word! Why didn't ya'll tell me?" Her hands land on mine. "How insensitive of me. You'll forgive me?"

I nod once, mouth still full, trying my best to keep living and not choke on the repeated news that my dad is the leader of some organization, and left me and Mom to fend for ourselves.

"Well, ya'll ... I gotta get back to my dealin's for the day. The work of a designer's assistant's assistant ain't gonna finish it itself. Stay as long as you want, and keep them clothes. You're totally rockin' that shade." She rises and starts walking away but turns back. "Miss Anna?"

I tilt up toward her.

"My daddy left when Marlena and I were just six months old. Mama, rest her soul, did everything right by us and instilled one thing we could never repay her with: creativity and independence. If it weren't for her, we'd probably be level zeros. But we aren't, and we both got good ideas. We just want a shot at reaching them. No way can we do that here. That's what a good mama does. She leaves us with a way to be better than everyone else." With a little salute, Lucie disappears from the kitchen.

"Hello?" a male voice calls from somewhere in the distance. "Lucie?"

Zane stiffens.

I, too, tense up. If Zane's worried, I probably should be, too.

A man walks into the kitchen area and stops.

A touch of gray colors his temples in otherwise black hair, but it's the eyes that I've seen before. Eyes that are a match for those of my sister.

22

Embarrassment washes over me. How could I think the man before me might be my dad? No matter what Zane, Mia or Lucie said about him actually being alive, he's not. He can't be.

My inner conscious doesn't believe me, though, and I want to ask *the* question, right now.

What if I'm wrong? What if they're wrong?

"Well ..." the Dad-look-a-like says. "I didn't know Lucie had company."

"We were just leaving, Sir." Zane drops the napkin he'd been using.

The man zips over to Zane, takes his chin in his hand and tilts his head left and right. "What the hell happened to you?"

I stare at the man. He looks so much like the memory I have of my dad, with long, deep cheek bones, a part on the left side of his head and Mia's green eyes. Broad shoulders could easily have carried me on them, in the park, to the swings. I'd even have sworn he is my dad, with a hand on the word of truth—if someone asked.

But my dad is dead.

"NARCA claims someone was spying," Zane says. "So Mia gave me the run signal, and I dragged Anna with me here."

Listening to Zane, I continue to eye the man, whose jaw flexes, but I don't see a release.

"Where's Mia, now?" the man asks.

Maybe Mia was right.

No, she can't be. This is just someone that looks like what I think my dad should look like.

"I don't know, Sir," Zane says. "She just told me not to go to her house, and after we almost got caught, too, I followed procedure number ten."

Old-guy waves his hand. "Did you take precautions to ensure no one followed?" A gold band surrounds his left ring finger. My dad, if married, would be at home with my mom. *No way this is him, then.* My brain is just making me think this is him, since everyone keeps talking about him in the present tense.

"Yes, Sir."

He keeps saying sir. So this is someone important. If my dad was important, he'd have Mom and me with him.

"We followed the circuitous route, as instructed, ensuring at each stop that no one remained in close proximity." Zane sounds all military and formal.

I'd have just said we took the long way around town to get here—which we did with over two hours of tram stops all throughout the inner district.

"Can you corroborate his story?" The man turns to me, eyes sparkling. So much like Mia's, but it just can't be true.

If he did leave, why didn't Mom tell me the truth? Why all the lies? Why didn't he support me with some credits? Why did I live in a shack in the dumpiest part of town instead of with him? Maybe he's poor. Maybe he doesn't have any money, either, and three poor people together is worse than two of us.

"Wind—"

"Anna ... Sir," Zane says. "She doesn't like be called anything but that, Sir."

Was he about to all me Windy?

Dad's doppelganger steps in closer, but I back away; it happens without my control.

"No," I say.

"No, what?" Zane asks.

Can't believe I said that out loud.

"I believe she's directing that to me ..." the man says. "But I believe this conversation might be best suited to my place."

His place?

He turns back the way he came in. "I'll meet you down the hall, momentarily."

Down the hall?

He stops, and without turning back, says, "Zane."

"Yes, Sir?"

"Go see Egan upstairs for some meds before that gets infected."

"Yes, Sir, Mister Keating." His footsteps fade off into the distance.

So, he is my dad.

An instantaneous sob explodes in my head, but I bite my lip hard to stop the tears that want to flow, the headache that wants to brew, and the madness that makes me want to scream.

"Come on, Anna," Zane says in a soft voice.

I don't move.

"Come with me."

I can't move.

Zane's touch to my shoulder makes me jump. "Come on, Anna." He nudges me a little, sliding his hand down my arm and taking my hand.

With a little tug from him, I stand and follow, but whatever I thought I knew about my life, myself has vanished.

Fifteen minutes after a visit upstairs to the medic, where Zane received treatment for his nose, we stand in front of a door. I point to the flat black barrier with the number one on it. When Zane said headquarters, I assumed some group owned the place. Certainly not that my dad would. That has to mean he gets a lot of credits. Has to. If that's the case, why didn't he take care of me? Of Mom? Of us? Why did he leave us to rot?

Zane's hand rests on the knob. "You okay?"

The headshake comes out involuntarily. I didn't mean to share, and I don't want his pity. No one needs to know how lost I am.

"Come on, Anna," he says again, with such softness that I want to melt against him, let him hold me like he did last night and cry into his shoulder.

I can see why his sisters used him so much as their teddy bear, if after one experience, I want another. Zane takes my arm, opens the door and guides me inside.

We continue on through the living area and to the kitchen, just like we did before.

Dad stands from his seat at the counter as we enter.

I walk toward the windows—long floor to ceiling glass surrounding the kitchen table—and cross my arms over my chest. With my back to Zane and 'Dad', I ask, "Mom works her tail off, trying to put food on the table, and you live ... you ... you live in this?" The place alone is three times the size of Mom's place.

I drop to a chair, keeping my focus on the buildings beyond the glass pane and horizon below, and try to think of all the people who have life worse than me, not about the man who didn't give a priority to his own family. I can't shut him off, though, and I don't want to see him or what he has. "She doesn't ever get a break. We've never gone on vacation. I've barely had clothes, and you're wearing the latest Armani. How is your family not a priority? Answer that for me. Just that question. How are we—why am I so unimportant?"

"You aren't—"

I yank at my hair on both sides and lean my forehead against the cool glass.

A shuffle sounds close to me; I jerk up and spin, bumping my butt into the window. Of course my choice of location has left me completely cornered, and he's decided to get close all of a sudden. Zane's not even in the room anymore for me to pull some support.

Dad sits in my chair, tilts up and meets my gaze. "Wind—"

"Anna," I say with firm insistence.

He closes his lids for a moment and reopens. "Anna. You were always my priority, as was Mia and your mother."

I want to remind him that I haven't seen him since he supposedly died, so he's obviously wrong.

"I never would have left you, if I hadn't been asked by the one person who mattered most to me."

"Who?" I don't mean to ask, but I want to know.

"Your mother."

"Mom would never make you leave. She wouldn't ever have asked you to." I know he's lying about Mom. She loved him. She'd even still wear her diamond ring, if she hadn't had to pawn it to buy food one month when everyone she tutored paid with dummies.

He angles his head down, shaking it a little. When he returns to me, red lines etch the whites of his eyes, and wrinkles and sags crease his face. Outside of that, he's expressionless. A blank face of nothingness. "I'm sorry, but I wasn't expecting this, and

I worked all night, so I'm fully and completely exhausted." He lets go of my hand and stands. "I can't have this conversation until I have a clear head."

I'll bet his head is pounding. *Traitorous sperm donor.* Especially with having to lie so much about what he did.

Whirling back to the window, I stare out, but without focussing anywhere as tears breech my lids and spill over. Everything in my life is falling apart, and I don't understand why.

"Anna—" he starts.

"Leave me alone. Please." There's nothing more to say.

Footsteps fade off into the distance.

At least he did what I asked.

Rather than look and see that I'm alone, I turn and inch my way to the living room—the one with the big rug and the blankets on the divans. The need to just cry and cry overwhelms me, and I curl up on the edge of the leather, tucking my knees against my chest and my arms around them.

I've never cared about being alone before, but the weight of all the revelations presses far too hard on me, and I wish Mom would just show up and tell me someone mixed up their life with mine, and she'll make everything okay if I just come home with her.

"Push me higher, Daddy! I want to go higher." The younger me, the one I'm pretending to be, in my four year old body, hair cut short to my head and looking more boy than girl, makes my heart hurt. "Higher! Higher!" Up and up and up I go until the swing is nearly even with the top of the set.

No, don't go higher, I try to tell myself. *You need to be safe, with Mom.*

"Higher! Higher!"

Up. Up. Up. I go.

"No! No! No! Not higher. You're going to fall! I'm going to fall!" My little self keeps asking for more and goes up and up.

The swing arcs.

It's going to go all the way around.

I'm going to fall out, and no one will catch me because no one is pushing me. I see that now. My dad's not there. Neither is Mom. No one is pushing me, yet the swing keeps going.

"Higher, higher, higher, Daddy!"

Why isn't he back? Why isn't he stopping this? Why doesn't he tell me how stupid I am for asking him to push me until I swing all the way around or fall off?

"Higher, higher!" My little self screams with glee.

Why doesn't he jump in and tell me that gravity is going to pull me down, that the swing won't go all the way over, that it can't, that as soon as I get to the top, the chains will buckle, and I'll fall, hit my head on the pole, collapse on the ground and die? Why doesn't he?

"Anna."

I look around for the source of my name, but no one is there, as my feet reach toward the sky and my head faces down.

My heart tumbles. My stomach lurches.

"*No!* Don't let her go! Don't! Don't let me go!"

No one is there. No one is speaking to me.

As my little hands grab and hold on to the ropes, the older me tries to stop with my feet digging into the ground. The little me gets mad at the older me, yanking my hands away, pushing me away.

Away.

Away.

Away.

"No, let me help you!"

"*Anna.*"

I reach out, wanting to take me in my arms, but I can't hold on and grab for myself, or I know I'll fall off. Somehow, I haven't swung back, I'm just hanging there as if I'm waiting to go all the way around, upside down, waiting, waiting to be pushed over or pulled back to safety.

To the ground. Get to the ground.

One little arm stretches out. My big arm reaches for the ground, but in doing so, I've let go and my entire body tumbles in a freefall toward earth.

"*No!*"

I move in slow motion. Going through clouds and blue sky, reaching the tops of the buildings, seeing my house and the ground coming at me. Flipping around, I try to climb back up, to grab the swing's ropes that are hanging on both sides of me.

Still, I plummet.

Toward the ground. Reaching. Grasping.

I won't be able to catch myself. There's no chance, even though I try, stretching as far as possible, as my own body spirals downward.

Tumbling into nothing—an abyss of darkness.

"Daddy, help!"

"Anna, I got you."

⊙━━◆━━⊙

I blink as comforting arms wrap around me. Not my dad's. His smell may have been there when we came in, but he's not filling me with the same. It's Zane behind me, holding me up in a mostly-seated position. On the floor. On the soft rug I wanted to wrap around myself.

How did I get down here?

Scrambling out of his arms, I turn and face him, sitting so

my back is against the other divan. "Wha—"

"You were dreaming."

Oh, gracious. I was.

"And talking in your sleep."

Embarrassment heats my cheeks.

"And then you fell off."

My eyes go wide. "I fell off the … the divan?" When had I fallen asleep? I must have, obviously, or I wouldn't have dreamed about the swing and fallen while swinging on the ground in the clouds. Shaking my head, I stare into nothing. Dreams are so real to me yet so impossible.

"Yeah. And you were saying not to go higher, or something, and then just rolled backward."

Heaving air leaves my chest. "Uh … thank you for … you know … catching me." *Note to self, never fall asleep in an unfamiliar room.*

"No problem. I'm sorry if the garbage riser scared you enough to give you nightmares. I didn't think about that; I just knew it would be a way out without being seen through every corridor and passage. I'm—"

"No." I shake my head. "I wasn't dreaming about that. I was swinging." I wave a hand at him. "You don't want to hear this."

"Probably not. I am a guy, and all." A smirk lights up his face.

The grin does me in. "You really want to hear it?" I make my way back up onto the divan, tucking my hands between my knees.

Zane withdraws two bottles from a small cold storage unit—one clear liquid, the other a bright red. "Water? Or Poke? He holds both out to me."

Water in a small container—not something I buy. Without credits, it's what Mom and I drink, but we take it straight from the tap.

The fizz of his drink sizzles as he opens it. "You sure you don't want one?" He takes a glass from a shelf above the unit and fills it from the bottle.

Shaking my head, I accept the offered drink. "You seem really ... comfortable around here."

Zane drops his drink to the small table, his gaze dipping, too. He lifts up and asks, "Can I just say something?"

Uh-oh. "Yeah, sure."

"Your da—Mr. Keating ... he's ... well, he's incredibly respected. I mean, everyone loves him. I don't know what happened when you were a little kid, but ... he's a really good guy."

My inner irked-o-meter begins its rise toward the hot zone.

"But at the same time, I want to say I'm sorry, too." Zane plays with his container, spinning it between his hands as he talks.

All my pent-up frustration washes away with his apology, yet he's not even the one that owes it. *He* hasn't done anything wrong.

"Why would someone who's a 'really good guy' leave his wife and two daughters for a new life? I was only four years old." I know Zane doesn't have the answer, but that's the question that plagues me as I press my shoeless toes into the super-soft rug beneath them, leaving an imprint.

"I don't know, Anna. I wasn't much older than you were when it all happened. So ... what you must see and feel is very different than what I see and feel. I know a warrior with a heart of gold. He doesn't slay a dragon, or fight with one of those old guns like in those old movies from two-thousand-twenty; he does it with words. One person at a time. One mind at a time. It takes credits, courage, discipline and ... perseverance. He tells us all the time—"

"All the time?" I get four years and he gets what? "How often have you—I mean, how much time have you spent with ... *him?*"

Zane shrugs.

I beat my fist on the table between the two divans. "How often, Zane?"

"A few times ..." His answer comes out soft and hesitant.

"That's a lie. A big fat lie. I can't believe, with everything we've been through, with the apology even, that you'd lie to me now. I've followed you. I was told to trust you, and I did. I let you stuff me into a garbage riser and trusted that you'd get me out. And you're going to tell me you've see that man *a few* times?" My fists clench as I heave air.

"Okay, weekly. A few times a month, maybe more, but that's only because I want to be a part of his organization."

"What organization?" I'm more adamant about that question.

His cheeks pink up. "Delta Street."

"Why, Zane? Why is he so important?"

With a big sigh, he says, "Because, Anna, your dad's leading the movement to overthrow the government."

23

"My dad's leading the organization that's planning to over-throw Osso?" I can't believe I just repeated the words Zane said, and I can't believe they're true, either. No one has successfully overthrown a government in hundreds of years. There have been splits of countries, but not takeovers of existing ones.

"Yes. With my uncle."

His uncle? Pain sears my heart. My own father planning treason should hurt worse than my greater realization. "So *your* uncle brings you to *my* dad, and you get to play in his life." I say it with a fury that keeps bubbling and fading but has now boiled over. "*You* got to spend time with *my* dad? *You?*" How could he do this to me? How could he leave me and Mom? "You got to spend time with my dad as you grew up, didn't you?"

Zane glances off to the side.

"Didn't you? Didn't you? Didn't you?" Each repetition gets louder and more forceful. "I didn't have a dad to grow up with, to look up to, to want to be like! I spent my whole life thinking he died! And you can sit here . . . and . . . how would you like it if you lost—" I freeze. My insensitivity hits me. "I can't believe I went there. That's not—I'm not—this isn't like me." I drop to the divan and lean forward putting my head to my knees. "I'm sorry." I have no idea if he hears me, since I mumble the words into the fabric of my jeans.

That pang strikes my heart again. *Don't do this, Eri. Geez, and you can't even call yourself by your new name. Maybe you should go back to normal. Go home and be a good girl and don't make waves, pretend your sister doesn't exist and your dad doesn't either.*

Zane sits next to me. "Did you know, in seventeen-seventy-six, when the U.S.A. started, they were trying to get away from government greed and dictatorships and laws and rules brought on by kings and queens with little or no consideration for their people?" Before I can answer, he says, "And that meant the creation of a whole new county in the new world."

He's glossed over my huge faux pas. My need to apologize builds until my hands tingle and my head pounds. "Zane."

"Someone has to lead that movement again because we've lost—"

"Zane."

"What?" The frustration is clear in his tone.

"I'm really sorry."

"For what?"

"For what I said. Forgetting about your parents. It was incredibly insensitive of me. It's not an excuse, but the feeling you had when you learned your parents died ... the ... pain?" I fist my hand against my heart, where it hurts like it did when Mia stormed out of our house and never came back. "I don't know how much more I can take."

Something weighty hits my shoulder. I reach and tilt up at the same time. Dad stands behind me with a stack of bound pages that are blurry from being too close, but are definitely paper. "What is this?" I ask.

"This," Dad says, "is why I haven't been in your life for fourteen years." He leaves them resting there. "And I think you should read them."

After a few seconds, I take the packet and slide it to my lap.

Paper envelopes of varying sizes, and at least ten inches thick, fill my hands. No one's used paper in fifty years or more, since the trees became a protected plant, and people decided recycling took too much effort. Since then, all letters, documents—any correspondence—has been done electronically.

"You don't have to read them now … or you can go curl up by a fire and read until your eyes close. Either way. Just know that there's a long story, and a short story, and many, many stories in between. If you want me to tell you, I will, but I only did what I was asked."

Dad moves around and sits on the divan across from me, his expression once again flat and unreadable. He's dressed in a T-shirt and jeans, comfortable, yet still fancier than anything I've ever owned—or had before all this began.

Zane spins toward Dad. "What's wrong, Sir?"

There's something wrong? How could he even tell?

"Mia's unaccounted for."

My intake of air is audible.

"What happened?" Zane asks.

Dad holds his PCD in his left hand, his right stuck to his hip. "She didn't check in at her post four hours ago, and again two hours ago, and not in the last ten minutes. I have a scout looking into it."

"Did she run?" Zane asks. "I know when they were after us in the facility they could see everything—until I dragged us to the garbage riser. Maybe she didn't get out?" He switches back to me, his eyes serious before returning to Dad. "She told me to go. She gave me the signal. She wouldn't have stayed, but I didn't think to check."

"Maybe she doesn't want to be a part of whatever you're doing." My words come out mumbled.

Dad shakes his PCD in my direction. "Your sister is stubborn and loyal. If she's not calling in, there's a reason. And it's not because she doesn't want to help us. She won her place in our group. She wouldn't give it up."

I totally get the stubborn comment. The fights she and Mom had over entering registration showed that. What I want to know can only be answered by Mia, though. Is she hurt? Is she okay? Is she stuck? Does she need us? What?

His device buzzes, and Dad taps his ear. "Eric Keating." He turns and walks toward the kitchen but stops with his hand to lobe. "When?" He goes silent again. "I'll be right there."

"Mia?" I ask, hope and worry competing for my tone.

Dad faces Zane as he says, "No."

Rude.

They seem to stare at each other forever. "Timeline's moved up. China's Economic Ambassador has just arrived on North American soil to meet with Osso."

"Which means, you gotta go meet with him. How long, Sir?" Zane asks.

Dad shakes his head. "Few days. Maybe a week. Two at most. You two stay here. Don't leave this building unless you hear from me. Understood?"

I nod as Zane says, "Yes, Sir."

"Good. Take care of my girl, Zane."

I want to say 'I'm not your girl' and 'I can take care of myself', but who am I kidding? When Dad disappears, Zane faces me again.

"Why does it seem like my dad doesn't really want anything to do with me?" I ask him.

His brow scrunches. "You get that from what?"

"He didn't want to talk to me. He handed me stuff to read.

He didn't explain anything. And it seems like he's doing life as usual when I'm sitting right here. A *daughter* he hasn't seen in years."

"I don't think he was uninterested. He's just really reserved and very good at controlling his emotions. Has to be."

"To meet with a guy from China? Don't you all know who is who and what you're doing and ...""

Zane's head cocks to the side.

"What?" I ask.

"Your dad's the A.U.'s Economic Ambassador."

"So?" My eyes wobble in my head as that information sinks in. *Wait ... he's what?*

"The Economic Ambassador for the A.U," Zane says again in the same flat tone, as if I'd asked out loud.

How do I not know this? Does Mom know? Working to get my mouth functioning again, I say, "Uh ... I thought he was the leader of the Delta Street thing."

"He is," Zane says.

"So, my dad's one of those powerful, secret-agent-double-agent kind of things and has to be blank-faced so people don't know which side he's on?"

"Yes. But it's even more important for him because he's *the* inside man."

With my dad gone, and Zane and I alone, I'm not sure what to do. I don't understand what's going on around me. I don't know why I should listen to the man who didn't care enough to be my dad. Mia said she planned to overthrow our leaders, but I never imagined my dad would be involved, too. How is he also in power? Why didn't I know these details about him? Sure, I don't know every member of the ruling party or our house of representatives, but wouldn't I know if my own dad had a role in it? Our last names, of all things, are the same. Wouldn't that be a clue?

Then again, I thought he died, and he didn't. How did I not know *that*?

"Why are you doing this to me, Zane?"

"What do you mean?"

What do *I mean?* "Why do you want to take over the country? I know you *said* we're out of money, but we have people to fix that. Why not just share whatever information you have and get them to correct it?"

Zane chuckles. "Because people in power don't want change, they want more power and more financial support to keep people down. You saw that with Lucie."

"But that's just one person." Two, if Marlena can't do her tattoo business.

Zane's head tilts left. "You really think this is about one person?"

"Okay, two." If I count Marlena.

He turns toward me and leans forward. "What did you want to be when you grew up, Anna?"

I look away. When I try to bring my gaze back to meet his, I can't. The only word that comes to mind is 'nothing'.

"What'd you say?" he asks.

Had I spoken?

"Did you know that no matter what it was … ballerina to mad scientist, you can't have it unless the main computing system that does all the analysis of your information decides your personality suits the profession. Your health profile and psychological eval give you your level. And that's it. People are *only* a part of the process to get you from one room to the other during registration. If even just one person was involved,

Lucie and Marlena might have a shot at the future they wanted and not what some intelligent piece of metal and code bytes picked for them."

Thinking on it for a moment, I say, "But doesn't that give everyone equality?"

"*That's* why we need someone else to pick our careers for us?"

I'm getting the impression I'm answering all wrong. "But ... um ..."

"How about you? Did *you* have enough credits growing up?"

I have no problem meeting his gaze. "That's different. My mom's a fluke."

"What if she wasn't?"

"She'd be a teacher ... or something, I guess."

"Okay, but a teacher doesn't make as much as say ... an attorney or an engineer, do they?"

"Well, of course not. The job isn't as hard or require as much training."

Zane's eyebrows go up. "So, if you're smarter you should get more? And if your job is easier, you shouldn't? And have you seen how much time teacher's put in that they don't get paid for? You. Me. Marlena. Lucie. All of us, not just one person, are put into a role based on profile data and a week of testing. I like cooking, but it's not what I want to do for a living."

I nod and bobble my head around. "Why is this bad, though, Zane? To me it sounds like it keeps everything organized. Less chaotic."

He closes his eyes and says, "We hold these truths to be self-evident ..."

Those are not words he made up. No way.

"... that all men are created equal, that they are endowed by their Creator with certain unalienable Rights, that among these are Life, Liberty and the pursuit of Happiness." Eyes open again, our gazes connect.

Nope. He definitely didn't make that up. I want to roll my eyes, but hold back. "Every time I make you mad or you have something to say, you start spouting off stuff like that. Why?"

"Because it's history, and we can learn from history." He says it with such passion I want to believe like him, but I don't get why it's something ancient that he keeps referring to. Why not something relevant to today? Before I can get up the courage to ask or the willpower not to, Zane says, "That's the Preamble to the *original* Declaration of Independence. What our leaders have done is take that all away. Don't want to be a life coach? Good luck changing. Don't care as long as you get a pay check? Then it doesn't matter. Two completely different philosophies. But ... if the powers-that-be let any of us change, jump levels or break in line, they'd have to let everyone do that, so instead ... they let nobody."

"Aren't *most* people happy, though?" Maybe not Mom and me, but we're the exception. "Marlena and Lucie might be held back a little, but I still don't get *why* that's wrong." Nope, no willpower.

Zane shakes his head. "Of all the people you know, are any of them actually happy?"

Hadley seemed to be when she got her assignment. Brie maybe not. Don't know about Vica. Me? Undecided. Zane? No. Mom? No way. Mia? I'd have to get to know her more to decide. So maybe he's right, but that's just a few people. Not a whole society.

"There's so much you don't know, Anna."

He doesn't have to tell me that twice. "Then, how do you know?" I realize, too late, I've asked him in a near yell. "How ..." I soften. "... do you know all this stuff, about all these issues, the money, registration, the sterilization ... if no one else ... knows this?" Even to me, my question sounds like it's being asked in a circle.

He takes my hand. "I can tell you, but it won't sink in like if I show you."

"So do. Prove something to me."

"Oh, ye of little faith." He chuckles.

The growl really does come out. Loud.

Zane holds up a finger. He stands and disappears, his footsteps somewhere on the opposite side of the room, softening and returning. Sitting next to me, he holds out a piece of paper.

"What's this?"

"Open it."

Unfolding the top and bottom, I find a list of stuff. Gowns. Syringes. Bulbs. Medical supplies it seems. Every one of them is struck through as if crossed off. At the top, it says, 'Monthly Acceptable Product Guideline for December 2131'. "What is this?"

"It's Dr. Richmond's cut list. He's the medic who fixed my nose. It's what he got last month to show him what he would not get this month."

"But, don't doctors need this stuff?"

Zane's lips curve up, though I don't think it's because he's happy. "When a business isn't making enough credits, it cuts costs. Think of our leaders as the owner of one giant business. Osso, though, the head honcho, he isn't hurting for credits, yet, but will be if he doesn't slash and burn. That, right there, is proof stuff is getting cut. Next up?"

I bite the side of my lip. We all know Osso and his family are wealthy, but I'm not here to run their lives.

Zane sighs.

I haven't even said anything.

Have I?

It's obvious he's passionate about our country being messed up, and Mom always says, 'When someone is set in their ways, there's no point trying to convince them otherwise, unless it's going to directly impact you', but as I rub my shoulder, where Marlena placed my temporary-permanent tattoo of a butterfly, I can't help but think about what he's said. "So ..." I start, "if letting people do whatever they want is right, why did it stop?"

Zane's lips curve high. "Two big reasons. During the nine-teen-thirties ..."

Here we go again with the history lesson. "That's like two hundred years ago, Zane."

He wags a finger in my direction. "The economy crashed and the government stepped in to help with something called welfare. It was a really good idea, but it was never supposed to be permanent. But, once people started getting money without the need to work as hard as they may once have, they stayed on it. And our leaders, wanting to keep everyone happy, began taxing the rich more and more until, one day, the rich weren't rich. Only those in power stayed rich and everyone else was ... not. *Just* ... like today."

"It's not right for people to make gobs of money when oth-ers don't even have enough food to feed their family, Zane. That's common sense."

"That attitude right there is why we have no money left in this country. Businesses aren't here to give jobs. Businesses are in business to make money."

"I don't understand." About our country. About my dad. About my mom. None of it.

Zane's finger keeps moving in my direction. "Think about someone who has everything ..."

Oh, shoot, I didn't realize I'd said that out loud.

"Don't they always want more?"

I think of Cam. She does, so I nod.

"What would they do if it was taken away?"

Pitch the biggest fit in the world. "They'd get really mad, 'cause that's … not … fair." My eyes go wide as the concept hits me.

Zane takes me by the shoulders. "Is it fair to have a society that lives off what someone else gives them? Especially when we have to take from the poor to give to the poor*er?*"

Everyone's going to throw massive-sized hissy fits. Cam. Jen. RK. Everyone with nothing? This can't be good. "Our leaders … why can't we—"

"They're protected. They've made laws that say they will always be paid, no matter what. And can't lose their jobs. Like the no term limits law passed in two-thousand-fourteen. They take care of themselves. They keep voting themselves in."

"But that's not fai—"

Zane smiles. "What were you going to say?"

That's not fair. That's not fair. "This sucks."

Zane claps his hands. "Exactly! You get it, Anna!"

"All because someone thought it was a good idea to help people in need?" It's come out a question, but it's really un-derstanding.

"Yes." Zane brings his drink to his lips. "Welfare led to so-cialism. Or, as our leaders call it, social capitalism, though it's a total misnomer. It's what your dad, my uncle, Mia, me and countless others are trying to fix."

"Fix it by taking over."

"Yes," he says. "*This* year, Anna."

"And they'll help for real? Not just help the people with the most money?" I don't think Zane could smile any bigger than he already is.

"Yes."

"And *my dad's* leading this group?" That's the most surprising of all of this.

Zane nods.

I kinda get what Delta Street is trying to do. The logic seems right. I think. Maybe. What I still don't understand is why my mom, who wants nothing to do with Osso or his leadership, wouldn't want to be right at Dad's side. Right there with him. This seems like the perfect group to be a part of. Perfect-perfect. Beyond perfect. Like a fluke's dream come true—if it is true. "I need to go see my mom."

"You can't, Anna. I told you before, she has to believe we're still in registration, and communication through a PCD is going to give away our location. That could jeopardize whatever's going on with Mia, your dad's role with the Chinese Ambassador. It's the domino effect. Not that all that would happen, but it could, and risking it isn't something we should do." Once again, Zane sounds all formal, as if he's reciting his instructions from a book.

Chewing on my lip, I consider my options. I have to talk to my mom, and if a PCD isn't going to work, I'll get to her the old fashioned way.

24

After an entire afternoon of talking—no, listening—to Zane, Dad still hasn't called to give us any instruction. As day turned to night, I feigned being tired and went into Dad's room, pulled his blankets up to my nose and breathed in his scent.

So many memories linger, but the stress of knowing my best friend might be in some foreign land for the rest of her life, that my sister is missing, and my dad could be taking over my country at any moment keeps me wide awake.

So much information. So many issues.

I inhale, bringing my dad into mind.

My dad.

My *dad.*

He's here, yet he's not.

That's good since I'll need to sneak out without him—without Zane, too. Of course, I've never had to get out of anywhere unnoticed before, but I figure since we had to run and go around in circles for hours that, at the very least, I should wait until it's more than just dark, but also when most people are asleep, Zane included.

To while away the time, I've brought the letters Dad gave me.

Paper has such a weird texture, especially older stuff that's been through the old postal service. It's a little brittle, bent and edgy. Tossing them from one hand to the other, they're heavier, as a bunch, than my PCD.

Slipping the first from the rubber band, I flip it over. It's light, not much more than a bird's feather. A letter, I'm guessing. I've seen them in history books but never actually received one. No one has in years and years. Before me, even. *How did he send these?*

My mom's name, Annabelle Keating, along with an address from a district to our west, is scrawled on the front. On the other side, the flap is sealed.

The second is similar—her name but a different address.

Envelope three is more of the same.

Four has our current address.

Five. Six. Ten. Twenty. More. All for my mom.

The last one has Mia's name on it, and the other side of it is open. I dig out the interior page; it lays even softer against my palm, folded in three, and I open the first and find Mia's name at the top in a neat handwriting.

Unfolding the bottom half, I find the entire page is full.

Darling Mia—

As you turn thirteen, I want you to know that I have always loved you and wish I could be with you, your mom and your sister.

From what your mother tells me, you've been a wonderful big sister, full of spunk and love.

Spunk and love? Who is my dad really writing about?

Sometimes, as adults, we don't have a lot of time to say the important words and because I can't live with you, I can't say them to you.

So from afar, from my perch in my kitchen, I look out upon the inner district and want to give you the fatherly advice any dad of a teenager would give.

First, big girl—

I smile at the nickname, having forgotten he'd called Mia that, and me Baby, just as Mom still does.

—know that all boys will want sex. Yes. With you. Trust no boys. They are your enemy. Okay, not your enemy, but the teenage years for a boy are transitional years from boy to man. Be careful.

Second, as you become a woman, you'll change, too. Your body will change. You'll want different things out of life. Different than me, your mom, even your little sister. Know that no matter what you want, I will always support you.

Third, take care of your little sister. She looks up to you, no matter what you think. She might be annoying. She might get into your things, but one day, she's going to need you, and you her.

Like now? Can you see the future, Dad?

Remember, if you do something, she's going to want to do it, too.

A grin splits my lips. I wanted to do everything Mia did, even when she yelled at me and slammed her door in my face as I stood in the frame, listening to her, her friends, her conversations, and watching her read and do her homework. I'd go in my room once she shut me out and sit at my little desk, pull out my reader and practice. I idolized my sister.

Fourth, I want you to know that when the time comes, when you turn eighteen, you will not be a documented citizen. I realize this will make limited sense to you now, but it will soon, and when it does, I want you to know I will be here for you.

So Dad told Mia about her future at thirteen? Talk about a little presumption. Way to go, Dad.

Your mother and I may not see eye to eye on this, either, but please try to understand her position. The worst thing you could do to her is not listen. Give her a chance to talk, but make the decision for yourself.

Independence is good. Cooperation is better.

I'm sure I could list hundreds of other things to tell you, but I'm taking risks just to get this to you.

Oh, goodie, Dad. You told her there's a problem, right there. Knowing my sister, she read that one line and immediately latched on to Dad. Mom would have no longer been interesting.

I love you always,
Dad

Yup. Now I know for sure that Mia's allegiance switched to Dad with this letter. That is, assuming Mia read it and not Mom.

Though, if Mom read it, there's no way it would still exist. That means Mia did read it.

Definitely.

A moment of sorrow hits me again.

Did Dad send me a letter? If he did, did Mom get it first? If not, why not?

I grab another from the pile, but realizing it's dated only two years ago, I decide to go back to the first and read in order. Shuffling through, I find one from right around the time he disappeared from my life. Sliding my finger under the edge, I manage not to rip it to shreds but to keep most of the container intact. With the interior page in hand, I open it like I did Mia's.

Belle, my love,

My heart does a flip-flop at the introduction. I remember my dad calling my mom Belle, but it's been so long that I'd forgotten; Her students refer to her as Ms. Keating—even Cam calls her that.

I miss you with all my heart and wish you would join me. Even just two weeks apart has been too long.

I imagine my dad sitting at a desk and writing out the note with a heavy heart.

There are days I don't even want to get up knowing you're not next to me in bed.

The letter goes on and on, with dad extolling his love for mom and sharing how much he misses her. Given my finger ripped up the top, I'm sure Mom never read it. Would that have changed anything?

Moving on to the next in the pile, I open it.

Belle, darling,

The opening is just as sweet.

What can I do to change your mind? Bring the girls. Join me. Live with me. Make love to me.

Eww.

This is our life and we need to be together.

He then also goes on and on asking her to join him. Join him in what? Obviously she knows, since he doesn't say. Is it with the overthrowing group? Something else?

The third envelope is more of the same. 'Please bring our family back together'.

The fourth, too.

Number five and six, as well.

If this is all I'm going to read, how am I going to learn why this is the story of their separation? Is it just to show me that the whole reason they aren't together is because Mom refused to reunite us? She hasn't even read the letters. Why didn't he try other methods? Why not send her flowers or take her on a date, or something active instead of just a bunch of begging and pleading in love-letter form?

Upon flipping over envelope seven, I find the lip isn't sealed like the others. I withdraw the thicker paper and open it.

Belle,

I don't understand your reasoning, but I can't keep trying to connect with you. You're my wife. I love you with all my heart, but I don't know what to do anymore. Our girls are growing up. It's not fair to them to have a mother and father living separate lives. We need to be together for them. For us.

Your ideals are grand, and I love that you believe so passionately in them, but living with nothing when you have two beautiful girls to raise is doing them a disservice.

I know you want to instil in them independence, an ability to survive and want nothing, but I want them to want for nothing. We are here, as parents, to make the world better for them, not take them out of it completely.

My home is your home. My life is your life. As we said on our wedding day, I promise to love you and care for you and that means even when we don't see eye to eye.

But we must try. We must merge our lives, for our children if nothing else. We can live well and still build in them a fierce desire for change. It's not necessary to live on nothing in order to prove the point that you can.

Please, Belle.

I know you love me but that your pride has gotten in the way. I know you want change, but patience doesn't mean poverty. You've returned every deposit I've made into your account, so I've set up credits for Mia and Eri separately. When they are old enough to understand, I'll explain to them that our separation came only from prideful differences of opinion.

We have the same goal, but your method is to the detriment of our children. I'll never disparage you, and I hope you'll do the same, but I won't lie to our children either.

Please, Belle. Please come to me. Together, we can be a force for change. Separate, we are nothing.

All my love,

Eric

Wow. So, Mom kept us from dad. Dad must have gotten a

job, or something, that Mom didn't agree with. If he thought Mia had the stubborn gene, he should have paid attention to where she got it. From Mom.

I move on to the next envelope and find it sealed.

So is the one after that.

Another four more are, too, until I find one that isn't.

Slipping the contents out, I find a legal document. From the fading, it seems to be a duplicate, not an original, and the date is just before my thirteenth birthday.

Petitioner: Annabelle Price Keating

Responder: Eric Thomas Keating

Decision: In the matter of Keating vs. Keating, the aforementioned Responder shall not have any direct connection with one Erianna Price Keating until such time as the minor child reaches the age of eighteen.

Both my mom and dad's signatures are on the bottom.

I'm shaking as I stare at the signatures.

As I realize just what my dad meant when he said he only did as he'd been asked.

When he said he'd done it for the most important person.

My mom forced my dad not communicate with me.

Is this why I don't have a letter from him telling me about registration? Is this why I became a documented citizen? Did he do that after Mom yanked us from the system? Is this why her anger spiked when I didn't tell her about registration but I wanted to go, anyway?

My fists clench as I glance at the clock and watch it blink two-fourteen in the morning.

It's time. Time to understand. Time to know why Mom walked away and kept me from Dad.

I open the bedroom door with my shoes in hand to save making more noise than necessary. Silence greets me. I don't want to wake Zane.

Tiptoeing through the hall, I come to the door I know will take me to the living room. There's not a bit of light in the room beyond, but luckily, the path from door to door isn't blocked by any obstacles, though I know I'll have to pass the divan to reach the only exit from the unit. Holding my breath, I place one socked-foot in front of the other across the floor.

At the door handle, I stop for a moment and turn. Even though I can't see him, I know Zane is sleeping just feet from me, and a moment of guilt reaches in and grabs me around the throat. I shouldn't leave. I should listen to him. My dad, too, but I can't. I have to get home. To Mom. I have to know.

A yawn hits me, but I bite it back, refusing to be tired. I have a long way to go.

Bye, Zane.

I'm coming back, but it seems right to offer him my thoughts.

Out in the hallway, the lights are dim but not off, and I stand in front of the riser. As the number counts up and the doors slide open, anxiety runs through me I glance back at the door two, three, four times.

It's been almost twenty-four hours since I had to travel by riser, and it's not like I'm claustrophobic, but my body denies the order to move when the riser arrives.

The entryway closes, and a touch to the button opens them again, but as I step forward, I freeze.

Go, Eri. Go.

Again the space before me closes up.

Another press and they open again.

Close.

Open.

Close.

I just can't get myself to pass the threshold.

"How many times—"

"Ah!" Whirling, I find Zane behind me, leaning against the wall just like he has so often since I met him. My heart pounds so hard, I'm expecting it will jump out of my chest at any moment. "You scared me."

Zane taps his foot on the floor and his finger on his crossed arm. "Going somewhere, Anna?"

"I—" What do I say? How stupid am I to think I could and should go talk with my mom?

"Where, Anna?"

Chin to chest, I say, "I need to talk to my mom."

"And you're going in the middle of the night, why?"

"Because I thought it was safer, you know, to not get ... caught."

"Not get caught? You made it five feet away." He chuckles.

"Well ... I ..." Rather than talk more, I spin and push the button. The riser doors open, and I walk in before whirling again and facing Zane. "I'm going."

He nods, and I am enclosed.

Alone.

The doors open again, Zane just outside. "You have to actually push the button for it to go somewhere." Still with his arms crossed over his chest, he steps inside, facing me, and behind him the barrier closes once again. "Going down?" He reaches behind him, his hand groping for the panel and presses '1'.

"You're not going to make me go back in?"

"Nope."

"Why not?" The riser lurches and begins its descent.

"Because if you're anywhere near as stubborn as your sister, you're going to find another way to go, so I might as well go with you."

"With me?"

"Yup."

"But, wouldn't it be better for you to just stay? To not get in trouble?"

Zane chuckles. "If I cared about not getting in trouble, I'd have left registration without you."

My mouth opens and closes. "You'd have left me?"

His grin widens. "Nah." He moves in closer. "Because I'm just as stubborn as Mia and you combined. So ... if you're gonna go, I might as well find out why it's so important to you."

"Oh ... okay." I stare down at my shoes.

"And pay for the transpo."

My head pops up.

"You didn't think about that, did you?"

I hadn't. In my head, I just needed to get out and go. How stupid am I? What would I have done? Walked? I don't even know where I am in relation to where my house is. Slapping my forehead seems appropriate but would also give away my entire internal conversation.

Zane moves next to me and leans into my shoulder, his touch sending tingles through my arm. "Don't worry about it, Anna. As long as we're back by ... oh ... tomorrow night, I doubt your dad will even know we left."

"Tomorrow?"

"Yeah. Whenever he's called to district one, it's usually a day, at least. My uncle's been there for two weeks for this meeting ... so I figure we have at least a day."

A day. Surely, I can get answers from Mom in a day.

The riser stops on the bottom floor and opens to the inner

lobby. *Now or never, Anna. Now or never.*

25

One very-well-paid-to-be-quiet private transpo service later, Zane and I stand in front of my house. The cold seeps through my shirt since, as a downright idiot, I forgot the temperatures would be so frigid. Rubbing my arms, I walk toward the door with Zane, but he stops and scratches at his temple.

"What? I'm freezing. Let's go in." Pointing to the door takes effort as my fingers go numb.

"Don't you think you're going to freak out your mom by, one: being here; and two: being here at three A.M.—not to mention having me with you?"

I rub my arms up and down trying to put some warmth back in them.

Zane takes off his jacket—one he obviously thought about before leaving—and puts it around my shoulders. I should give it back, since it's me who brought us out here in the cold. "Don't you think we should find a way to come back at a normal time?"

I start to shake my head and open my mouth to answer when the front door flies open.

My mother stands there, her face ashen, eyes crazed. "Erianna!"

"Mom!" Both our exclamations come out more like questions.

"Get in here. Both of you." She motions for us to join her *and quick*, wrapping her robe tight around her. "Hurry, before you let all the heat out."

When I hold out my hand, Zane takes it, and we walk in. Mom shuts the door behind us. "Sit, sit. The two of you."

"Mom—"

"Not yet. Just get in here and get warm." She shuffles into the kitchen and fills a pot with water, placing it on the two-burner stove, on the front one since the back one doesn't work. "I'll make us some tea."

Her greeting seems really odd given how intensely mad she'd been.

Slipping Zane's jacket off, I hand it to him and move to the divan. Mom's P-Comm, an older model than my last one, and one that barely works with the visual and audio requirements she has with her students, rests on her desk as usual; a mug of tea wafts steam into the air. That has to mean she was already awake—probably tutoring some kids in some other part of the world when the transpo drove up. No wonder she spotted us the moment we arrived.

Zane and I sit on the divan side-by-side. For some reason, despite being in my own house, I have this vague sense that I'm nothing more than a visitor. It's weird, like I know the place, but it's not mine anymore. Can having been gone for two days have done that? Is that part of growing up and moving out? That fast, though?

Mom returns with two steaming cups and hands them to Zane and me. "Now, baby, please tell me why you've just shown up at my front door in the dead of night."

Is it odd that she asked why I'm here and not why am I not at registration?

She sits on the footrest of a table we have in front of our

divan—right at the corner edge. Any closer to the center and it'll snap in half. Even putting our hot cups on it could melt it.

While the mug, a cracked one I made in level one a decade ago, warms my hands, I'm struck with the thought that I shouldn't tell Mom what's happened. Not exactly, at least. "I ... had a panic attack."

Mom's head cocks to the right, but her lips stay sealed. That's her 'keep going' face.

"Around midnight."

Still, she says nothing. Can she tell that I'm lying?

"I woke up with that dream I've had since I was little."

That earns me a righting of her head, but her gaze bores into me. There's truth to that dream. I've had it all my life, but in the last three days, I've had it over and over, with it getting more and more frightening each time as if my unconscious mind is grasping for something from my childhood.

"And ..."

"And," Zane starts, "without a male escort, the women of registration aren't allowed out of the grounds. Since Anna met up with my resident medic, I was assigned to escort her. We apologize about the time, Ms. Keating, but sometimes, when a student hasn't left home very often, they need that solid reminder of what home is to ground them for their return."

I force my lips shut. Just listening to him makes me want to lean into him and let him hold me like he did when I cried buckets in our room.

"That's very kind of you ..." Mom says toward Zane, in that tone that says, 'fill in the blank of your name'.

"I'm Zane Warren." He holds out his hand, and Mom shakes it.

"I appreciate you taking care of my daughter. Perhaps you'd both like a bed for the night, and we can regroup in the morning?"

So many questions run through my mind that I want to ask right now, but if Mom's talking bed, she must have been on the last bits of her own energy. Running on fumes as she says.

"Anna?" Zane asks. "Would you like to sleep?"

"What did you call her?" Mom asks, her tone tight and clipped.

Zane's hand on my back firms up. He must have forgotten I'd changed my name, even as I had. Mom called me Baby, so it didn't click that I should remind Zane, but then again, why should my heart lurch because I want to use a different part of my name? I bring my gaze up to Mom's. "I go by Anna now."

Those lips tighten into a purse as she faces away.

"Mom." I reach out and pull her back. It's a move she's done to me countless times. A tear slips down her cheek. "Why are you crying?"

She wipes her cheek and rises, pulling out of my hold and walking to her P-Comm. Mom stands at it for a moment as the screen goes dark. "You're welcome to stay the night," she says, still facing her unit. "I'll let my daughter get extra blankets and whatnot for the divan." With that, she turns and heads toward the hallway.

She's doing it again. Shutting you out. Just like before you left. "Mom, stop." I can't believe I've said it with such authority.

I can't believe she stops either.

Or that she turns and faces me.

The tears, though, they break my heart into a million emotional pieces.

She says nothing.

I rise, leaving the warmth of Zane's side and setting my cup near the corner edge of the table. "What's wrong?" I ask her as I reach her.

Her fake smile appears—one that shows up on her face but doesn't reach her eyes. "You're just getting older and growing up, and I'd always hoped I'd find a cure for that." She's a worse liar than me. Especially because a sentiment like that would earn me hair tucked behind my ear, a pat to my cheek, or a tweak to my nose.

"Mom—"

"Why are you here, Erianna?" She asks with that same expression, bold, false but serious all at the same time.

"I told you."

"You told me what I wanted to hear." She's right, but I know enough not to admit it. "You're not prone to panic attacks. You're not the kind of girl to let a boy lead you. You're not even the type to walk out on an organized program that has your name on it." She's right on all of those facts.

I try hard not to break our connected gazes, but my eyes want to dip down, to look away, to not give up all the inner details by staring into hers.

"I don't know what I've done to lose your trust." She gives a little shrug.

Oh, Mom, don't go there.

"Maybe it was the same with your sister. But all I've ever done is for you, not against."

All she's ever done? Like keeping my dad from me? Making us poor for no good reason?

On a deep sigh, she pats my cheek. "Is it too much to ask that I be treated with the respect that I deserve as a parent? As a mother. To have both my girls listen and answer when asked a question."

Inside, I'm seething. Eighteen years of believing in my mom comes crashing down on me. "You want the truth, Mom?"

"Always," she says in monotone.

"I want to know why you told me dad died when he's alive and well."

She only flinches but doesn't gasp or put her hands to her mouth or faint dead away, like I'd imagined she might in my head.

"Well?" I ask when she hasn't said anything for three breaths.

After a few blinks she says, "I never told you he die—"

"Yes you did!" My tone ratchets up a vocal notch.

She shakes her head.

"Yes!" It's all I get out before her laser-glare returns.

"I most certainly did not. I never once said he died. You presumed, and it was easier to let you believe." She says that without a hint of emotion.

"Why?" That comes out a plea.

She runs a hand over her head and hangs on, covering half her face with her arm. "Because ..." The arm lowers. "... sometimes, adults have to do what they have to do."

"But we're poor, and he's not, and I saw that you made him stay away, and I know you could have lived with him."

"No, Erianna, that's not how it works."

I throw up my hands. "Yes, Mom, it is. Why did Dad leave? Tell me. From your perspective, why did he leave?"

Her lips firm again as her chest rises and falls. "Sometimes ..."

"No, Mom. Tell me. No excuses." I've never been so forceful with my mom. Ever.

"Well ... you see ..."

"No. I don't." I want to say 'spit it out already' and push her along, but that's never worked with her before, and trying it now seems like it will only make her mad.

"Your Dad and I ..."

"He loved you. You made him leave. You took him away

from me."

Her eyes widen. "How—"

"The letters. All the ones he sent and were returned. Did you open them? Read them? I know about the court order that he signed agreeing to stay away from me. He did, too, didn't he? Why would you let me believe he died and then make him stay away? What did he do that was so bad you couldn't live with your own husband?"

"He's a traitor." She says it with calm fury, with that underlying hint of steel that implies anything I say in my dad's defense will go unconsidered.

"Why?" I don't think I've asked 'why?' so much since my toddler years.

"You wouldn't understand." With a wave, she turns toward the hallway again.

"Did he cheat on you?"

She spins back. "Who told you that?"

"No one. I'm guessing since you won't tell me."

Mom glares over toward Zane, and a momentary panic that he might turn and run has me shuffling over to him.

"I know what's going on now," I say.

"You know nothing. You're a child."

The sword in the heart pierces deep. I've always been Mom's child. I've always been the kid who didn't make waves, who did everything anyone asked, who picked up the messes without complaining. Mom, though, never said that to me. She'd tell me how mature and strong and resourceful I've been. Only since she found out about registration have I been the child of the house.

"I'm eighteen. I'm not a child. In the eyes of our country, I'm an adult with adult responsibilities. I deserve the truth."

"If you're an adult, then you'll know how to walk out that

door." Her arm raises, finger pointing toward our front door.

I storm toward her instead. "Tell me why Dad's a traitor."

"You can let yourself out."

"Tell me!"

"No."

"Tell me!" This time, it comes out a scream.

"Erianna—"

"No! Tell me. Now!" I sound like some whiny five year old, but I don't care. "Now, Mother. Now!"

"You want the truth?" Her nostrils flare a little.

"Oh, my goodness, yes! All of it." Standing my ground takes concerted effort as my legs shake and hands tingle with whatever adrenaline's running through me.

"Your father is a traitor because we decided—" Her breath breaks. "We decided that we'd never, ever take money from the A.U. We made a pledge. A promise to my grandmother. To his mother. That we'd never take money from the government, and then he goes off and accepts a position."

"But that was before Mia and I were born. Why kick him out when I was four?"

"Because of the promotion."

"What promotion?"

"He went to work directly for Osso. He broke every rule we'd made. He broke our pact. He broke our belief system. We had a plan from the time we married until our deaths, to work to change the system by not taking from the system, but your father couldn't bear to not have money, to not live well, to not sponge off the filth that operates our country."

"But—" I start and her hand goes up.

"You wanted the truth, so you're getting it. When he came out and encouraged Mia to sign up, I made sure he couldn't do that to you. I made sure you'd get every opportunity for freedom. Osso and his family are brainwashing people into subservience. The only way to combat that is to not take, and by not taking, we don't live under their rule." Mom starts to shake as she explains.

I walk up to her and hold her arms.

She doesn't pull away. "Why are you smiling?" she asks.

"Because, Mom, Dad's not what you think. He is doing what you said, but he's the leader of—" A weight on my shoulder stops me.

"I'm sorry," Zane says with his hand there. "But, Anna, you can't share that information."

I whirl to him. "What?"

Zane gives me a quick headshake. "We're already risking a lot to be here, and I can't let you risk your Dad's reputation, or position."

Wiggling out of Zane's hold, I say, "This is my mom, Zane, not some street lady looking for a credit for dinner. She's not—"

"You can't." His eyes plead.

"But, if I can't share, how am I going to get her to understand that what she believes, he does, too? That her ideals and his are the same, just the execution is different? That we all want the same thing, Mia included, and that I want her to have more than this?"

"Some other way."

"But—"

He gives me that same left and right with his head. "Remember what I said about registration and your sister. All that. I can't let you."

"You can't let me?" Back to Mom, I stare, wanting to tell her everything I've been through, about my sister, about Cam, about registration, too. About Marlena, Lucie and Dad. I want her to know what I know, and about Delta Street and what they're trying to do.

"Less is more, Anna. It's not safe."

"But this is my mother." Information jumbles up in my head. "As a fluke, she should—"

"She's not a fluke."

I'd forgotten he mentioned that, but at the time, I thought he said it as a suggestion based on circumstances, not an absolute. "I thought you just meant that like *if* she was."

He points to Mom. "You'd have to ask her to know for sure."

My heart flip-flops in my chest. On my heel, I make the turn, facing Mom again. "Are you a fluke?" The question is timid, with a hopefulness that he told me wrong.

Mom says nothing again.

"Are you?" Head cocked to the side, I wait. "Mom? Are you, or aren't you, a fluke?"

After what seems like forever, she says, "No. I'm not."

My hands fly up. "Then why did we live like this?" I ask in a screech far too loud for the space around us. As thin as the walls are, I expect the neighbors will hear me. As if on cue, a dog howls outside. "Tell me, Mother. Why?"

She blinks a few times, I presume at my tone, but it could also be the use of 'mother' instead of 'mom'. I never call her that, and now I've done it twice—in one night.

"You've changed, Erianna. In two days, you've become someone else."

Stunned into a frozen stupor, I don't breathe, don't move, don't respond.

Zane's warmth defrosts my right side. "Come on, Anna. Let's go back to your dad's place."

"Eric's? You've been to his home?" There's fury in her eyes as she asks, "Since when?"

"Since I found out you've lied to me all my life. Since I

found out my dad is alive an-and—" I want to tell her just what he does, but I'm not sure I know the woman standing in front of me, anymore. The fight two days before registration is nothing compared to the mixed emotions, anger and despair and full-out confusion running through me. "Not since I was four, Mom, so don't think you can go after him."

Her shoulders stiffen. "There are things you don't understand, Bab—"

"Anna. Call me Anna."

Her mouth stays open for a second before she says, "There are things you don't understand ... Anna. And you're too young—"

"Stop!" I hold out my hands as if to tug on the words she's saying and force them back in. "Stop saying I'm too young. I'm an adult. I'm duty-bound to the A.U. I have a job." If I can get back into registration. "I have a future." Unless what Zane says is true. "You need to be honest with me."

Without even a blink, she says, "You want honesty?"

"Oh, my goodness, Mom, Yes! Isn't that what I've been asking for this whole time?" Why doesn't she get that?

"Then here you go." She steps forward. "I went off the grid, became a fluke as you term it, took no more money, lived my own life, indepedent, free, whatever you call it, when I turned eighteen. So did your father. Or so he said. I went off because I was pregnant with Mia, which wasn't supposed to be possible, and surely couldn't be possible for one of Osso Senior's own grandchildren."

I jerk back. Did she just say Osso? As in our current CEO? As in the one who'll probably be replaced by his son Osso Jr, in two years when he retires from service? Mom's his granddaughter?

"And because I wanted nothing to do with my family, I

chose to get out completely. To do what any self-respecting citizen would do when they don't support those in power. I don't support them in any way. Flukes don't have a choice, but I did. I opted to be like them. So I changed my name, married your father and then he took that job. He *took* it. He broke every rule we had. I tried to convince him to get out for four years, and when he started filling Mia's head with possibilities, I made the break."

"But—" One hand goes up, and I hush.

"Your father broke the biggest promise he made to me—to stay out of Osso's coffers."

"But what about Grandma?" I ask it fast to get it out. "You said you did it for her, but she was family."

"Not by blood. Only by marriage. Though her husband died, the Osso family supported her until she passed. She supported whatever *I* wanted to do. I never took money from her. I never took a dime from your father. And, in doing so, I helped bring up two amazingly strong daughters. What do I get in return? Both of you run after your father like he's some saint." With that, she turns around, finishes the walk to her room and slams the door.

I can't move. I can't breathe. My lungs and heart have stopped functioning; there's no other reason why I can't get air.

At the touch again, I whirl.

Zane stands there. He says nothing. He doesn't have to. I get it now. He knew.

Tears burn my eyes, but I don't want them to fall. I don't want to break as my entire life gets turned upside down. I want to be the strong girl Mom thinks she brought up. I don't want to fight with her, but why couldn't she have just told me? Why? "*Why?*" It comes out on a soft whisper.

Zane tugs me into his arms, into his scent, into his comfort, and the tears spill, though not as heavy as I thought they would, just a river of sorrow falling onto his shoulder.

"Why?" I manage through hiccupped air. "They're on the same side."

"She doesn't know that."

"Why not?" I mumble into his shirt. "Why didn't he try harder?"

"These are questions you should ask him yourself."

Rubbing my forehead against him, I say, "I should stay with my mom. I should make it up to her."

Zane pulls me off him and holds me at arm's-length. "Or, you could help your dad and show her just what kind of girl she did bring up. It's your choice."

My choice. That's what I wanted from the very beginning. A way to change.

That path stands right in front of me.

"What happens with registration? With my job. With—"

Zane tucks a hair behind my ear. "I don't think any of that's going to matter soon."

That's right. Our country's out of money. "What about my sister?"

He smiles. "Have you met your sister? She knows how to take care of herself. Someone in this very house taught her that."

Mom did. He's right on that, too.

"If I were to ... um ... go with my dad ..."

"He'll work you to the bone, but you'll love every minute of it." Zane's lips curve into a smirk. "Or hate it. One of the two."

"Um ... if I go ... can I still find out about my friends? They went ... um ... to other houses."

His head cocks left. "Still? Anna, if you don't, they'll be off the grid worse than your mom. The only way anyone's going to give you information is if you get out of here."

"Oh." I hadn't thought of that. More names and faces flash through my mind: Hadley, Vica, Brie. If I walk away from the A.U.—if I go off the grid like Mom—I may never see them again. "What about the others ... from the red house?"

Zane's head angles down. "I don't know, Anna."

"What about my mom?"

Zane sighs but lifts his head. "I'm not supposed to tell you this, but your dad's always had eyes and ears on her ... and you."

"Huh? But—"

He holds a finger to his lips. "I just know he's done what needed to be done. And she'll be fine. Maybe you're the one who can get her to join Delta Street."

"So, I go with you, back to my dad's, and then what?"

"The path is wide open with possibilities. Probably gonna be a big war, of the minds maybe, and maybe fighting, too. We could all die. Or go broke. Or be a huge success. It could all end tomorrow, or our kids' kids might be the ones who benefit from what we do today. Who knows?" His hands land on my biceps. "The idea is that no one gets to control any part of what you do or who you are from now on. From what color you wear to how many kids you have, to how much money you make, to when you die. Do you want true freedom? Or do you want to go back to what you had and let everyone else tell you what to do?"

Those who enter the red house are never the same when they come out.

I asked for change, and I got it.

Staring up at Zane again, a question bubbles up inside me, along with heat to my cheeks. His head tilts the opposite way as if he understands I have more to ask. "Um ... Zane?"

"Yeah?"

"Will you ... um ... will you be staying ... I mean, if you're going to be around me ... are you going to keep spouting off all this history?" That sounds horrible. "I mean ... telling me stuff is one thing, but showing me ... well—"

"I'll show you more, Anna. I will." He gives me one firm, emphatic nod. "No way on God's green earth I won't be there with you, and I will show you whatever you want to help you understand this. I want our country to get better, not worse. And yes, I think one person can be the point of change. Maybe that's me. Maybe that's you." He holds out his hand to me. "Come on, Anna. Come with me. Let me show you what's really happening, why our country doesn't even know what's going on and what we have to do to fix it. Let's do this. Together."

Together. In an unwritten, unplanned, unknown future. It's actually what my mom wanted, just in a way she never expected. The only one in my family that won't get what they thought out of life will be me.

Instead, I'll have way more.

Maybe.

Or maybe not.

ACKNOWLEDGEMENTS

To the one, and only, God above, my thanks for the inspiration, drive and firece determination that has been given to me, as well as the opportunity to write this book. I can only hope, that in 2132, you really aren't referred to as 'Oz'.

To the most amazing man that is my husband, thank you for being who you are, for guiding me when the idea struck and for having my back when I said, 'you know, this book is really going to tick off some people'.

To my kids, who have their own minds to make up about this country. Go in with open eyes. Never let others tell you what to think, and if they do, question it. Every day of your life, question authority, but live within the rules. If you don't like the rules, work to change them.

To my most amazing friend and cheerleader, Julie B., you know this book wouldn't have happened without your repeated remarks to 'get this published now'. And to 'hurry up' and for the moment you said you actually had nothing, at all, to criticize. That shocker of a moment had to be the final act that pushed me forward.

To Amaleen Ison, Brooke DelVecchio, Julie Reece, Terri Rochenski, Kelly Said, Wendy Seagondollar, and Danielle Smiley. You didn't all agree, like or hate the same parts, but what you did was completely make my point. We are all different. In our personalities, beliefs, desires and hopes for the future. Without a single one of you, your gut reactions and your comments, I wouldn't have known that my own 'gut' feel on this book was solid. I can't thank you all enough for taking the time to read the early drafts.

EMI GAYLE

Emi Gayle just wants to be young again. She lives vicariously through her youthful characters, while simultaneously acting as chief-Mom to her teenaged son and searching for a way to keep her two daughters from ever reaching the dreaded teen years.

Ironically, those years were some of Emi's favorite times. She met the man of her dreams at 14, was engaged to him at 19, married him at 20 and she's still in love with him to this day. She'll never forget what it was like to fall in love at such a young age—emotions she wants everyone to feel.

EMI GAYLE

Dawn *conceals*
what the dark
of night *reveals*

AFTER DARK
Book One of the 19th Year

AVAILABLE NOW

EMI GAYLE

His life is no longer
the stuff of *fiction*

DAY AFTER
Book Two of the 19th Year

AVAILABLE NOW

Choose him,
or let him *go.*

DARKEST DAY

Book Three of the 19th Year

JANUARY 2014